ALL THIS TIME

By the Author

All This Time

Writing as Jordan Meadows:

Proximity

Not Just Friends

ALL THIS TIME

by

Sage Donnell

2024

ALL THIS TIME

ISBN 13: 978-1-63679-622-2

THIS TRADE PAPERBACK ORIGINAL IS PUBLISHED BY
BOLD STROKES BOOKS, INC.
P.O. BOX 249
VALLEY FALLS, NY 12185

FIRST EDITION: MARCH 2024

CREDITS
EDITOR: BARBARA ANN WRIGHT
PRODUCTION DESIGN: SUSAN RAMUNDO
COVER DESIGN BY TAMMY SEIDICK

Acknowledgments

I'd like to thank the entire Bold Strokes Team for bringing this book to life with particular thanks to my editor, Barbara Ann Wright, for your encouragement, suggestions on making the book stronger (and she felt things), and the many snips that helped to make my writing flow.

As always, my thanks go to my daughter, Haley. Without you, there would be no books. It was your encouragement and the example you set that got me here.

Thanks also to my high school friends. Our reunion weekend, while not nearly as exciting as the one depicted here, nevertheless provided the creative spark that resulted in this book.

CHAPTER ONE

C an we watch *A League of Their Own* for girls' night, mom?"

Darcy's question startled Erin out of her wandering thoughts, and she dropped the shirt she was folding.

"Sorry," Darcy said.

Erin smiled at her youngest, still in her practice clothes. "You surprised me. I didn't hear you come in. How was practice?"

"Good. We scrimmaged with the Wasps and held our own." The Wasps were the fast-pitch team of 18U's, one level above Darcy's 16U team, the Stingers. Erin was so proud that at newly fifteen, Darcy was one of the youngest on her team.

"That's awesome. And, sure, we can watch *A League of Their Own.*" She couldn't help but tease by adding, "Again."

"Not the movie. The TV show." Darcy had the corner of her mouth pulled between her teeth like she did when she was nervous about something.

Erin couldn't imagine what she was nervous about. "There's a TV show? Really? Sure. Why not?" She paused, examining her kid. Her feet were bare, presumably because she'd left the slides she would have worn home by the front door. Her practice pants were dusty, with patches of ground-in dirt, par for the course. Her practice shirt was also dusty and dark in spots from having been sweated in while practicing under the hot summer sun. Her messy brown ponytail was sticking up through the opening of her visor. Even as tan as she'd gotten this summer, her cheeks were pink from the sun or exertion. She looked after-practice normal, aside the corner of her mouth. "Is something wrong?"

Darcy shook her head. "Nope. Nothing's wrong. All is good. Can we order pizza?"

"Why not?" Erin turned back to folding the laundry piled on her bed. There was a lot less to do now that only one kid lived at home. But the three people who lived here still produced copious amounts of clothes between all of their activities: everyday clothes, workout clothes, Air Force uniforms for Grant, softball practice and game uniforms for Darcy, tennis clothes for Erin. It added up. In some ways, though, Erin wouldn't have minded a little more. Brad had just gone back to college for his junior year, and she missed him already. He'd told her he wouldn't be around much next summer because he needed to get an internship, so these last couple of months of having him at home had probably been the last. Meanwhile, Lindsey had long gone and would no doubt be folding clothes for her own kids in the not-too-distant future.

"Great." Darcy hung out in the doorway, making Erin wonder if there would be more. She picked up the shirt she'd dropped and started folding it, taking the pressure off. Usually, Darcy was more forthcoming if she was allowed to talk on her own. "Um, Dad won't be home tonight, will he?"

Erin snuck another peek. She wasn't sure why Darcy was concerned about Grant. He was a decent dad, showing up to games here and there. He was busy with his Air Force career that included plenty of nights out with the other officers for bonding and career development, plus lots of gym time, so he wasn't a super present dad like some on the team, but he was around and supportive. "No. It's poker night. The whole reason we have girls' night on Thursdays."

It was Erin's favorite night of the week in general. It was so low stress. No pressure to cook a big meal, no dinner conversation about doing better in school, improving in sports, or plans for after high school. It was a time they took a deep breath and just chilled out together.

"Right. Just making sure."

"Just you and me for the movie and pizza. And maybe ice cream? You could walk to the store if you're feeling ambitious. I've got a few more chores to finish but will be ready to get started in about an hour or so. Just enough time for you to shower and make a quick run for ice cream."

"Sure," Darcy agreed, smiling. "Family card, right?"

Erin laughed. "Absolutely." Darcy had a credit card for when she was doing something Erin and Grant were paying for, useful when she was traveling with her softball team, and Erin wasn't one of the chaperones. Admittedly, that didn't happen very often. Darcy also had her own debit card that Erin loaded up with her monthly allowance. She was good about not abusing the family card, but she did like to use it when she could.

Darcy patted the doorjamb, then left. Erin could hear her going down the stairs; she must have decided to go get ice cream before showering. Erin went back to folding clothes. This time, her thoughts weren't wandering but rather focused on why Darcy didn't want her dad around this evening.

"Ready for this?" Erin asked, lifting the remote. Pizza was ordered, ice cream was in the freezer, clothes were folded, Darcy had showered, and they were both wearing soft clothes.

"Wait. Mom?"

Erin lowered the remote. "Yes?"

Darcy didn't speak right away, just sat, staring at the home screen on the TV. Erin kept the remote in her lap and waited. She loved conversations with Darcy, but getting them started required a certain finesse. Each of her kids was different in that way. Lindsey rarely confided in her, preferring to keep her own council. They talked more now that she was twenty-six and living a flight away in Denver than they had when Lindsey was a teenager living in the same house. Brad was a talker but had to be drawn out with questions. Darcy told Erin plenty about her life, but it had to be on her own terms. If Erin asked too many questions at the wrong time, Darcy would spook and stop talking.

Erin was a talker, so it hadn't been her instinct to allow the space. It was still a little challenging, but she tried to take these moments to work on her breathing, a relaxation technique she'd picked up at the woman's retreat at their church.

After a few long moments, she said softly, "I heard there are LGBTQ characters in this version." Even more softly, she added, "Is it still okay to watch it?"

Erin was a little taken aback. She had complicated feelings about people who were gay from the church she'd grown up in, her own teenage experiences, and their current church. It didn't exactly preach hellfire and brimstone for people who weren't straight, like the church she'd grown up in, but they didn't exactly welcome them with open arms. Grant had some homophobic tendencies and had said things about *those people* over the years. Erin had always just stayed quiet. In her experience, those sorts of comments were only to be expected.

Darcy's earlier question about if her dad would be home or not this evening now made sense. Was she questioning her own sexuality, or did she just really want to watch this show that her teammates were probably talking about?

Erin's heart twisted at the memory of what she'd gone through as a teenager. One day in particular flashed in her head:

Erin was sitting in the church pew next to her mother. Her father was on the other side. She was daydreaming about Jodi and not paying much attention to the sermon until the preacher sneered the word gay. He went on to tell them all for the next twenty minutes about how it was a sin, how parents needed to guard against any tendencies in their children to deviate from girl things for girls and boy things for boys, how people struggling with impure thoughts needed to get them under control. If they couldn't, they needed to come to him for counseling.

Erin did her best not to squirm in her seat, which would only draw attention to herself.

When he finally wrapped up, when Erin's father had finally dragged her mother out of the basement post sermon gathering for bad coffee and stale cookies, when they were all three in the car driving home, they passed a group of goth teens. Erin's father said, "Those little queers could use that sermon from today, couldn't they?"

He laughed. Erin's mother shook her head sadly. Erin told herself for the thousandth time that she and Jodi needed to stop doing what they were doing. It had gone way too far.

Trying to make sense of her sexuality had been one of the biggest challenges of her life. Erin hoped that she wasn't putting Darcy through the same thing she'd gone through as a teenager. She loved her kid and would support whatever journey she was on, even if it was just accepting teammates who weren't straight.

Refraining from asking probing questions, she went with, "Yes, honey, it's okay. We can still watch it."

Darcy looked relieved. "Okay. Ready, then."

Erin started the first episode. Three hours later, they were still on the couch. They'd paused for the pizza, to clean up the box since Erin liked things taken care of and had a hard time relaxing with a mess in front of her, and paused for ice cream. But mostly, they'd let it play.

"There are my two girls."

Erin started at the sound of Grant's booming voice and paused the episode. It wasn't that she was afraid of him. He'd never raised a hand to her or to the kids. He wouldn't be happy about her and Darcy watching a show with LGBTQ characters, though. He'd tell them to turn that crap off or some such thing. It wouldn't help Darcy to open up about whatever was going on with her. Luckily, it was currently on a game scene, nothing to particularly draw his attention. He came into the room and leaned over to kiss each Darcy and Erin on the temples.

"Hi, Dad," Darcy shot a nervous glance at the TV.

Erin's heart broke to see her kid not feel safe in her own home. She drew Grant's attention by asking, "How was your poker night?"

"It was fine. The usual. I'm going to go take a shower and go to bed. It was an early morning." He turned to leave, then paused at the image on the screen. "Are you two watching *A League of Their Own* again?" He shook his head and chuckled. "Girls."

In the silence, Erin could hear his tread up the staircase. She listened for the sound of the bedroom door before saying anything. Darcy must have been waiting for the same thing because as soon as Erin heard it, Darcy said, "He didn't even notice they were different people."

"Maybe he'd have noticed if it was Max playing?" There had been no Black characters in the original movie.

"You'd hope," Darcy said, rolling her eyes. "I guess we should stop watching?"

Erin looked up, considering. "That's probably best. He's going to be gone all weekend. If you have time, we could watch more then."

"I'll make time. Thanks, Mom." Darcy gave Erin a hug before running off upstairs to her room.

Erin clicked the remote to the TV off and switched off the lamp that sat on the side table but sat there for long minutes more. She considered the whirlwind of emotions watching the show had set off. She'd married a person who was perfect on paper. He was a good Christian man with a secure career. But had she ever loved him romantically? Was she even capable of loving a man that way?

And aside from all that, there was Jodi.

She'd swept so much under the rug for so long, she'd come to believe that the rug was a fairly secure place. How was it that three hours of watching a show with her teenage daughter could rip that rug right off the floor, letting everything she'd crammed underneath swirl out into the air?

CHAPTER TWO

When Carson's husband showed up in episode seven, Erin started shifting uncomfortably.

"You okay, Mom?" Darcy asked. "Do you need a break or something?"

She was probably shifting about like a little kid needing to pee. She couldn't tell Darcy why she was uncomfortable. This scene was hitting a little too close to home. How Carson explained her feelings about her husband nailed how Erin had felt about Grant during the first, oh, ten years of their marriage. He was a good friend, usually fun to be around, and she didn't mind the sex. It was nice. Pleasant, even.

They'd started growing apart during the next ten years as Erin was busier and busier with their growing family while Grant made being a provider and somewhat-present parent an art form. And in these last ten years, their relationship was entirely platonic, and it felt like they were staying together because that was what was expected of them. They had kids together, their religion said they should stay together, their extended families considered them both family members, and they were a team when it came to the kids: Erin doing nearly all of the parenting labor while Grant supplied the funds to make it work.

Was that still enough?

Erin had had a taste of more as a teenager. Goofing off with Jodi had turned into...more. She had a hard time labeling it because she'd been told that being gay was wrong. But that relationship had given her all the feels, as Darcy would have said. She'd grown used to marriage with Grant, but now she was reminded of what she was missing out on. Sitting here watching *A League of Their Own* that was full of women—or maybe not all people who identified as women, it seemed—who were all living true to themselves as much as possible, she felt like she'd taken a wrong turn somewhere. She'd done all the things she was supposed to do. Found a man to marry, had children, stayed home to take care of them, and now?

Now she was in this shell of a marriage. She wouldn't trade her kids for anything, of course, but this was not a full life. Still, could she possibly start over at fifty-one? Wasn't it better to just stay at this point?

"Mom?"

Darcy's question jolted her out of her thoughts, and she realized she'd missed a chunk of plot. "Yes?"

"Do you…do you think it's wrong? Carson and Greta? Not the cheating part, of course, because that's wrong, but at all?"

Erin pushed the pause button and shifted on the couch. It wasn't wrong. Erin believed that with all her heart, despite the life she'd chosen to live. It was the fact that she'd chosen a life that wasn't true to herself and done it for so much longer than Carson had that was making her uncomfortable. But what Darcy was asking was more about the fundamentals of if loving a person of the same sex was wrong. That was what Erin had to address.

Darcy was looking at her hands and chewing on the corner of her mouth. It was a big leap on her part to even ask this question. It was likely that no one in Darcy's family or even friends of the family had ever given her the slightest idea that being gay was okay. Between Grant's casual homophobic remarks, their St. Louis church, and the outright anti-gay stance of both Erin's and Grant's parents, nearly everyone in her life would think it was wrong.

Erin wasn't sure what the message at school was. Darcy went to a public magnet high school in central St. Louis, which meant a liberal leaning neighborhood, at least. Erin had to assume there were out and proud kids there. Maybe that was why she was asking.

Erin wasn't completely naive. She knew that a lot of lesbians drifted toward sports, particularly softball. Maybe some of Darcy's friends were gay. Maybe she wasn't questioning her own sexuality. If she weren't gay, her life would likely be easier. Erin's would have been easier without the attraction she felt toward women, that was for sure.

Either way, Erin knew what her answer was, even though it went against all she'd been taught. "No, honey, I don't think it's wrong."

"But Dad does." There was no question in her voice.

Erin sighed. "I think that's true."

"What do you think Dad would do if a kid of his turned out to be gay?"

Erin stilled. That question solidified for her that Darcy probably identified as gay. Darcy was gay. This was really happening. Erin simultaneously felt a surge of pride for her working through it all and a stab of worry. There were so many aspects of Darcy's life that were not gay-friendly. That was mostly on Erin. Guilt joined the party thinking about it.

Right now, she needed to focus on Darcy. While she didn't think Darcy would ask that question if she weren't gay, she needed to let Darcy get to any reveal that might be coming at her own pace.

Still, Erin couldn't help her mind straying to forthcoming difficulties. Darcy's life was going to be filled with obstacles because of her orientation. She was going to have to make decisions about when to come out and when not. Those choices were absolutely going to affect her relationships with family. Either many family members were not ever going to really know her or their relationship would be altered forever.

Erin pulled her attention back to the here and now once more and finally answered Darcy's question. "I'm not sure."

"But you must have some idea."

"He'd probably take y…any of his kids who told him they were gay to talk to Pastor Mike. I think."

"You don't think he'd disown us?"

Erin really couldn't be sure. Her mind was swirling with so many different thoughts. He might, but there was no way that Erin would. Erin would be the support she wished she'd had as a teenager. She could help smooth the path for Darcy, and she would. There was her marriage and what she really wanted from a partner now taking second fiddle to her daughter's distress about the possibility of being disowned by her father and searching for acceptance. This couldn't be their life, hiding who they really were and what they wanted. She tried to pull her thoughts back to answer. "I honestly don't know."

Something was going to have to change.

By the time Grant was due home on Sunday, Erin had done a lot of thinking and knew it was time for a talk. She was pretty sure the end result was going to be divorce. She worried about going through it, telling her parents and her kids, what her fellow congregants would think, how Grant would take it, and the financial fallout.

She wanted what she hoped would be on the other end, though. She wanted the freedom to find a relationship that felt fulfilling to her. She wanted Darcy to have a safe home. If Grant wanted to try couple's counseling, maybe she would agree. If they could get back to a warm, friendly relationship, that would be a reason to stay married. But only if she also was able to believe he would be willing to accept Darcy, should she be gay. Otherwise, it was time to forge a new path.

While all that sounded planned out, Erin was desperately trying not to feel overwhelmed. Her nerves buzzed mostly with dread and anxiety. She hadn't gotten much sleep the night before for thinking about everything. She'd made it through the day thanks to copious amounts of coffee, which didn't help with the buzzing. Talking to Grant was the right thing to do, and some of the buzzing was excitement about what a new life could hold, but she'd have to get through this difficult part to move on to the scary but exciting part.

She planned on suggesting that she and Grant have dinner alone the next night. That way, he'd have a chance to get a good night's sleep and be clean and rested. But she was still glad when

Darcy announced she was going out for pizza and a movie with some girls from the Stingers. However, with her out, there wasn't much to distract Erin while she waited. She had too much nervous energy to just sit and wait, so she took her racket and some tennis balls out back.

Erin had taken up tennis to fit in with some of the officers' wives when she and Grant were first married. She'd found a passion for it and had gotten pretty good. She wasn't great, by any measure, but good enough to hold her own at the club. But it wasn't until Brad had gotten into tennis after they'd moved to St. Louis that they gotten a rebounder net for the backyard. Erin had probably ended up using it more. Certainly, she was the only one who used it now.

As she smacked balls into the rebounder over and over, she was able to focus on the movements needed to keep the ball in motion, and that left little room for her anxiety. She should have bought this rebounder for herself years before, rather than inheriting it from her son. But it was here now, and she was realizing more and more that she needed to take her own needs into account. She'd spent too long putting what others wanted first. Initially, it was her parents, then Grant and the kids. Change would be hard on everyone, but she needed to live an authentic life, to be true to herself.

She was out there hitting balls until dusk. When she realized she couldn't see the ball very well anymore, the choice was to turn on the backyard light or go in. She was surprised Grant hadn't shown up yet and went inside to see if he'd come home without her noticing.

She went through the garage to drop her racket off and pick the top towel off the stack she kept there to wipe the sweat off before going into the dark house. She found her phone on the kitchen counter. She chided herself. She usually kept it close in case one of the kids needed something, but she'd been so distracted, she'd forgotten to grab it. There was one message, and it was from Grant: *Getting dinner with some of the guys. Home late. Don't wait up.*

This was typical of Grant and usually didn't matter to Erin, but it did this evening. She'd been all ready to tell him they needed to have a talk. Now she wasn't sure what to do with herself.

Actually, she did have one idea, but she'd been resisting it. She continued to resist while she took a shower and put on pajama pants and an old T-shirt. Then, she gave in.

She went downstairs to the nook beside the kitchen where she kept her laptop. She sat at the small counter and opened the computer. She paused, looking around as if she was doing something shameful. Not only was she home alone, but she wasn't doing anything untoward, really, just looking up an old high school friend. Anyone would do that.

Still, before going any further, she glanced at her phone once more. There was a text from Darcy asking if it was cool if she slept over at Flo's with several of the girls. Erin sent a quick affirmative, and relieved of chauffeuring duty, she placed her fingers on her keyboard.

After hesitating there for a moment, she typed Jodi Swanson into Google, wondering if Jodi went by something else now. Had she gotten married and changed her last name? She probably hadn't married a guy, but nothing was out of the question. And now that gay marriage was legal, maybe Jodi had married a woman and changed her last name. It was ridiculous, but Erin felt a jealous pang about the idea of Jodi getting married.

The first thing she learned was that Jodi Swanson was a pretty common name. When she added their high school into the search, she found Jodi on Facebook.

Huh. Apparently, Jodi was the cohost of two different podcasts, both about books. One was about science fiction and fantasy while the other was about...oh. It was about books about lesbians. Jodi had a lot of podcast and book related stuff on her Facebook account, which wasn't a surprise at all. There wasn't really anything in terms of personal stuff. Checking the same username on Twitter and Instagram, Erin found Jodi there, too, with mostly the same content.

Going further down this rabbit hole of cyber stalking Jodi felt both exciting and shameful. It felt almost like cheating on Grant because Erin felt more about the idea of Jodi than she did for him, but a bit of that shame came from the fact that the person she felt that way about was a woman. She didn't want Darcy to feel that way about herself, and she really did believe that love was love, but there were a lot of people in her head telling her otherwise.

Her curiosity won out, shoving the voices aside. She figured out how to listen to podcasts. She knew of their existence, of course, but had never gotten into them and wound up with a new app on her phone. She picked one of the *Lesbians on Books* podcasts at random, plugged in her earbuds, and pushed play.

Jodi's voice was immediately familiar, even after thirty-plus years. It was a little rougher but still her. She sounded happy and engaged as she bantered with her cohost. Erin wondered if they were a couple. The idea of Jodi happily coupled up made Erin feel both happy for her and a little jealous. The jealousy wasn't reasonable. Jodi was a woman decades removed from the girl that Erin had known. But Jodi, or at least the idea of her, was someone Erin had held secret in her heart of hearts all these years.

Three episodes later, Erin had cleaned most of the house and knew Jodi and her cohost, Val, weren't together. Val was happily married to another woman and had kids. Erin knew people did that, but the normalcy of it struck her. The idea that such could have been her life ricocheted around in her head until she realized she'd missed about fifteen minutes of the podcast. She stopped it and turned off the vacuum. She took out her earbuds, sank into a chair in the living room, and put her face in her hands, overwhelmed and not sure how to deal with it.

She didn't know how long she'd been sitting there when she heard two things. One was the grandfather clock striking eleven, the other was the garage door going up just after that. Grant was home.

Erin stood and looked around, slightly panicked, before she realized she wasn't doing anything wrong. Odd, sure, that she was vacuuming at nearly midnight but not wrong. Grant couldn't know what podcast she was listening to or why it mattered. Still, she ripped the cord out of the jack on her phone and shoved it in one of the pockets of her pajama pants, putting the phone itself in the other pocket. She felt very underdressed for the conversation she was about to have, but there was no fixing it.

She walked her Dyson back to the closet on her way to meet Grant in the kitchen. He was already there, having come through from the garage, and was hidden by the door of the fridge, apparently looking for something.

"Hi," she said.

He popped up above the fridge door holding a can of seltzer water and looking surprised to see her. "Hey. What are you doing up?"

"Oh, I just got into some stuff. But it works out because I wanted to talk to you. How was the training?"

"Fine. The usual. Not a lot of sleep." He did look tired.

"I won't keep you up, but I did want to suggest we have dinner, just the two of us, together at home tomorrow evening."

"Why?"

She was taken aback. As much as she knew there were major flaws in their relationship, asking why a married couple might plan dinner alone together was a strange question. Sure, she was going to be bringing up the possibility of divorce, so there was definitely an agenda, but asking shouldn't have resulted in scrutiny. She tried to think of when they had last done something, just the two of them, that wasn't accidental like eating dinner together when Darcy was out. She really had no idea.

"I think we have some things to talk about."

There was a flash of something like panic across Grant's face before it settled into resigned with hints of belligerence. He straightened his shoulders and said, "I guess that means you know about Tami. I don't know what you expected when we haven't had sex in years. Of course I was going to find someone else. I did the honorable thing and stayed married for the sake of our kids, supporting you and them. But now that you know, how do you want to handle this? Separate rooms here in the house so we keep up appearances or divorce?"

It was delivered so matter-of-factly. Erin didn't know how to react. What was she feeling? Shock? Oh yeah. Anger? Yup. Hurt? Some. Their marriage was a sham at this point, sure. She knew it was, but Grant should have tried to fix it first or asked for a divorce before starting up with someone else.

What surprised her the most was the flood of relief.

It took her a minute to reply, but when she did, she calmly said, "Divorce, I think."

He nodded. "I'll go get a few things before I go. I'll come back for the rest later."

She didn't even watch him leave the room. She leaned against the kitchen counter and considered how quickly things had gone from what she'd thought was a workable enough marriage to her being relieved that Grant was leaving tonight.

This was…more than a little overwhelming. There was so much to figure out now, not the least of which was how she was going to support herself. She supposed there would be child support and alimony, at least for a little while, but would it be enough to stay in this house? How long would it last? She didn't have answers, but what she did know was that her future was now wide open in a way she hadn't experienced maybe ever.

CHAPTER THREE

One Year Later

"Can we watch *A League of Their Own* for girl's night tonight? Because it's the one-year anniversary from when we watched it the first time." Darcy was once again leaning on the door frame of the room Erin was in, wearing her dirty practice clothes, but that was where the similarities with the first time she'd asked that question ended.

This time, Erin was sitting at her desk in the office of their apartment, doing the books for one of her clients, the very fast-pitch organization Darcy had just finished practicing with. She turned in her fancy swivel office chair and smiled at her grinning kid. "Sure. Seems fitting. Want to get us ice cream again?"

"On it," Darcy said. "When will you be ready?"

Erin glanced back at her monitor, considering. "Six o'clock?"

"And we'll get pizza, right?"

"Absolutely."

Darcy shot a double thumbs-up while grinning to show she didn't take the gesture seriously, then disappeared. Erin turned back to her computer but didn't go right back to work. Instead, she marveled over the changes of the past year. She was a year older, sure, but the differences between fifty-one and fifty-two were pretty negligible. More importantly, Darcy was now sixteen, a leap from fifteen, if in no other way than that she was now driving. She'd also come out to Erin. She was out with some of her friends, too, but not to her wider family yet, including Grant, nor to everyone at school.

Grant had gone the very night he'd left to Tami's, where he now lived. When Darcy had come home and found him gone, she'd been worried that Erin had kicked him out because of her questions about how he would take having a gay kid. She had explained that they just weren't suited for each other anymore but wasn't sure if she should tell Darcy she'd have divorced him to protect her, too, so she'd left that out.

When Darcy had realized that he'd actually left for another woman, she'd decided not to go to dinner when he came to pick her up. She'd barely seen him since. He still occasionally showed up to some of her games, but that was about it.

Erin was relieved he was so far out of her life, but she felt a little sorrow for Darcy, who now had only one meaningful parent. Erin had to admit that she was probably projecting because Darcy seemed lighter and happier now. She'd gone through some rough periods with all the changes, but she was settling into their new life so well that Erin had to accept it had been the right decision for Darcy as well as herself.

Just two weeks ago, he'd notified Erin, as required by the newly minted divorce settlement, that he'd gotten new orders and would be moving in a few months. Erin figured he would just fade completely from Darcy's life after that, aside from the childcare payments and his share of her college costs, also as dictated by the court. That was an even bigger relief.

Erin and Darcy had moved out of their big house and into an apartment just a couple of months after Grant had left so the house could be sold. There'd been another house they'd kept as a rental from a previous assignment that had also been sold. They'd split the equity of both. Until that happened, Erin wasn't sure how finances were going to settle out. Now that it was done, she felt more secure, but they were happy enough in the apartment. Although Erin did miss the rebounder in the backyard.

There was also alimony, but it would only last until Darcy left for college, so Erin had started doing the books for a business here and there. She'd had to learn some new programs, but her accounting skills were still there if a little rusty. She was currently working about thirty hours a week and figured between that and her share of the equity, she'd be fine on her own when the alimony ended.

Their older kids had come down on Erin's side, joining Darcy in outrage when she'd told them about their dad moving directly into his much younger girlfriend's house. Lindsey was the only one who really had any contact of substance with him anymore. Brad had stayed with Erin when he was briefly home for breaks over this last school year. He had, indeed, gotten an internship this summer in Austin, Texas and loved it. He'd just gone back to college for his senior year.

So here they were, down from a family of five to two. It would be just Erin soon because Darcy was only a couple of years away from leaving the nest. Erin was happier in ways she hadn't expected, even without finding anyone to date. She hadn't realized how much tension Grant had brought into the house until he was gone.

She had just gotten back into the Stinger's books when her phone lit up with a text. She clicked on it. It was from Meredith.

Meredith, Sally, Jodi, and Erin had been a tight group of four in high school. Erin had fallen out of touch when they'd scattered for college. When she'd done her cyber stalking of Jodi last year, she had also looked up the other two. She couldn't find hide nor hair of Sally, but she had found Meredith's not much used Facebook account and DMed her. She'd wanted to reach out to Jodi, but it was too fraught. Plus, what if Jodi wasn't the one who monitored the account but Val?

No. It was too hard. Meredith was much easier, so much less baggage. The message had sat there unanswered for a couple of months, but then, Meredith had replied with enthusiasm. It turned out she wasn't much of a Facebook user and hadn't checked until then. They'd been texting regularly since.

Still feeling good?

Erin chuckled. Meredith was now so much a fixture of her life that she knew the one-year anniversary of Grant walking out was just days away. *Great. Darcy and I have a girls' night planned, and if anything, it feels like a celebration.*

Awesome! Have any other celebratory plans?
No. I should. I feel like it's time to have an adventure.
Like an African safari? Because I haven't made it to Africa yet.

Meredith loved travel and was working on visiting every continent. Erin had traveled some; that was par for the course for a military wife. She and Grant had even lived in Germany when Lindsey was little, but she didn't really have the travel bug. *I was thinking something more like a weekend at the beach with friends. Only, it turns out, my friends were really only the wives of other officers and church friends.*

It had hurt a little, figuring that out. When Erin had stopped going to the Officer's Club for tennis and stopped attending church, she'd realized all her friends were gone. No one had reached out. And texts she'd sent either sat unanswered or were answered with ambiguity and never followed up. It had taken some time, but she'd found a new inclusive church and a community tennis club. But those were all fledgling relationships, not people she'd invite for a weekend away.

We should do that, then. Maybe a reunion weekend. Jodi would be in, I bet, and we can ask Sally, too.

Erin had found out early on in their renewed friendship that Meredith was still in touch with Jodi and to a lesser extent, Sally. She'd asked after both but had been reluctant to ask too many questions. While it'd be normal to ask after high school friends, Erin had been worried her interest in Jodi would be too obvious. She simply hadn't been ready to navigate those waters yet. She'd just accepted any scraps of information Meredith happened to mention.

Now, her heart raced at the thought of seeing Jodi. It was stupid. Jodi wouldn't be interested in her anymore, surely. But she did know that Jodi wasn't dating anyone seriously. She'd spoken about it on her podcast. It felt like Erin kind of knew her from those weekly podcasts, but that was a one-way relationship at best, a para-social relationship, which was an embarrassing thing to admit about one of her best childhood friends. If Erin wanted to date a woman, she really needed to find someone new, not someone she'd been involved with in high school and fangirled over now. Still, her heart beat faster at the idea of spending a weekend with her. Would there still be a spark?

She tried to text casual. *That's an idea.*

I'll send a group email. This'll be fun!

Erin wasn't sure fun was the right word, but what she did know was that there was no way she was going to be able to concentrate on the finances of her daughter's fast-pitch team right now. She decided she'd finish in the morning. For now, she'd go find her kid and see if she was ready for their evening.

The rewatch of *A League of their Own* brought up more thoughts of Jodi. Erin was sure it was because Jodi was the only woman she'd ever acted on her feelings of attraction with. But as much as she told herself that she might not even like her anymore, she couldn't help fantasizing about how a reunion might go. Nothing would happen, of course. They were very different people from when they were teenagers. Still, the thought of just being around an out lesbian of her own age was thrilling. And a little scary. But mostly exciting.

What if Jodi said no?

CHAPTER FOUR

A nd it's over." Jodi was taking her usual post-lunch walk around the neighborhood and had taken the opportunity to call Sal.

"What? Already? It just started," Sal said.

"A few weeks ago, to be fair." Jodi hurried across busy Cesar Chavez so she wouldn't get hit.

"Did you call me before you got to the quiet part again?" Sal sounded slightly amused and slightly annoyed.

"Think of it as a compliment. I just can't wait to hear your dulcet tones."

Sal barked out a laugh. "Sure."

"Do you have time to chat, or is work actually busy today?"

"Oh, I've got time."

"You sound annoyed."

"More bored. I have no idea why these…hang on. You talk for a bit. I'm going to go for a walk, too. Tell me about why it's over with Kathy."

Jodi sighed. "It'll just bore you more. It was nothing. That was the problem. No spark."

"Maybe you need to date and see if something can grow rather than needing a spark right away," Sal said.

"Eh. I gave it three weeks. How long is it supposed to take?" Jodi stepped out into a quiet residential street to go around someone who was walking three dogs, all interested in some different scent. Ambitious.

"Sometimes more."

"Oh yeah? And how long until you felt the spark with Brit?"

There was a long enough pause that Jodi started to pull her phone out of her pocket to see if the connection had been lost. Before she actually got it out, Sal said, "Okay, I see your point. But that's not how it works for everyone."

"Whatever. Are you outside yet? Tell me about all your work-related woes."

"The thing is that I have no idea why they even wanted to hire anyone. There's nothing for me to do." They groaned. "I've asked, and my boss just said, 'Yeah, it's not a busy time of the year.' And yet, I have to sit here all day, looking like I'm doing something on the computer. It's crazy. I need something to do with my time aside from endless online crossword puzzles."

"Have you considered reading a book? I could recommend a few," Jodi said innocently.

"First of all, I have to look like I'm working, so I can't just pull a book out and start reading. Second of all, I am aware of your recommendations."

"Aw. I didn't know you listened," Jodi teased.

"Please. I have to do something while I sit here doing nothing."

"Well, you don't have to limit yourself to my podcasts. I can also give personal recommendations, and you know you could listen to audiobooks or read in your browser. But more seriously, maybe it's time for a career change. Your graphic design stuff is really coming along. You too, could work in the glory and splendor of your own home."

Jodi had turned her second bedroom into a recording studio of sorts. She recorded her two book-centric podcasts in there and rounded out her income puzzle by producing some other podcasts. It was an entirely work-from-home situation, which was sometimes great and sometimes a little lonely.

"Eh. I don't know if I'm ready to make the leap."

"I get that, but I think you are. Val and I love our new logo." Sal had created a logo for their podcast, and it was one of Jodi's new favorite things.

Jodi could practically hear them shrug. "Maybe."

After they'd walked and talked for another half an hour, Jodi was nearly done with her loop. "I've gotta get back to work, unlike some people, who apparently don't have any work to do at all," Jodi said.

"Rub it in," Sal grumbled. "Oh, hey, Brit wants to know when you're coming up to Seattle next."

"I dunno, will you guys take me to Pike Market for cinnamon rolls?" Jodi unlocked the condo building's front door and started up the steps.

"It is tradition."

"Then how about this weekend? I'm unexpectedly free." She plucked her water glass off her desk and carried it to the kitchen to fill it.

"Because you dumped Kathy." Sal made it more a comment than question.

"Pretty much." Jodi took a drink.

"Okay, then, Friday?"

Jodi wiped her hand across the side of her chin where she'd dribbled a little. "Yeah, if it's cool, I'll drive up in the morning and work from there in the afternoon to beat the Friday afternoon traffic. Seattle has a lot of nice qualities, but rush hour isn't one of them."

"True story."

They said their good-byes while Jodi topped off her glass and went back to her computer to get to work. When she opened her email, she nearly spat a mouthful of water back out. After regaining control, she called Sal back.

Sal didn't bother with a greeting. "Miss me already? Or you just realized you've got plans this weekend after all?"

"Check your email."

"This sounds serious. What's...oh." Sal had clearly found the email in question. They read quietly for a minute. "Meredith wants to do a reunion weekend?"

"That's what I'm seeing. Holy hell. We can't, right? I mean, that's a whole weekend of being misgendered for you and..." Jodi trailed off, not sure how to put into words how it would be to be around Erin for a weekend. She hadn't seen Erin since after their freshman year of college. There hadn't been a falling out exactly, but their lives had gone in drastically different directions. Erin had seemed to double down on church and her family, whereas Jodi had come home from her first year of college out and proud. Would Erin even come? Jodi had to admit that she was a little curious about what she'd be like these days.

"And what? You're thinking about saying yes, aren't you?"

"Maybe a little. But you wouldn't have to come if you didn't want to. I know it's hard for you to be around people who knew you before college."

Sal was not out to their family and therefore, not to anyone who spent time back home. Their family had never had the pleasure of meeting Brit, who was awesome. They all thought that Sal was single when in actuality, they'd been paired off since their sophomore year of college. Jodi could admit that she was a little jealous that Sal's first love had turned out to be their only love, whereas Jodi had gotten her heart broken a couple of times before she'd learned to guard it.

Anyway, Sal did still go home sometimes. Mostly, they hadn't wanted to cut ties because they'd worried that one of their siblings' many children would find themselves in a nearly untenable situation like Sal had. They wanted to be a lifeline if that was happening, so they made the pilgrimage back home for all family reunions and spent the entire time feeling like their skin was too tight.

"It's not exactly the same with those two as it is with my family. I could maybe come out. Meredith is okay with you, so she'd probably be fine at least about Brit. I just don't really spend time with her. Also, I know that she and my mom go to the same hairdresser, so I've been playing it extra safe. I imagine she'd keep it to herself if I asked her. Although, I don't know how she'll react to the enby thing. Erin…"

"Erin might be ultra-religious," Jodi finished when Sal trailed off. Jodi wondered if that was indeed where Erin had landed. When she'd gotten even more involved in the church in college than she had been growing up, she might have been overcompensating for what had happened between them in high school. She might have mellowed from her ultra-religious stance. "I'm finding the more I think about it, the more curious I am. I think I want to say yes. But I don't want to force you into anything that would be uncomfortable."

"I'm curious, too, I think, but…I'll have to think on if I'm curious enough to actually go. I may just wait for your report."

"That's fair enough. Although, if you did come, we could sneak off and talk shit about the others, which might be fun." Jodi couldn't help cajoling just a little bit.

Sal laughed. "Maybe. I'll think about it."

They said good-bye again, and by the time they did, Jodi had already sent her reply.

I'm in.

CHAPTER FIVE

Jodi threw open her door. "You're here!"

Until Sal knocked on her door, Jodi wasn't sure if they'd actually show. They'd agreed when the other three had, but Jodi felt the ongoing reluctance rolling off them in waves. On the other hand, they'd seemed keen to speculate with Jodi about what it would be like to get the four of them together again.

Sal dropped their bag in the hall and hugged Jodi. "I'm here."

"I'm so glad."

"Well, the jury is out about how I feel about it."

Jodi leaned over to pick up Sal's bag, but Sal glared at her and picked it up themselves. Jodi stepped back so they could enter her condo. She knew Sal wouldn't let her pick up the bag, but she liked to tease and try. Sal had a real this-is-my-job attitude about carrying stuff. Jodi and Brit liked to tease them about it but always deferred because it seemed to mean a lot to them.

Sal set their bag next to Jodi's couch and shrugged out of their backpack. "But I am excited about this evening. I miss Kati more than I can say."

Kati was both Sal and Jodi's favorite Thai place, and luckily for Jodi, it was a twenty-minute walk away from her home. "Oh, sure. You just use me for access to Kati. I understand." Jodi flopped on the couch.

"Like you don't use me for access to the cinnamon rolls at Pike Market, not to mention my pho place."

Jodi waved that away. "Phst. You know I use you so I can be friends with Brit."

"She is the best part of us."

Jodi mock glared. "Listen, don't sell yourself short. Also, sit down. You're making me nervous towering over me like that."

"I've been sitting for the last three hours. Let's walk to Sweet Hereafter for a drink. I could stand to take the edge off my nerves about this weekend."

Jodi popped up. "You got it. Need the bathroom or anything first?"

"Actually, yeah. Be right back."

Jodi flopped down again and pulled out her phone, ostensibly to check messages. When there weren't any, she checked Erin's Facebook. Erin had friended her official account after they'd arranged the reunion weekend, so Jodi had friended her back. It was a little cheating because Jodi did have a personal social media account that she hadn't shared with Erin. So Jodi got to see Erin's personal account, whereas Erin only saw Jodi's podcast account. It was a little stalker-y. There was a new post. It was a picture of Erin's teenage daughter making a catch at first base, along with a statement about how proud of her Erin was.

Jodi had discovered through this stalking that Erin was recently divorced and had gone back to her maiden name, Hess. She had three kids, one of whom was still living at home. The divorce had been a surprise. Jodi figured that mostly churchy, rule abiding Erin would stay married for life, happily or not. It had made Jodi even more curious about what she would be like now.

Sal came back, and they walked the six or so blocks to Sweet Hereafter, chatting about the drive down, Jodi's workday, Brit's upcoming performance that Jodi would be coming to Seattle to see. Brit was a choreographer and director with an aerial arts studio, and Jodi always enjoyed her shows from when she'd premiered as a performer so many years ago to now when it was mostly others performing her ideas.

"If you were to get into graphic design and start your own business, you could work whenever you wanted, and your schedule would line up better with Brit's," Jodi pointed out.

Sal said, "I actually have news on that front."

"Oh? Do tell." Jodi leaned in.

"I created a website and some social media accounts and all that jazz. I didn't think much would come of it, but I already have a client."

"Amazing. What's the job?"

"Creating a book cover for a self-published book. I've been offering services at a huge discount because I'm unknown, so I guess this person thought, why not? I figure if I let it grow organically, maybe I'll get to the point where I can do it full-time."

"That's awesome, Sal." Jodi gave them a one-armed hug.

Sal looked both pleased and embarrassed about being pleased. After Jodi removed her arm, she lifted one shoulder in a half shrug. "It's a start."

Once they'd ordered their drinks and were sitting out on the back deck of Sweet Hereafter, Sal said, "So we pick them up at noon tomorrow, right?"

Jodi nodded. "Meredith's flight is supposed to get in at eleven fifteen and Erin's at eleven fifty-five. No checked bags, so…"

"So." Sal nodded slowly for a while.

"Okay, what's the most anxiety producing thing about this weekend?" Jodi asked. They'd discussed this before, but contrary to how Sal had been through most of high school, they were both talkers. Once Sal and Jodi had come out to each other the summer after their first year of college, Sal had shown an unexpected tendency to talk everything out. Jodi had been pleasantly surprised. They'd been offering friend therapy to each other ever since. In fact, Jodi had been the first person Sal had asked to use they-them pronouns ten years ago.

"I'm worried that if I come out to them, they'll say hurtful things. And if I don't come out to them, I'll be uncomfortable all weekend. I'm also a little worried that one or the other of them will be malicious or careless enough that word will get back to my family."

Jodi took a drink of the eponymously named drink, the Hereafter, a mix of vodka, bourbon, lemon, and iced tea. "Okay, let's start with that last bit first. Of course, people change, but they were both good at keeping secrets in high school. Or at least keeping them outside of the four of us. I'd be surprised if they changed so much that they'd blab anything you didn't want them to."

Sal sighed and took a drink of their choice, the house mule. Considering how quickly Sal had thrown off the shackles of her upbringing when they'd found Brit, it had been a little surprising to see how long it took them to try drinking. Jodi would have thought that would have been an easier thing to do, but it had only been in the last dozen or so years that Sally had taken up occasional drinking. They still liked drinks on the sweeter side, like the house mule, which had simple syrup in it.

"It's just real close to home, you know?"

Jodi nodded, acknowledging the point. "Which would feel better to you? Keeping quiet and allowing them to believe you're still the high school you and staying safe in terms of your family or telling them so they can know the real you and address you properly?"

"I want to be me, but it's no small thing to come out to someone with Erin's religious background." Sal set their glass down heavily. "I have religious trauma, dammit."

They said it in a kind of joking tone, but Jodi knew that it wasn't really a joke. Sal had been brought up Mormon. They'd suppressed so much about themselves growing up that they'd barely even talked to Jodi, Erin, and Meredith. Erin wasn't Mormon, but her church had also been mired in deep homophobia.

Jodi wanted to tell her that Erin might not be as bigoted as her upbringing might indicate, but that would mean explaining how she knew. To this day, Jodi had never spilled the secret of the short-lived relationship she and Erin had shared at the end of their senior year of high school. They'd loved each other. At least, Jodi had loved Erin without a doubt. It had been her feelings that had made her realize she was a lesbian. Jodi was also pretty sure that Erin had loved her back, but it had been too hard for Erin to overcome her religious upbringing and to do something she knew was against everything her family wanted for her. Erin had ended it over the summer before

Jodi went away for college. Erin had stayed at home and gone to the local college.

Since Jodi couldn't say any of that without betraying Erin's trust, she just said, "I know. You can still skip out if it's all too much."

Sal sighed. "If I can go back home by myself with no support, I can get through this weekend with you there. I am curious what it'll be like. And who knows? Maybe Erin will surprise us. She did with the divorce."

"True story."

Sal took another deep breath. "Okay, then there's Meredith. While I know she's always been fine with you, and she's not at all religious, I'm also pretty sure she voted for Trump."

"Right? Like, what the fuck is that about?"

"Indeed. She could start talking about, I don't know, stollen elections and shit, and then what?"

"Well, it'd be interesting to see Erin's reaction to that. Maybe it'll end up being a tale of two weekends where you and I just stop talking to them and vice versa."

"I swing wildly back and forth between curious and wondering why the heck we're doing this."

"Seeing if it makes sense to still be friends? Maybe we're judging them too harshly, and they'll be cool? We were all pretty tight in high school."

"Well, to be fair, I was kind of on the outside of all that tightness, but I take your point."

Aside from Sal being the least talkative amongst the four of them, they'd also just hung out less with the other three. They'd had more family obligations but also had spent a lot of time by themselves. As they told Jodi later, they'd always known something was different about them. At least when they'd been alone, they didn't have to pretend. They liked having a group to be a part of but had never felt like they could open up. Meanwhile, the other three had practically lived in each other's back pockets, although who was close to whom had shifted at various times.

"Well, it'll be interesting," Jodi finally said.

They both took sips of their drinks.

❖

Erin exited the plane with a mixture of nerves, excitement, and a desperate need to pee lending a swiftness to her steps. She'd had a window seat next to mom with a toddler. The toddler had cried for the first half hour of the flight—which Erin was sympathetic about, having traveled with her own children over the years—and then had conked out for the remainder. Erin had needed to go for the last two hours but hadn't wanted to disrupt the sleeping boy.

After finding a bathroom, she fished out her phone to see if Darcy had replied to the text she had sent saying she'd landed. Sure enough, Darcy had sent a celebratory emoji, said she was fine at Flo's, and to "have a good time with your little friends." Erin chuckled at the role reversal joke. It was Thursday, and the team was off to a tournament the next day, which meant that Darcy was only at Flo's for one night.

That taken care of, Erin made for the exit, hoping she'd see Meredith before finding the others just because Meredith was a more familiar touchstone right now. To her relief, Meredith was waiting right there for her.

"Hi," Erin called, giving an enthusiastic wave.

"Oh my gosh, hi! It's so good to see you," Meredith said, opening her arms for a hug.

Erin towered over Meredith as she always had. She was by far the tallest of the four, the rest of them were all just a few inches over five feet. "You too." They made their way outside, and Erin asked, "Do you know what kind of car we're looking for?"

"I'm pretty sure Jodi drives a Subaru." She shot Erin a knowing look, but Erin had no idea why. She laughed anyway, pretending.

Before they got any farther, a silver Subaru stopped at the curb right in front of them, and Jodi and Sally spilled out, grinning.

Erin's breath caught at her first sight of Jodi in over thirty years. She looked so much like the high school girl that Erin remembered but seemed more comfortable and somehow more alluring. She wore glasses now. That was new, and it was hot. She wore her hair in a pixie cut now instead of the ubiquitous ponytail she'd sported in high school and looked good with dangly earrings highlighting her exposed neck. There were soft lines around her eyes and mouth, mostly laugh lines. She wore a pair of shorts that Erin was pretty sure she recognized as Title Nine, a catalogue that came in the mail regularly. Erin had never ordered from them, but she did like looking through the catalogue with all the women doing active things.

Jodi went to the back to open the hatch and then come around, still grinning, to hug Meredith. Erin finally broke her gaze free to see Sally looking at her speculatively. She blushed and held out her arms in the offer of a hug. Sally had been the least touchy of the four, but it would be weird to hug Jodi without hugging Sally, too, right? And Erin did want to hug Jodi.

Sally surprised her a little by taking her up on the offer, although it was a loose hug. Sally was wearing cargo shorts and a baggy T-shirt. She was just as thin as she'd been in high school, but she didn't have the hunch she used to have. She held herself straighter, and Erin was surprised to realize that she was actually a fair bit taller than Jodi or Meredith. Erin had always lumped the other three together as short.

Jodi took Meredith's bag and tossed it in the back before offering Erin a hug. Erin wanted to pull her close and feel the changes she'd seen, but she restrained herself. She returned a hug that was not quite as loose as the Sally one and maybe lasted a beat longer but was still a perfectly normal friend hug. Sally put Erin's bag in the back, too.

With a little awkward shuffling, they all ended up in the car, Erin behind Sally on the passenger side, and Meredith behind Jodi on the driver's side. Jodi pulled away from the curb. Erin felt like they were just starting a roller coaster ride like they had at the amusement park in Denver every summer just before school started. The excitement was high, voices tumbling over one another in greetings, inquiries about flights and plans, but there were also nerves. Erin was feeling them for sure. Jodi and Sally were showing signs, too. If anyone was immune from the nerves, it was Meredith sitting next to her and looking for all the world simply excited to see her friends and at the idea of a few days on the coast. Erin envied her a little.

CHAPTER SIX

A re you guys hungry? We can get lunch in Portland before the drive. Sal and I shopped this morning, so we have some basic groceries if we just want to have lunch at the house. If we want to eat out, there aren't any good restaurants after we leave Portland until we get to Cannon Beach. Unless you're in the mood for fast food?" Jodi craned her neck to look at her passengers in her rearview mirror as she spoke.

When her gaze fell on Erin, she didn't want to look away. She'd have recognized her anywhere. She wasn't too surprised to see that Erin wore her hair in the same style as she had in high school— high bangs and wings giving way to long flowing hair—because she'd seen pictures on Facebook. Jodi would have scoffed about the throwback style, but it suited Erin. It had been nearly black back then, and while that was still the predominate color, it was also streaked with silver. That part was nothing but an improvement. Silver hair was dead sexy.

Jodi mentally shook herself and paid attention to the road and the cars around them. Meredith and Erin had both snacked on their flights, and Jodi and Sal had eaten a rather late breakfast, so they decided to wait until they got to Cannon Beach.

They talked the whole drive. Sal was much quieter than Jodi was used to. It was a little jarring, but Jodi didn't push them. They needed space to make their own choices about how they wanted to engage with the weekend.

When they got close, Jodi suggested that Sal pick a place to eat. "I think I remember a pub that has an eclectic selection. Somewhere on the north side of town."

Sal found it on her phone without difficulty and guided Jodi there. They got out of the car stretching and complaining about stiffening up and old bones. Inside, the hostess showed them to a half booth. Jodi held back, not sure if it would be easier to share the bench seat with Erin—where there would be nothing between them—or sit across from her where she'd have to try her best not to be a creeper and stare. The decision was made for her when Meredith slid in next to Erin on the bench, leaving Sal and Jodi to the chairs on the other side. Jodi selected the seat across from Meredith. That would make easiest to keep from staring.

After they ordered, Erin looked between Sal and Jodi. "Are you both vegetarian?"

Erin had ordered the salmon while Meredith had gone with the fish and chips. Jodi had decided on the margherita flatbread after considering just going with an appetizer and dessert, while Sal got the cauliflower steak.

Jodi nodded while Sal mumbled, "Most of the time."

Sal was mostly vegan, thanks in large part to Brit's influence. The exception was when they went home, where they ate whatever was served and where they hid so much of themselves.

"Seems a waste not to eat fresh fish at the coast, but you do you," Meredith said.

Her tone was good-natured, but Jodi felt prickly about it anyway. If Meredith was judging eating habits, what else was she going to judge? Would Sal feel comfortable expressing their true self if Meredith insisted on making snide comments about things like food? Jodi glanced at Sal, wondering how they took it. Maybe she was being unnecessarily sensitive. Sal was sitting very still, looking at the table in front of them.

Jodi decided to push back gently. "It's only a waste if you have any interest in fish. And some of us never have, as you well know, Meredith." She grinned.

Meredith's eyes sparkled with amusement. "I remember when my parents took us to Long John Silver's, and you ordered chicken."

"I mean, what should I have ordered? What I remember is we couldn't figure out which meal was the chicken when we got them to your house. To this day, who knows if we ate chicken or fish? And what does that say about Long John Silver's?"

Everyone laughed and went on to other reminiscing. It was like they were thrown back into their old high school dynamics: Meredith, Erin, and Jodi practically talking over each other, Sal observing rather than participating. It was so different from how they were now that it was jarring. Jodi wanted to pull them into the conversation like she would have done if they'd been having dinner with some of Jodi's Portland friends. And there, that would have worked. Here, Jodi felt like they were making a choice to hide and wouldn't appreciate being drawn out. She felt horrible all over again that she'd encouraged them to come.

There was a pause when the server brought the food, and they all took their first few bites. Erin said, "How's the cauliflower steak? I've wondered if they'd be any good."

She sounded genuinely curious, and Sal responded in kind. "You can try a bite if you like. It's not bad, but it's just cauliflower. If you like that, you'll probably be okay with the steak. If not, well…"

Erin laughed. "I'm okay with cauliflower, but it sounds like it's not something I'd choose as my main dish."

"Very much the same," Meredith agreed.

"I know that Meredith is a fancy finance person with an MBA, Jodi is a famous podcaster, but I don't think I know what you're doing these days, Sally," Erin said.

Sal looked like a block of granite again. But they didn't protest, and Jodi didn't want to out them. This was exactly the sort of situation she'd known would be difficult. Despite that, she couldn't help snorting at the famous podcaster bit. Her podcasts were medium at best. It wasn't like she was the host of an NPR podcast.

Erin smiled at her snort. Her smile hadn't changed. Jodi's traitorous heart gave a little leap. She was transported back in time to when Erin's smiles were special ones meant just for her.

"I've recently started a new job, actually, but it's mostly boring office stuff," Sal said, their tone even.

"I think we all do boring office stuff, aside from Jodi," Erin replied.

"Speak for yourself," Meredith said. "I love my spreadsheets."

Erin smiled again. "I actually enjoy doing the books for small businesses myself." She addressed Sal, "Do you like your new job?"

"I'm still figuring out my place," Sal said diplomatically.

Jodi wanted to step in and talk Sal up but also didn't want to put words in their mouth. She settled on, "Sal is also starting up a graphics company. It's good design. One of my podcast logos was Sal's work. So if you know anyone who needs graphics done…"

Sal gave Jodi a small smile but waved it off. "I wouldn't call it a company. It's more of a hobby than anything."

"That's cool." Erin waited a beat, maybe to see if Sal had anything more to say about it, before turning to Jodi. "You seem like you like your job."

What did that mean? Had Erin listened to one of her podcasts?

When Jodi didn't answer right away, Erin continued, "You sound like you're enjoying yourself."

"You've listened to her podcasts?" Meredith said. "Who has time?"

Jodi felt pleased that Erin was interested in her enough to listen to a little bit. She also felt slightly annoyed that Meredith was so dismissive of her work. Podcasts weren't for everyone, certainly, but that was a broad statement. Before she could decide how to respond, Sal spoke up. "Lots of people. I, for one, love both of Jodi's and listen to several that she produces, too."

"I mean, if that's not going above and beyond as a friend, I don't know what is," Jodi said, grinning.

"You produce, too? What's involved in that?" Erin asked, and they were off on that topic for a while.

After lunch, they got checked in at their rental and dropped off their things. It was a cozy little unit amongst several. The front door opened into an open floor plan kitchen and living room combination. On the other side of the living room, there was a door that led to outdoor seating that, past a stretch of hardy-looking grass, sort of overlooked the ocean. There were two bedrooms, so they'd be doubling up.

"We'll take this one, if it's okay," Meredith said, claiming the room to the right of the living room and clearly including Erin in the "we."

"Sure." Jodi went into the other room to check it out. Sal followed. Softly, so as not to be overheard by the others, Jodi teased, "I'm not going to get in trouble with Brit for sharing a bed with you, am I?"

"Not so long as you keep to your own side, bed hog. If I go home tired from being forced to sleep on a sliver of mattress, you may find yourself on her bad side. You don't want to be on her bad side."

Jodi held her hands up in surrender. "I'm well aware. Remember when I visited you in college on that family weekend, and we got so into playing foosball that you forgot to meet her for dinner with her parents?" Jodi shuddered. "I thought I was never going to get to hang out with you again."

Sal laughed. "Well, yeah. At least it wasn't the first time I was supposed to meet them. They already liked me at that point."

They each claimed a spot for their luggage, then Sal went out to grab the groceries. Jodi poked around the kitchen, seeing what was there. She was opening the fridge when Erin said from surprisingly close, "Is that a bottle of wine? Think it's any good?"

Jodi chided herself for the traitorous swoop in her stomach. Single or not, Erin was not available. She had made her intentions to only date men clear back when they'd broken up in high school. "Seems unlikely, but we should try it anyway, don't you think?" Jodi didn't really know what to look for in wine. She wasn't a big wine drinker, but it seemed the thing to say.

Meredith joined them. "Try what?"

She held the bottle up. "This wine."

"All right, break out the glasses." Meredith started looking through cupboards. Sal came in carrying two bags, and Meredith said, "I imagine you don't want wine?"

Sal set the bags on the small counter. "Actually, I do drink some alcohol these days."

Meredith looked surprised but pulled down four glasses. Jodi opted to join in on the wine this time. It felt like the group thing to do. She pulled the corkscrew she'd seen in a drawer out and started opening the bottle while Sal and Erin each unloaded a bag.

"We should take these outside," Erin suggested as she accepted her glass.

Once they were settled looking out over mostly grass, Meredith lifted her glass. "A toast, to the four of us and how far we've come."

That was a toast Jodi could drink to, even if not everyone knew how far some of them had come. She was so proud of Sal. She was also sad that they were in a position where they felt they had to hide who they were. But it was good to see her old friends. Erin was... interesting to get reacquainted with. She just wished it was easier for Sal.

CHAPTER SEVEN

Erin felt like she was tingling all day from Jodi's proximity. It was exciting but also a little tiring. At meals, Meredith had assumed a natural pairing of Erin and Meredith on one side and Jodi and Sally on the other, which had made things easier. Erin couldn't imagine how much worse the tension she already felt being around Jodi would have been if she had to share a bed with her.

After dinner, Meredith mentioned the hot tub they had access to and jokingly suggested they recreate Jodi's seventeenth birthday party. Erin shot a reflexive look at Jodi at the suggestion, but she was looking resolutely out over the ocean. That birthday party had been the first night they'd kissed. It had started as a demonstration to one another of their ideal kisses with boys. They'd all practiced with one another except Sally, who'd kept her distance. After Sally and Meredith had gone inside, Jodi and Erin had practiced one more time but without a hand between their lips. It had taken Erin several sessions before she was able to acknowledge that it wasn't just practice anymore. They had started a several-month clandestine relationship.

Erin had called it off in the end. She was too scared about going to hell, too scared about her parents disowning her or sending her to a conversion camp and too sure it wouldn't work out anyway because Jodi was going away for college in the fall. Erin would be living at home while she went to school locally.

They all agreed to go hot tubbing and walked out with towels or robes over swimsuits. Erin couldn't stop shooting glances at Jodi.

She really hoped no one noticed. She was dying at the idea of Jodi dropping her towel. Her mind was painting all sorts of pictures of what sort of suit she might be wearing.

No one else from the complex was in the tub when they arrived. They set their plastic cups around the edges and then, in a flurry, everyone was disrobing and getting in. Erin only managed to get a brief look at Jodi's tankini before she was submerged.

She couldn't help but hope that Jodi had at least looked in her direction. Even as a mother of three who lived in St. Louis, Erin hoped that she'd retained at least enough appeal that Jodi would sneak a look, but if so, she hadn't caught it.

Erin eased her back against a jet, sighing at how nice it felt. Everything was different from that time thirty-six years ago. It was early fall now, not the middle of winter. They were in Oregon, not Colorado. They'd all changed a great deal. They'd lost the ease with one another they'd once had. Even before Erin and Jodi had had their fling, they'd all—aside from Sally—been very physically affectionate. Now, the only time they'd touched since Erin had arrived was for hugs and squeezing in for a picture this afternoon. In the past, they'd moved with the ease of youth; now, they were all gingerly settling themselves. Then, it had been cans of soda around the hot tub. Now it was wine or some mixed drink Jodi had whipped up and offered after their first glasses.

But here they were again, practically recreating the scene of her and Jodi's first kiss. There wouldn't be a repeat tonight. They weren't teenagers who could casually suggest that they try out kissing techniques.

"So who wants to practice kissing first?" Meredith said, jolting Erin out of her musings.

They all laughed, but Erin felt like it was a little forced, aside from Meredith's.

"Speaking of, who is everyone kissing these days?" Meredith asked.

Erin darted a glance at Jodi, who was darting a glance at Sally. Were they…no. No way. Sally was buttoned up and had been raised in a strict Mormon family. There was no way.

Jodi spoke to the whole group when she said, "No one currently." She laughed. "My last girlfriend only lasted three weeks, and that was a few months ago. How are things with Tom?"

"Good," Meredith said. "Although, I have to admit that I've never liked his style of kissing."

"Seriously? Even after ten years?" Jodi asked. "Seems like that should have been corrected by now."

Meredith waved it off. "He has other things going for him. Like serious lasting power."

Everyone laughed again.

"What about you, Sally?" Meredith asked. "Anyone special?"

Sally started to shake her head, then squared her shoulders. "Actually, yes. I've been with the same person for over thirty years."

Erin was shocked. Sure, she'd been out of touch with all of them for a little *over* thirty years, but she'd have expected to have heard about such a long-term relationship before now. What she noticed most was the proud look Jodi gave Sally.

But Jodi had just said that she wasn't in a relationship with anyone. Or was that a cover? Erin's insides turned cold with jealousy at the thought that Sally had gotten the part of Jodi that Erin had always wanted but hadn't let herself acknowledge until recently.

"What?" Meredith's mouth was gaping. "Who? Are you secretly married?"

Sally nodded. "I am, actually, at least as far as anyone in Colorado or my family is concerned, and I'd appreciate it if none of you told them."

"But why?" Meredith asked. "Is he not Mormon or something? Wait. Do you have secret kids?"

Sally laughed a little. "No. No secret kids. She is also not Mormon. Neither am I, not anymore."

The only sound was the bubbling jets. Jodi put her arm around Sally, which made Erin's gut clench, and said, "Thanks for trusting us all with this."

Sally, not only allowing the contact but seemingly comfortable with it, said, "You're welcome, but I should say that Jodi has known all along."

Erin tried not to wilt as she anticipated the next words. It would probably be, "Because the person I'm married to is Jodi." She almost missed it when Jodi said, "And Brit is great. They're very cute together."

Erin sagged in relief.

"Well. That is news. I wish you and Brit all the happiness." Meredith sounded a little falsely cheerful.

Erin realized she should be replying. "I'm so happy for you." She was utterly sincere and hoped she sounded it.

"And how about you, Erin?" Jodi asked.

She started. What was the question in reference to? She had to think about it before she realized Jodi was throwing things back to the question of who everyone was kissing these days. It had seemed like a natural time for the conversation to move on, so for Jodi to bring it up, did that mean she was invested in the answer? Erin looked directly at her and said, "No one. Not since the divorce. Well, really for quite a while before that, to be honest."

Jodi looked a little flushed, probably from the heat of the hot tub. With her fair skin, she had always had a tendency to go a little red from heat, too much sun, embarrassment, or as Erin remembered a little too well, passion. It was weird to both know someone so intimately and also not really know them at all. Jodi and Erin had both had too many experiences to be the same people they'd been in high school.

"And that is a shame," Meredith said. "Any prospects?"

It took Erin a moment to figure out what Meredith was talking about. She'd gotten rather wrapped up in thoughts of Jodi. Again. "Oh, um, not really. I'm mostly trying to just be a good mom for Darcy these days."

"Only for Darcy?" Meredith asked wryly. "What about the other two?"

Erin waved a hand. "They hardly need me anymore. Brad just started his senior year of college and was only home for a week over the summer. Lindsey is grown, married, and living in Denver." That wasn't completely true. Lindsey did seem to need her more now that she was an adult. She'd been the sort of child to spend a lot of time in her room and not the sort to confide in her mom. Now, they spoke every Sunday evening and texted regularly.

"Denver? Really? What drew her there?" Sally asked.

Erin took a moment to marvel that it was Sally asking. Maybe now that she'd shared her secret, she was opening up in other ways, too. "Her husband's job. Well, hers, too, I guess, but he was the one who got his job first. It doesn't hurt that Grandma and Grandpa are right down the freeway."

"And what does she do?" Jodi asked.

That led to Erin getting to brag about her kids for a while, which was always fun.

After the hot tub, everyone was relaxed and sleepy, so they all headed to bed. As Erin slid under the covers, her thoughts were drawn to Jodi, who was lying in bed in the other room. She wished she was brave enough to get her alone and tell her what she'd realized about herself.

Meredith slid into bed next to her a few minutes later. "Kind of wild that two of the four of us turned out gay, right?"

"Um."

"Are you freaked out? I'd get it if you were."

"I'm not freaked out." Erin was very freaked out, but it was more to do with her attraction to Jodi and the fact that she was also gay. She wasn't completely sure if she was a lesbian or a bisexual. She hadn't minded sex with Grant, particularly in the beginning. It was fine. Intimacy with Jodi had been so much more than fine, though. Was that because it was Jodi, or because Jodi was a woman? Erin didn't know. Those were the only two people she'd ever made love to. So, yeah, she wasn't freaked out about Sally also being gay. That was fine. She was freaked out about herself and if she should come out.

"Did you know that Peter is gay, too? I had such a crush on him in high school. Man, just everyone turned out gay. Was it something in the water?"

Erin started laughing. She knew there was a little bit of a hysterical edge to it, but she couldn't help it. She didn't know that Meredith's high school crush was gay. It did seem that the LGBTQ world was closing in around them.

Meredith started laughing, too, but she also said, "It wasn't that funny. Are you okay?"

Erin waved, still unable to stop laughing. Finally, she said. "I think I'm just really tired. I didn't get a lot of sleep last night, and it's been a long day. Plus, it's about two a.m. at home."

"Yeah, it's about one for me, and we're getting too old to stay up this late. Well, good night, then."

"Good night."

Meredith drifted off almost right away, and it was only moments before the room was filled with the sound of snoring. It was alarmingly loud. Why hadn't she mentioned she was a snorer? Between that and her thoughts of Jodi, Erin didn't get a lot of sleep.

Chapter Eight

When Jodi woke up, she was alone in the bed. She wondered if Sal had gotten up and gone for a run. They were into stuff like that. Jodi enjoyed walking, even a good long way, but she was not a runner.

Her next thought was about Erin. It had been a little discouraging to see her slump in disappointment about Sal having a wife. Jodi had hoped that even if she didn't acknowledge her attraction to women, she'd at least be an ally. That led her to think about Meredith and what seemed to be forced cheerfulness in her reaction. At least no one had jumped from the hot tub in revulsion. It could have been worse.

What was worse was that Jodi was still drawn to Erin. She wished she wasn't. It would have been easier, but she seemingly had no control over it. When Erin had looked right at her while answering the question about who she was kissing? Well, Jodi had felt that. Thinking about those expressive brown eyes locking on hers had her squirming in bed a little.

Annoyed with herself, she threw off her covers and went into the bathroom to get ready for the day.

There was no one in the main room, but she could see the back of Erin's head on the porch. She poured herself some coffee, doctored it up, and carried it outside to join her.

Erin looked up at the sound of the sliding glass door. She looked tired, but she smiled, causing Jodi's stomach to swoop. "Good morning."

Oh God. Her morning voice was a little rougher than it had been in high school, but that only made it sexier. Jodi tried to smile back, but her natural reaction to that sexiness was a desire to bite her lip, so the smile probably got a little lost in translation. "Good morning. How did you sleep?"

Erin groaned and dropped her head back. "Very poorly. Meredith has developed a loud snore."

The groan and thrown back head had Jodi feeling a little weak in the knees, and she sat in the chair next to Erin, looking out toward the ocean so she could hide her expression a little. "Oh no. I'm sorry. Brr. It's chilly out here."

"Here. Have some blanket. I found it in one of the closets, and it's clearly meant for a bed, not a chair. There's lots." Erin threw part of the blanket that was covering her lap over Jodi's. She warmed up immediately, both from the blanket and the intimacy of sharing, even though there were the arms of the chairs between them. "And it's not your fault."

"No, but I feel like we're all partially responsible for everyone's comfort and sleeping situation since we're all in this together."

Sal came around the corner of the building decked out in their running gear, confirming Jodi's guess about where they'd gone off to. "This looks cozy. Also, if we're all in this together, I'd like to mention that somebody was a bed hog last night."

Jodi cocked her head. "Certainly not me. I've never been accused of such a thing."

Everyone else snorted. Jodi was surprised that Erin would admit to that sort of knowledge for a split second, but she realized that they'd all had the opportunity to share a bed with one another in high school on sleepovers everyone knew about, not just the clandestine sleepovers she and Erin had. Sal had always taken the floor back then.

It wasn't until Sal and Jodi had come out to each other after their freshman year of college that Sal had explained why they'd kept to themselves so much. "You guys all always seemed so comfortable with each other, and I just felt like if I let my guard down, everyone would know I wasn't like the other girls."

"Did you have a rough night, too?" Sal said to Erin.

"Yes. Meredith snores."

Meredith came through the door from the cottage and grimaced. "Yeah, sorry. Tom has told me it's gotten pretty bad some nights."

"Not to pile on, but he's not wrong. It varied between loud and louder."

"Maybe we consider a shift in sleeping arrangements," Meredith said. "I'd say I could sleep on the couch, but I think I'd keep everyone up with only one door between me and you guys. Erin is much too long to fit on the couch." She winced. "Sorry, Erin. I'm not sure what to do."

"I'd take the couch," Sal said. "Brit has been known to snore, so it probably won't bother me, at least with the closed door to dampen things. But that leaves Erin with the bed hog."

Jodi went still at that idea, but she didn't need to worry about it. Erin would never agree.

"That might work. I've had to bunk with Darcy on tournament weekends, and she's quite the bed hog, so I'm used to that. I've found the best solution is to just move to the other side as needed."

Jodi was surprised that Erin would be willing, considering how she seemed to feel about queer people. Something of her surprise must have shown because Erin faltered as she added, "If that's okay with you."

"Oh, um, sure, that works." Jodi would get no sleep, but how could she say that? How could she explain that all she would be able to think about was Erin lying in bed next to her? She couldn't. Not with how Erin clearly felt about gay people.

"Great," Meredith, who now had a bed to herself, which probably counted for at least half of her cheerfulness, exclaimed. "Now, how about we go out for some breakfast?"

Everyone agreed to the plan, but Sal said they needed to shower first, and Meredith, who was still in her sleepwear, went in to change and get a cup of coffee while she waited.

"Is that okay?" Erin asked softly once they'd gone.

"Going to breakfast?" Jodi asked, deliberately misunderstanding to give herself time to think about how to respond. "Sure. I like breakfast."

"I mean, sharing a room."

Jodi thought it wasn't the room so much as the bed, but she could see why Erin would couch it in those terms. It gave a little distance to the situation. "Yeah, it's okay. If it's okay with you."

"I suggested it. Why wouldn't it be okay with me?"

Jodi's mouth got ahead of her brain. "Because you were disappointed or something when Sal said they had a wife." She kicked herself for outing Sal more than they'd already outed themselves. She hoped Erin didn't notice.

"Oh." Erin went quiet for a minute, then she softly continued. "I wasn't disappointed or anything like that. I was relieved."

Jodi faced her. "What? Why?"

"Because I'd been worried she was married to you."

Jodi was still gaping when Meredith came back through the sliding glass door, dressed for the day and mug in hand.

❖

Jodi found herself looking at Erin even more often during breakfast than she had the day before. Sitting at the table, all she wanted was to get Erin alone and get to the bottom of what she'd meant by being worried she and Sal were married. What kind of sense did that make? But it was not a conversation for the whole group. Not by a long shot. So Jodi just kept sneaking looks. She often found Erin sneaking looks back. On these occasions, their eyes would lock briefly, and Jodi felt those looks to her core. How was she possibly going to sleep next to Erin?

The conversation over breakfast started with talking about what kinds of food they each ate now compared to high school, then went on to talk about school lunches compared to what they each liked to do for lunch these days. Jodi didn't know about the others, but she was feeling like food was a safe topic of conversation and did her part to keep things on that level.

After breakfast, as they strolled back to their rental along the waterfront, Jodi suggested that they go to Ecola State Park to see the lovely beach and maybe even play in the waves a little.

"Is it warm enough to go in the water?" Meredith asked.

Sal shuddered. "It is not. The Pacific is freezing. Most sane people don't put more than their feet in." They gave Jodi a pointed look.

"That's what wet suits are for," Jodi said.

"You brought a wet suit?" Erin asked, looking like she was trying to figure out where Jodi would have hidden one.

"No, actually. I figured this wasn't the trip for it, but I do have one."

"Do you surf?" Erin asked.

"I tried it, and I like it, but it's challenging, and I don't get to the coast often enough to work that hard, so, no. I bodyboard. It's easy and fun."

Sal shuddered again. "But freezing. She took me out with her once. Never again."

"Yeah, I'm out on going in the water, either," Meredith said.

Erin said, "I'd be interested in trying. That's where you just lie down on the board, right? Brad and Darcy did it in Hawaii when we went on vacation, and I wanted to try but felt, I don't know, too old or something."

"Yeah?" Jodi said. "If you're serious, we could rent some gear and try it out."

"Yes, I think I am." Erin smiled.

Jodi was impressed that Erin wanted to try it, especially given all the protesting Sal was doing. She was also pleased. She wanted to spend more time alone with her, to hear more about why she'd been relieved Jodi wasn't married to Sal. And because she'd been enjoying her company generally. It was a dangerous road to go down, getting attached to Erin again, but she couldn't seem to help herself.

Meredith said, "I saw some sand chairs back at the cottage. Sally, you and I can do the smart thing and watch these two fools from the safety of the sand."

Sal nodded. "That sounds like a plan to me."

"You'll miss out on all the fun," Jodi teased, "but I guess that's your choice."

Erin looped her arm through Jodi's. "It's just us brave ones, then."

Jodi was very surprised to find Erin's arm in hers. Sure, it was just elbow to elbow, but no one had been very touchy-feely with each other until then. Jodi felt super aware of her. Given their height difference, Jodi's hand nestled in the crook of Erin's elbow. She marshaled her thoughts enough to make a plan. "Okay, well, I saw a rental place just up the street. Do you guys want to stop in with us, or shall we meet you back home?"

The latter was addressed to Meredith and Sal, who looked at each other.

"Home?" Sal asked. "I think I'll give Brit a quick call."

Meredith shrugged. "Sure. I can call Tom, too."

When they got to the surf shop, they walked on, waving good-bye while Jodi and Erin went in. It didn't take long to rent wet suits and boards, and soon, they were on their way, gear under their arms.

Jodi couldn't hold it in any longer. "What did you mean that you were relieved that Sal and I weren't married? How could you even think we were?"

Erin's step faltered. "Um, maybe we should sit for a minute?"

There were benches here and there along the beach side of the street, so they sat, looking out over the water. Jodi waited for Erin to speak. It was hard not to anticipate what she might say. The only thing that made sense was that Erin was jealous of the idea of her and Sal together. Why else would she be relieved?

The idea sent a jolt of pleasure through her. She wanted Erin to want her. Being in her presence snapped her right back into that teenage desire for Erin to think she was special. But what if she was wrong? What if Erin found her repulsive? Jodi told herself that was ridiculous, but her mind was filling in the gaps and swinging wildly back and forth.

Finally, still facing the waves, Erin said, "I've realized a lot of things in the last fourteen months or so."

Jodi waited again. When Erin still didn't speak, she wondered if she was waiting for some encouragement. "What kind of things?"

"This is going to seem like a non sequitur, I'm sure, but have you watched *A League of Their Own*?"

Jodi snorted and Erin shot her a vulnerable look. "I'm sorry. I didn't mean to laugh at you. It's just that, yeah, of course. I'm not sure there are any self-respecting sapphics who have not. I take it you've seen it?"

Erin smiled a little. "I have. It was my daughter, Darcy, who wanted to watch it at the end of last summer. I really identified with Carson."

"Oh." Realization sunk in. "Oh. Like, Carson's marriage?" Jodi was invested now. Did this mean that Erin was still, or rather *now*, identifying as women-loving?

Erin nodded. "Exactly like that. In the course of a few days, I went from being fine enough in what was a marriage of convenience to moving out. Of course, it turned out that Grant wasn't interested in staying, or I'm sure it wouldn't have been so quick." She paused and looked at the water for a moment before adding, "He'd had a girlfriend for quite a while, turns out."

Jodi put her hand over Erin's on the bench. "Erin, I'm sorry. That sucks."

Erin froze, and Jodi started to pull her hand back, but Erin turned hers over and grasped Jodi's. Erin met her eyes again, and Jodi thought her heart would burst. She'd had one other serious girlfriend…

No, calling Erin a serious girlfriend was not even really accurate. They'd been together only four months in high school. But Erin was absolutely Jodi's first love and only one of two women she'd ever been in love with.

So, okay, for Jodi, it had been serious. And she'd had one other serious girlfriend in college. She'd dated plenty without any of the relationships turning into love. It was like something in her had been waiting on Erin to hold her hand and smile at her like that. That was trouble. Jodi was going to get her heart broken again. She considered pulling her hand free but didn't want it to seem like she was taking her support away.

"It wasn't all that much of a blow, to be honest," Erin said. "We had been in what was a roommate-business relationship more than anything for many years. That doesn't mean it wasn't quite an adjustment, going from a stay-at-home mom living in a big house to single mom living in an apartment and trying to resuscitate a dormant career."

"But you did it, Erin, and that's amazing. How's Darcy holding up?"

Erin looked away and then back, seemingly deciding something. "She is thriving. I feel like I can tell you this because if nothing else, our time together proved that I can trust you with important things. I'm not going to out her to anyone else, although, I'm honestly not sure she'd mind, but Darcy is a lesbian. It was why she wanted to watch *A League of Their Own* in the first place."

"Oh. I see."

"Yes. Grant is...maybe not a homophobe, but he told homophobic jokes from time to time, and it was clear he didn't approve of gay people. So when Darcy started hinting to me about her sexuality, it pushed me to divorce him so she could be true to herself in her own home." Pause. "Me being free to figure myself out was a bonus."

Grant sounded like a full homophobe, but Jodi chose not to push. Instead, she addressed the latter of what Erin had said: "I think that's super important." She squeezed her hand.

Erin smiled. "Me too."

They looked at each other for a while, and when Erin's eyes dropped to Jodi's lips, Jodi dreamily thought about leaning in and...no. She needed to protect her heart. At least as much as it was possible around Erin. Also, Erin hadn't actually said she was interested in dating women, much less Jodi.

She dropped Erin's hand and looked back at the waves, not really seeing them. "And with Sal? You still haven't explained why you thought we were together. I'd told you guys about my latest girlfriend." She could feel Erin looking at the side of her face, but she kept staring at the water resolutely.

Erin sighed. "It's stupid."

That made Jodi turn. "You're not stupid, Erin."

"That's debatable. I've made some questionable choices. Not that I would change anything that meant I didn't have my kids, but…" She sighed again. "In this case, I was thinking like a jealous teenager. You're mine. In the context of our high school friend group," she hastened to add.

The brief soaring feeling dashed to the ground by the additional context. Jodi was pretty sure that, while Erin was owning up to her high school feelings, she wasn't interested in Jodi now in any way beyond friendship.

Erin continued, "I mean to say that it would have hurt my feelings a lot to think you'd had a romantic relationship with either Sally or Meredith, much less a long-term one. I would feel like there hadn't been anything special between us."

"Oh, there definitely was something special. You were my first love, Erin."

Her mouth parted, drawing Jodi's attention to her lips. She tore her gaze away and realized what she'd just said. She bit her lip. Shit. Was that too intense?

"Jodi?" Erin's soft tone pulled her to look back into her eyes. "Thank you."

Jodi jerked in surprise. "For what?"

"For your honesty and confirmation that what we had was special. I'm sorry I wasn't in a place to really see what it could have meant for us."

Jodi felt like she might cry. She'd held on to the memory of those months with Erin in a way that had probably hampered her from finding a long-term partner. The love and connection she'd felt then was so strong. She'd told herself over and over that it was just teenage hormones, but she still couldn't let it go. And she was scared that it had been completely one-sided, that she'd misjudged Erin's feelings completely. To hear now that she hadn't, well, that unleashed a whole flood of emotions she'd bottled up for a long time. She took a deep breath and ran a finger under her eye. "Thank you."

"For what?"

"For also verifying that I wasn't alone in my feelings. I've wondered over the years."

Erin held her gaze, and Jodi couldn't look away if she wanted to. What she did want was to drown in those warm brown eyes until she got so close that she would have to close hers in order to kiss her. Erin's lips glistened with the gloss she'd reapplied after breakfast. Jodi wanted to taste the flavor.

She couldn't tell who leaned first, but all of a sudden, their lips met in a soft kiss. It only lasted a moment before Erin pulled back.

"Sorry," Jodi said, looking away.

"I'm not."

Jodi looked back to find Erin looking sincerely at her. Well, that was…interesting. Was that just a kiss to put a seal on their high school relationship? The start of something new? What did Erin want? What did Jodi want? Did she trust Erin enough with her heart to try again? What would that mean when Erin lived more than halfway across the country?

"We should probably get back to the others before they send out a search party," Jodi finally said instead of voicing any of her actual questions.

Erin nodded. "Okay."

CHAPTER NINE

As they stood in the sand just beyond the reach of the waves, Erin felt both excited and nervous. The water contained a number of surfers and bodyboarders already, plus kids splashing in the shallows. She told herself it would be fine. Jodi was watching her, making her feel warm all over in spite of the cold water playing around her feet. Of course it would be okay. Jodi was with her.

"Ready?" Jodi asked.

Erin nodded. "Let's do this."

The wet suit rental hadn't included booties, and Erin's feet burned with the cold as soon as they stepped in. She marveled at the kids out there with only their swimsuits for protection. Did they develop some sort of ability to withstand cold water just by living here?

When they were about waist high—Jodi was probably rib-high—and a wave was headed their way, Jodi said, "Turn to the side and hold your board above it so there's less for the wave to catch."

Erin did as directed, and the wave went on by. "How do we know when to ride one?"

"We watch and wait. First, we want to get to where they're actually breaking. Not way out there where the surfers are. Can you see the two kinds of breaks?" Jodi pointed. "Watch that wave. See how it broke out there? Watch it as it comes farther in."

Erin watched as the wave made its way toward them, started to peter out, then broke one more time and picked back up.

"There. That's where we'll go. We'll still be able to stand, which makes catching a wave easier, and the waves will be less powerful."

"Do you go way out there when you come alone?"

Jodi laughed. "No. I'm not that serious. These close waves are really mild right now, though, and when the tide is different, sometimes, they're stronger. I will still go out in those, even though I wouldn't take a first timer for that. Even when the waves are stronger, I always stay where I can stand. I'm a wimp."

Erin didn't think she was a wimp at all. She'd been incredibly brave the whole time Erin had known her. She'd come out to her mom in high school and had lived the way she'd wanted ever since. Erin only wished she had that kind of strength.

"Okay, this is as far as we'll go," Jodi said, breaking into her thoughts. "We'll wait for a good one, then try to catch it together, okay?"

Erin nodded.

"When the time is right, turn toward shore. Then, just as the wave comes by, I'll say, now. When that happens, put your board down and flop on it, kicking to catch the wave, okay?"

Erin nodded again, less certain.

Jodi squeezed her arm. "It'll be fine. You might not catch the first few. It's a timing thing, but it's not hard. You'll get it. And I won't go without you. If you fall behind the wave, I'll stop and come right back."

"Fall? Am I going to get caught underwater? And how do you stop?"

Jodi let her board dangle by its wrist strap while she held both of Erin's arms. "Don't worry. Nothing like that will happen today. It's very mild out. You won't get rolled, you'll just find that the wave has gone on without you, and you're not moving. That's what I mean by falling off the wave. As for stopping, I'll just put my feet down or roll off my board, which will stop my forward momentum. I won't leave you, okay?"

Erin stood stock still, ignoring the water moving around them. Jodi wouldn't leave her. The thought reverberated through her brain. She tried to tell herself that her reaction was outsized, but she couldn't help the way the words made her feel. She wished there were some way they could give them another try. It just seemed hopeless. Their life experiences didn't match up, and they didn't even live in the same region of the US, much less the same city.

"Are you okay?" Jodi looked worried. "We don't have to do this. We can just go back in."

"No." Erin shook her head, resolute. "I want to try. I'm ready."

It took a few tries, but when Erin finally caught a wave with Jodi right there beside her, it was amazing. She was gliding along, feeling like she was soaring across the water with Jodi laughing by her side. They stayed out for a couple of hours, and Erin didn't even care that her feet had stopped feeling the cold. Although, that didn't seem like a good thing when she really thought about it.

After one long ride in, Erin struggled a little to get up. She was pretty fit from all the tennis, but bodyboarding used a different set of muscles for sure.

"Maybe it's time to call it," Jodi said, watching her.

"Maybe. This was great. Thank you."

"Thank you for doing it with me. It was really fun."

"Yes."

They stood in the shallow water, looking at each other for probably too long. Jodi's cheeks were pink from the cold. Her hair was wild with salt water and wind. Wet, her hair looked darker than its normal blond. Her blue eyes were glowing, Erin presumed from having had a good time. Although as she looked into them, they shifted, becoming darker. Erin's free hand started moving toward her of its own accord.

"Did you guys have fun? You were out there a long time." It was Meredith.

The glow in Jodi's eyes dimmed slightly at the interruption. Erin wanted to think it was because she'd been right there in the moment. Jodi said, "We had a blast. Or at least, I did."

Erin smiled at Meredith, trying not to feel resentful about her interrupting what felt like a moment. Probably, she should be grateful because in front of their friends was not the best place to revisit the kiss from earlier. Erin wished she knew what Jodi had made of it. It had been so soft, so brief, but it had curled Erin's toes in a way they hadn't been curled since…well, since the last time Jodi had kissed her.

Maybe not the very last time. They'd known then that it was over. Erin had been pulling away, unable to bear the secrets and deviating from what she'd been taught was normal, acceptable. Their last kiss had been tinged with sorrow, regret, and shame.

So, no, not the last kiss, but still, it was Jodi who'd last curled her toes. And she'd done so again with a mere press of the lips. Erin knew for certain now that she was extremely attracted to her. She'd known before, sure, but hadn't really known how much of that was remembered attraction versus current attraction. Erin's reaction had made it abundantly clear. She wished she could whisk Jodi away to a hotel to spend the night alone.

However, she also didn't want to start something that would leave her heartbroken. Nor did she know if Jodi felt the same way. She seemed to have a fear of commitment, which meant she was not Erin's type. If only her body, brain, and heart agreed.

All these thoughts only took a split second to flash through her mind because they traveled down paths that already felt well-worn. She'd thought them as they'd walked to the rental, as they'd gotten ready to go, driven to this lovely beach, walked down the bluff to the water, as she'd struggled into her wet suit, and in between waves.

"I did, too. It was great. You should try it," Erin said to Meredith, trying to shove the thoughts away for the moment, even though she didn't really want Meredith to go out in the water with Jodi. She wanted to be Jodi's adventure partner, no one else.

That was not realistic. Ugh.

"I think I'm good with watching the waves and reading a book. Although, I think I'm getting a little burned. I might be ready to pack it in. Is that okay with you guys?" Meredith pushed on her nose and winced. She did look a little red. "And I think Sally is getting cold. She has all the towels piled on her."

The Oregon coast wasn't exactly warm most of the time, Erin was learning. Although Jodi had said that September and October were supposed to be some of the mildest. Still, they'd all been wearing layers over the last two days.

"Sure," Jodi said. "Let's head back. It'll be time for lunch soon, anyway."

"Yes." Meredith nodded seriously. "We must take the next mealtime into consideration. Always."

"This is what I'm saying," Jodi replied.

"Breakfast was both huge and about three hours ago, you guys," Erin noted.

"Which definitely makes it near lunch. Particularly by the time we get back and cleaned up." Jodi was already starting up the beach.

Erin followed and heaven help her, enjoyed the view.

CHAPTER TEN

When Meredith pulled Erin into a store to check out some earrings they'd been exclaiming over, Sal held on to Jodi's arm, keeping her on the sidewalk. "What is going on between you and Erin?"

Jodi glanced inside, then back to Sal. "Nothing? I don't know."

"Are you sure? Because she asked to share a room with you."

Jodi shook her head. "Just because it made the most sense."

Sal gave her a skeptical look. "And all those long looks I've seen you two give each other?"

"What long looks?" Jodi was dissembling. She knew. Over lunch, she'd caught Erin's eye often. When someone had said something funny. When she'd thought about their kiss. When the server had flirted with Erin, and Jodi had wanted to see how she was reacting. Politely disinterested on that last one, which had given Jodi a satisfied feeling. "Sorry if I'm ignoring you."

"You're not. But about half the time I went to exchange looks with you about something, you were looking at Erin. It was just a surprise is all."

Jodi had never told Sal about Erin, even though she'd wanted to. After all, Sal was her best friend, the person she had the most history with. However, Erin had not wanted anyone to know. Jodi had respected her wishes and kept their relationship close to her chest. She wasn't about to spill the beans after all this time, even though she really, really wanted to analyze what was happening with Sal.

"We were pretty close in high school. Maybe we're just finding we still have a lot in common."

Sal looked through the window at Erin, who was leaning over a display case inside. "Do you really? I mean, like what? An interest in jewelry?"

"No, of course not. Just, I don't know. A certain sensibility. A sense of humor? A similar way of thinking?"

Sal put their hands on their hips. "Like religion?"

"Okay, okay. I know there are a lot of differences, but I'm enjoying her company. I feel like we've just clicked back into a friendship. Well, not just. It took, I don't know, until this morning, I guess. I just like her. She's a friend. Is that so bad?"

"No. Of course it isn't."

Both of them looked in the shop again. Meredith was holding some earrings up to her ears and looking in a mirror.

"But do you feel the same way about Meredith?"

Jodi didn't even have to consider that. "No. I mean, don't get me wrong, I don't dislike her. I think she's smart and funny. But, no, we haven't clicked back into a deeper friendship. There's a bit of a vibe, you know?"

"I do. It's that vibe that's keeping me from asking them to use the right pronouns for me."

"I don't think she'd tell your family or anything, but I do think it could be awkward. If you want to tell them, I'm here for you. Awkward be dammed. If she freaks out, I'll take you home, even. I could always drive back out for them. Or they could take the bus."

"Is there a bus back to Portland from here?"

Jodi shrugged. "I have no idea. But you come first."

Sal hugged her. "Thank you."

Jodi squeezed them back. "Of course."

Sal stood back. "I think I want to tell them. I want to be myself."

"For what it's worth, I think Erin might be cool."

"What have you guys talked about that would make you think that?" Sal narrowed her eyes, back in detective mode.

"I can't really say, but I think if you are yourself with her, she might be herself with you, too."

Sal looked speculative. "I think I might have been on the right track with suggesting there is something going on there."

"Going on where?" Meredith asked as she came back out, bag in hand.

"Over there." Jodi pointed to where someone was using chalk to draw on the sidewalk. A small crowd was gathering to check it out.

They walked over to look. Jodi found herself walking next to Erin with Meredith and Sal in front. Erin brushed her arm against Jodi's, deliberately, she thought. There was a questioning look in Erin's eyes. Jodi smiled at her but didn't say anything. There were a lot of secrets to navigate.

"I was grateful for the booming housing market when we sold two properties last year," Erin said before maneuvering a chip with salsa to her mouth.

They'd been talking real estate, a subject that their teenage selves would never have even considered. "Two?" Jodi asked, watching the progress of the chip closely. She was a little surprised Erin was living in an apartment if there had been two houses to sell and share the profits from when she'd gotten her divorce.

Erin nodded. "Yes. There was our primary residence, but we'd kept the house we'd bought in San Antonio, our previous base, and we'd been renting it out. As part of the divorce settlement, we sold both and split the equity. It was easier than figuring out who should get which one. We basically liquidated everything and split the money."

Meredith shook her head. "Sounds like a mess. That's part of why Tom and I never got married. If we ever go our separate ways, it'll be easy to each take what is ours."

"You might find that trickier than you think. Colorado is a common-law marriage state, and you two have been together a long time," Jodi pointed out.

"We've been careful to keep our finances separate, and the house is only in my name. I did check on what would qualify as a common-law marriage, and part of it is mixing finances. Otherwise, people who really are just roommates could be considered married." Meredith picked up the saltshaker and added more to the chips in the basket. Jodi thought that was a little rude. She could have asked everyone if they wanted more first.

"When did you and Brit get married?" Erin asked Sal. "Was it right after the supreme court decision?"

Sal shook their head. "No, we got married in 2013. Washington voted in marriage equality in 2012. We had a spring wedding."

It had been lovely. It had been small, all found family and other close friends. About twenty attendees. One of Sal and Brit's friends in Seattle owned a small art gallery and had offered it up for their use. They'd gotten married among some gorgeous, queer-centered art with all their closest friends, everyone still so excited and happy that they even could get married. "Probably my favorite wedding I ever attended," Jodi said, smiling at Sal.

"That's great." Erin was smiling a little dreamily.

Meredith, on the other hand, was smiling a tighter sort of smile. "Sounds lovely."

Jodi wasn't completely sure where the tightness was coming from. To give Meredith the benefit of the doubt, she supposed it might be from hurt about not being invited, but Jodi worried there was something more. They'd stayed in loose touch over the years, and Meredith had never seemed fussed about Jodi being a lesbian.

On the other hand, Meredith had also recommended a blog her brother was writing. Jodi had skimmed a few entries and found it to be pretty libertarian leaning but not too horrible. That had been when libertarian thinking was lots of "freedom" and "personal responsibility." There had been a time in Jodi's life when that seemed like it wasn't the worst idea. Then, Jodi had come to realize the privilege associated with personal responsibility, and the libertarians had gone off the fucking deep end.

Anyway, his blog had seemed fine enough until she'd gotten to his take on marriage equality. He'd said that his issue with gay marriage was that it imposed on the freedoms of others: businesses would have to pay for insurance for their employees' same-sex spouses, which they shouldn't have had to do. That was an appalling enough take, but then he'd equated marrying a same-sex partner with marrying a dog. While that hadn't been Meredith's stated opinion, even the fact that there was an article like that in a blog that she'd recommended had left Jodi with the idea that Meredith was maybe not as chill about LGBTQIA+ folks as she'd seemed. And as for her brother? Jodi went out of her way to avoid him.

Jodi and Sal exchanged a look. Sal looked resolute, and Jodi wondered if now was the time she was going to come out. Sal was quiet and hidden when they went back to their childhood home. It was a huge weight on them to endure that periodically. They were a very different person among friends in Seattle. It made sense to share their truth so they could be themselves with these friends, too. However, it also wouldn't surprise Jodi if they'd changed their mind and didn't want to risk word getting back to their family or hurtful things being said. Jodi nodded, hoping to convey that she had their back, whatever their choice was.

"It was one of the best days of my life. One of the others was when I announced to my friends that my pronouns are they-them, and they started using them. It just felt right, and I felt really seen."

Erin said, "Wait, so you prefer to be referred to as they? Is that right?"

Sal nodded. "And I prefer Sal to Sally."

"Okay, Sal," Erin said simply. "Sorry for misgendering you."

Jodi's mouth dropped open while Sal said, "It's okay. You didn't know."

Erin seemed amused by Jodi's reaction. "I have a teenager. Don't look so surprised. I know a few things. Darcy has a teammate who uses she-them pronouns."

Jodi's expression morphed from surprise to delight. Erin was keeping her on her toes in the best way possible.

Meredith went quiet. Jodi watched her meticulously unwrap the napkin around her silverware. Her lips were pressed together. Jodi suspected she wasn't taking it super well from the way her gaze was focused on the simple action and the lack of response.

The server came with their food, giving them all something to do for a few minutes.

Jodi exchanged a look with Sal, trying to silently ask if Sal wanted Jodi to push the issue with Meredith. When Sal shook their head just a little and shrugged, Jodi decided to just get the conversational ball rolling again. She asked Erin, "Darcy has a tournament this weekend, right? How's it going?"

Erin beamed at the question. "Good. They won their first game today and have two more tomorrow. Depending on how that goes, there will be the semifinal and final on Sunday."

"That's awesome. Good luck to them." Jodi took a bite of her fantastic mushroom and spinach enchilada. After swallowing, she said, "Sal and Brit play in an adult kickball league."

Sal laughed a little. "But it's just for fun. We don't have tournaments. Games, yes, but sometimes, no one even keeps track of the score enough to know who won."

"You guys do some strange things here in the Pacific Northwest," Meredith said, sounding too serious for it to be a joke.

There was a pause while everyone decided how to take that. Erin broke the silence by saying, "It sounds like fun. I like playing tennis, but it's sometimes a little too serious. What else do you guys do to keep fit these days? Aside from bodyboard, of course." She nodded at Jodi.

"I don't do that very often, to be clear. A few times a summer is all. Mostly, I walk. Sometimes actual hiking but mostly just walking."

Sal scoffed a little. "She makes it sound like she takes strolls around the block occasionally. Let me tell you, she walks. One of her ideas of a fun Saturday is to walk all day, following her whims. I've joined her on a couple of those sorts of days and had the sore muscles the next day to prove it, even though I run regularly."

"How about you, Meredith?" Jodi asked, trying to be inclusive.

"Oh, just the gym." Unsaid but seemingly implied, was "like a normal person in their early fifties."

After a brief moment of quiet again, Jodi said to Erin, "So tennis. What made you pick up a racket?"

The rest of lunch was mostly Jodi, Erin, and Sal chatting while Meredith was a slightly sullen observer. It was both odd because that had never been the group dynamic before but also because it felt natural. Jodi was quite used to having conversations with Sal, of course, and had clicked right back into a connection with Erin. It would have been great fun without Meredith sitting there, acting so out of character. Jodi told herself that Meredith had no one but herself to blame. She didn't have to be bigoted.

CHAPTER ELEVEN

Erin was looking at the not-quite ocean view after dinner. When they'd returned to the rental, everyone had split in search of a bathroom or to check in at home or whatever. Erin had settled out back with the blanket again. She was tired and thinking about just going to bed. It had been an active day, a late dinner, and she hadn't slept much the night before. But thoughts of going to bed meant thoughts of lying next to Jodi.

She didn't know what had come over her earlier when she'd blithely suggested she and Jodi share a bed. It was tantalizing, sure, but it was also fraught. What if Jodi thought it meant Erin wanted sex or something, especially after they'd kissed earlier?

Did Erin want sex? She didn't *not* want sex, to be honest. She'd been checking Jodi out all day, and her libido was making itself known in a way it hadn't for years. However, she also wasn't a casual sex sort of person. Even if her body did want it, she wasn't ready.

Her desires would make sleeping next to Jodi but not sleeping with Jodi very challenging.

"Can you believe that?" Meredith surprised Erin out of her thoughts as she sat.

"What?"

"Sally wanting to be called 'they.' What? Is she more than one person? It's bad enough that it's a fad with teenagers. Why does someone our age need to get involved in that?"

Erin considered how to reply. Meredith had been a good friend after the divorce. She'd been supportive. She'd been funny when Erin had needed distraction. Heck, she was the one responsible for this weekend. Erin knew that some people their age had a hard time accepting new ideas. But they could adjust. It had been easy for Erin to accept Darcy being a lesbian, but she could admit to herself that if Darcy had announced she was really a he, that would have been more of a challenge for Erin to wrap her head around. She liked to think she'd have gotten there, even so. Carefully, she said, "I think that it just feels right to some people, and it doesn't hurt me to call Sal they."

Meredith sighed. "It's just silly. What does your church say about all this?"

"Well, after the divorce, I changed churches. Darcy and I go to one that is very inclusive. A Methodist Church that preaches acceptance. We have a woman preacher who is married to a woman."

"That really surprises me."

"Why's that?"

"Because the church you grew up in is so anti-gay. They're in the local news sometimes about it."

Erin shrugged. "That doesn't mean I am."

"Guess I'm outnumbered, then," Meredith said a little sourly.

"Maybe in more ways than you know," Erin said under her breath. She wasn't sure if she'd have explained if Meredith had heard her or if she'd have dissembled. Erin had never come out to anyone. She had never said, "I am attracted to women," or "I am a lesbian," or "I am gay," or even "I'm in a relationship with Jodi." The first was definitely true. The second was something she was still considering. She might have been bi. The last had been true for a while in high school. But nevertheless, she'd never said any of it. She'd watched with awe as Sal had expressed her pronoun preference with grace and dignity at dinner. She hoped she could use that as a model for her own coming out, but she wasn't sure she was ready.

And things were already awkward with Meredith. Would it make things worse to admit she was gay, too? Quite likely. Of course, Meredith's comfort shouldn't have been the top priority.

She was saved from making the decision by the fact that Meredith hadn't seemed to hear her over the noise of Jodi and Sal coming through the door. Jodi eased into the empty seat on Erin's other side. Erin was hoping Jodi would catch her eye again, as she'd done repeatedly all day. When she did almost as soon as she was settled, warmth spread through Erin's chest.

"I don't know about you guys, but I think I might need to call it an early night," Sal said. "I didn't get a lot of sleep last night with the bed hog over there." They hooked a thumb at Jodi, who huffed.

"It's like you think I did it on purpose."

"Just keep shoving her back onto her half, Erin. If you wake her up, it's just desserts," Sal said, leaning past Jodi to address her.

"I'll just put my cold feet on her. That'll keep her on her side."

Sal and Meredith both laughed, while Jodi crossed her arms and mock scowled. "I'm kindly giving you an alternative to sleeping with Snorey McSnorerson, and this is the thanks I get? Next time, we clearly need a four-bedroom place."

Sal nodded fervently. Meredith looked away. Erin figured she was not interested in a next time and wondered if she was even regretting suggesting this reunion.

Erin stood at the foot of the bed. They'd all ended up staying up a little longer, moving into the living room to chat when they'd gotten cold out back. Meredith had rallied some, and they'd all chatted amicably for a while, mostly reminiscing about high school. While that was fun, it wasn't too long before Erin had been nearly nodding off. She figured that was all for the good. If she was really tired, she'd just fall asleep once she was in the bed. When Sal had started yawning more than talking, Erin had been the first to take the hint, retrieving her things from Meredith's room and getting ready for bed.

Now, here she was, actually looking at the bed she would be sharing with Jodi, who would be out of the bathroom soon, no doubt feeling wide awake. Would it be weirder to be standing here waiting for her or in bed? God, both options seemed ridiculous.

And the bed loomed.

Erin finally got in, hoping she chose the correct side, and looked at her phone, pretending to be engrossed in the messages she'd exchanged with Darcy throughout the day. While she had been happy to hear the team was doing well and that Darcy was having fun, her mind was preoccupied with the bathroom door. She wasn't taking in any new information in her for-show perusal of her phone.

Until a text from Lindsey came through. Erin was surprised. Sure, Lindsey was in her twenties with no kids, and it was a Friday night, but it would be midnight in Colorado, and Lindsey and her husband Todd were usually in bed by eleven, even on the weekends.

How's your girls' trip going?

It was innocuous enough, aside from the timing. If anything, Erin had heard from Lindsey more since the divorce than before it. She debated how to answer. *Mostly good. There have been some surprises. Is everything good there? You're up late.*

We went to a movie with some friends, and I'm just still winding down. What kind of surprises?

Erin thought about what she could and couldn't say. Lindsey was the most religious of her kids and the one Erin was the most concerned about regarding her own sexuality. If she knew Erin was on a weekend trip with a lesbian and a nonbinary person, she might freak out. Erin carefully worded her message so as to not alarm her *and* not misgender Sal. *Sal used to be really quiet in high school but is actually talking a lot this weekend, for one.*

That's good, right? Unless it turns out she's boring or something.

No, not boring.

The bathroom door opened, and Erin quickly sent one last text. *Gotta go. Talk soon. Love you.*

Jodi paused in the doorway.

Erin swallowed hard, taking in her thin loose T-shirt and sleep shorts. She was a little surprised Jodi still had her glasses on. She obviously needed them enough to wear them to bed. Erin had taken her contacts out and was wearing her glasses, but she'd needed them since she was little. If she wasn't wearing them, she wouldn't have been able to see her phone. "Um, if you want this side of the bed, I can move."

Jodi shook her head and looked like she was refocusing. "No. No, you're fine there." She cleared her throat and moved toward the bed.

Erin looked away, thinking that watching her approach was a little too intimate, as much as she wanted to watch her every move. Even with her eyes averted, she was very aware of Jodi's progress. She could hear her, feel her getting closer. The covers shifted, the bed dipped a little, and Jodi was in bed beside her.

The last time that had happened was the summer before college, when they'd been in a relationship, secret as it was. They'd spent the night at one another's house regularly under the cover of friendly sleepovers. Well, it was possible Jodi's mom had suspected there was more going on because Jodi had come out to her but had never told her she and Erin were involved so there was plausible deniability.

Anyway, the point was that the last time this had happened—Jodi slipping into a bed Erin was already occupying—they'd moved seamlessly into each other's arms and started kissing and touching. Now, they were both keeping careful space around them.

Erin looked at her phone again.

"Important messages from home?" Jodi picked up her e-reader.

"Oh, um, just texting with Lindsey a bit." Erin put the phone aside, feeling slightly embarrassed, like a teenager who didn't know how to interact with people IRL, as the kids said. But if Jodi was going to read, maybe she should pick her phone back up.

"Is everything okay?"

"Oh, sure, she was just checking in."

"Ah. I thought for sure you'd be asleep by the time I got here. You were practically sleeping on the couch."

"I was. I'm feeling…more awake now." Erin felt like every nerve was alive, so, yes, she was awake.

"Um, yeah. So…about that kiss earlier…"

Erin looked up quickly.

Jodi was sitting up, back against the headboard, looking at the e-reader in her lap as she plucked at the blanket.

"I'm sorry if it was unwanted."

Jodi raised her head, and their eyes caught. Erin saw surprise, wariness, and, yes, attraction there. She was pretty sure. Jodi said, "No." She cleared her throat. "It wasn't unwanted."

"Oh." Erin sighed. "I'm glad."

"It's just that it left me...confused."

"Yeah. I get that. I'm a little confused, too."

Jodi grinned. She put her e-reader aside, took off her glasses, set them on the nightstand, and scooted down, shifting to her side to face Erin. "Well, glad I'm not the only one. Tell me all about your confusion."

Erin had been propped up on the pillows into a semi-seated position. She tucked one pillow between her knees—it helped her back but also felt a little like drawing a line for herself—and shifted to mirror Jodi's position. She kept her glasses on so she could see Jodi clearly. "It's not about if I'm attracted to you. Because I'm seriously attracted to you." She was rewarded with a huge grin that made her want to pull Jodi to her and kiss the daylights out of her. Instead, she nodded. "I know. Embarrassing to admit."

"No, please don't be embarrassed. If I admit I'm seriously attracted to you, too, does that help?" Jodi put a hand on her arm.

She sucked in a breath. "Yes and no, to be honest. I mean, it does help with the embarrassed part because at least we're in this together. However, us being attracted to each other opens a whole can of worms I'm not sure I'm ready to deal with."

Jodi pulled her hand back, and Erin missed it. She made an abortive move to put her hand on Jodi's, pulled it back, unsure, then moved with purpose to rest her hand on Jodi's arm. Jodi looked at the hand but didn't pull away. "I'm getting mixed signals."

Erin sighed. "I know, and I'm sorry about that. I just...don't want to have casual sex, especially with you because I suspect there would be nothing casual about it, given our history." Also given how Erin felt about Jodi right then. She worried that if they shared themselves in that way, she'd fall head over heels. Jodi seemed like a casual dater and again, lived nowhere close. It would be a one-way road to heartbreak for Erin. At the same time, she wanted to touch her. Like, all the time.

Jodi nodded. "It wouldn't be casual sex for me. I don't know how much of what I feel is leftover, wanting what we had back then, and how much is here and now. It's hard to untangle, but you matter to me, Erin."

The sound of Jodi saying her name in that low tone, coupled by the words, were Erin's undoing. She tightened her hand on Jodi's arm and pulled. Jodi offered no resistance, and this time, when their lips met, while it started soft and tentative, it deepened quickly. Erin tasted the mint of Jodi's toothpaste, something fruity she couldn't quite identify but was probably lip balm, and then, as they opened to each other, Jodi herself.

There was a pulse in Erin's center that she answered by scooting to align her body to Jodi's. She was stymied by the pillow between her knees and broke off the kiss to deal with it.

Jodi breathlessly asked, "Are you sure you want to do this?"

That did give Erin pause. She didn't want to just sleep with Jodi once and then be long-distance friends. That wasn't her. That wasn't enough.

Jodi shifted back to her own side. "I see you're not." She paused. "Is it because you think it's wrong?"

Erin shook her head. "No. No, I don't think that. I just worry it won't be enough." She put a hand over her mouth, worried she'd said too much. Did she want to try to have a relationship with Jodi? If Jodi were open to that, and if she didn't live so far away, the answer was clear to Erin. She did want that. If anything, she wished they could have been together all along. If only she'd been brave back then. If only she'd gone away to college with Jodi, and they'd let their relationship grow in the light of day. Who knew if they'd still be together, but with the way that Erin felt when she was around Jodi, she suspected they would be.

It was the thought of her kids that pulled that train of thought to a quick stop. If that was what had happened, she'd never have had them. So there was no use wishing for a do-over. This was where they were, what their lives were. The question was, what should she do now? Should she jump at the chance to have sex with the lovely, charismatic person who made her feel all sorts of ways and was in her bed right now? Or should she stay true to the concept of herself as a person who didn't have one-night stands?

"What are you thinking?" Jodi brushed a thumb across Erin's forehead. "There's a lot happening behind those eyes right now."

Why not just be truthful? Erin was too old to play games. "I'm thinking about how I wish I'd been brave and gone away to college with you thirty years ago, but how that would mean I wouldn't have my kids. I was thinking about how much I want to make love to you but also about how I'm not sure that there would be a future for us, and I'm still not sure how I'd feel about myself if I went ahead and slept with you without there being a possible future. I've always said to my kids that sex is like superglue. It bonds people to one another, and it's hard to keep feelings out of it."

Jodi looked thoughtful, and Erin hoped she hadn't overwhelmed her. She had faith in her, though. They'd always tackled tricky topics in high school. They'd told each other everything back then. At least at the times they'd been close. They'd been friends a lot of years, and there had been some ups and downs. But again, Erin had no time for games at this point in her life. It was best to lay her cards on the table and see what happened.

"I haven't always experienced sex that way." Jodi held up a hand to ward off any comment. "I have but only with two people. I think that if there are feelings, sex does tend to cement them. That was certainly my experience with you. I've had sex with people, and it was just fun. I am the sort of person who is open to casual sex with the right person. As I said earlier, this is different. It wouldn't be casual for me. I worry that if we were to make love, I'd get my heart broken because you…"

"Walked out on you before?" Erin felt sadness and regret all over again to have been the person who'd caused the pain she heard in Jodi's voice. She had been miserable about the breakup, too, without a doubt, but knowing she was the reason they'd both been heartbroken had been quite a burden.

"There are so many obstacles to us having any sort of relationship beyond friends. I feel like we're both interested in that…" She trailed off uncertainly.

Erin hurried to reassure her. "We are. I am. I wish we could, yes."

"Yeah, exactly, we both wish we could." Jodi flopped onto her back and stared at the ceiling. "But we live in different places. I feel like we'd need to start slow and see how it goes, but that's hard with distance. You have a family who it might be hard for you to be out to. I don't think I could take being in a relationship I have to hide again. I don't know where you are in your process of getting over your, what, nearly thirty-year marriage, much less how you identify."

"I hear those concerns. I share the one about living in different places. I…yes. I haven't come out to my family. That's true. I have been thinking about what will make me happy, and I think it's being able to be open about my true self. I'm pretty sure I'm…Jodi?"

"Yes?"

"I'm a lesbian." It felt right. It felt true. Erin had only ever been interested in men because she was supposed to be. Sex with men hadn't been horrible for her, either, but she'd also never been in a position where she couldn't help touching a man, not even Grant. Yet, here she was with Jodi, unable to not kiss her, to not move into her space, even after only a day together. It was wildly different. Her body reacted not just to Jodi but to women in a different way.

She was a lesbian.

Jodi turned back onto her side. "That's big. How do you feel?"

"Good. Scared."

Jodi nodded, understanding. "Is that the first time you've said it?"

Erin nodded. She felt her lips curl into a smile. "I like it. It's right."

Jodi kissed her, just a brief kiss, no pressure. "Congratulations. Felt like you should celebrate that with a kiss with a woman."

Erin grinned at that. "Indeed." They smiled at each other for a few moments. Erin broke the silence. "I want to tell people and let the chips fall where they may."

"How do you think the people in your life will handle it?"

"Well, Darcy is gay, so I expect that will be no problem. I think Brad and Lindsey…will be a challenge. My parents may disown me, but I'd honestly rather be that lightning rod so Darcy will have a map for how to proceed."

"Will you advise her to keep it a secret if it doesn't go well for you?"

"No. How she wants to handle it is completely up to her. I'm pretty sure she's decided not to tell Grant. Maybe ever. So she may not want to tell others, but I expect she'll tell her siblings." Erin sighed. "I hope they are kind, even if they don't enthusiastically embrace the idea."

Jodi squeezed her arm. "I'm sorry it's hard for you and her."

"In some ways, with marrying Grant, it's the bed I made, and I have to lie in it. But Darcy didn't choose."

"You didn't choose to be raised the way you were, either, and you're putting a halt to generational trauma as much as you can now by creating a safe home for Darcy. Erin, that's huge. I'm so proud of you."

Erin squirmed a little at the pleasure of those words of affirmation. She kissed Jodi. "Thank you."

Jodi smiled. "Just saying true things, but if I get kisses for it…"

Erin kissed her again. She couldn't help herself. They got a little carried away with this one. Erin pushed her glasses up on top of her head. Their mouths parted and tongues collided, then caressed. It was so sensual, so good to kiss her. Erin felt like she could do this all night. Except for the fact that it woke up other parts of her body with a vengeance, and she still wasn't ready to go there. She pulled back.

Jodi touched her mouth with her fingertips. "I…I thought this feeling was just because it was the first, you know? I mean, back in high school. You being my first kiss, first love, first everything, sure spoiled me for others." She flopped back again. "Oh my God. I keep saying these things aloud."

"If it comforts you to know that I'm feeling it, too, well, I'm feeling it, too."

Jodi's expression was sincere as she asked, "Should we actually try this? What would that mean?"

Erin's heart felt like it would explode at the idea of actually trying with Jodi. Actually making a go at being a couple. That would be…she didn't have words for the feeling of excitement and pure pleasure the thought brought. "I have concerns, too. The distance issue hasn't gone away in the last ten minutes. But also, you seem to go through girlfriends pretty quickly. It would break my heart if that happened with us."

"Erin, I…" Jodi looked away and seemed to gather her thoughts. "I'm not closed off to being in a relationship. It just hasn't worked out for me yet."

Erin processed that. It was perhaps a flimsy idea to hang her hat on, the possibility that Jodi might really want a relationship. But her body was crying out for contact. It had been so long since she'd experienced any pleasure with a partner. She wanted this. It was enough.

She was done worrying about tomorrow. Jodi kissed her, and when her body cried for more? She moved closer.

CHAPTER TWELVE

Jodi couldn't believe this was happening. She'd resigned herself to a night of torment brought on by her proximity to an untouchable Erin. Instead, Erin was in her arms, warm and clearly craving this as much as she was.

Without breaking their kiss, Jodi sank her hands into Erin's long, thick hair. She took the glasses off the top of Erin's head, setting them carefully aside. Then she was stymied by the braid. That was new. When they were teens, Erin had always slept with her hair loose. It had been Jodi's favorite place to hold while they kissed, and only at night, when no one would notice Erin's stiffly held 'do in disarray. Jodi released the braid and ran her fingers through Erin's hair until it was free around her, then cupped her head.

"I'd forgotten how much you like to do that," Erin murmured against her lips.

"Is it a problem?"

"No. I like it."

"Good." Jodi went back to the important business of kissing her. There was too much space between them. She pushed until Erin lying on her back, and Jodi was on top. Erin groaned, and it was all Jodi could to do stop herself from sliding a hand into Erin's pajama pants. But, no, she wanted this to last, wanted it to be good for Erin. She pressed her leg between Erin's and enjoyed the rocking of Erin's hips.

Erin slipped her hands under Jodi's T-shirt and flattened her palms on her back. Jodi arched, pressing herself even closer. She kissed her way down Erin's neck. "Can I take this off?" Erin asked, pulling on Jodi's shirt.

In answer, Jodi pulled back to give her space, watching to see what Erin's reaction would be. Jodi wasn't young anymore, neither of them was, and Jodi was well aware that she had a round tummy and sagging breasts. She considered them badges of age but felt a little vulnerable to be shirtless in front of a woman who had last seen her naked at seventeen.

But Erin looked at her with something close to reverence. She pulled Jodi close and took one nipple in her mouth. That cleared up any doubts about if Erin would hold back or be shy after not having been with a woman in over thirty years. She was clearly ready and willing to take what she wanted.

Jodi stopped thinking about anything except the sensation of Erin's mouth licking, sucking, lightly nipping. She gasped and felt Erin's lips curl into a smile around her breast.

"Your nipples were always super sensitive."

In response, Jodi threaded her fingers in Erin's hair, guiding her. Erin wrapped her arms around Jodi's back and shifted to her other breast, giving it similar attention.

When Erin kissed her way to the valley between Jodi's breasts, Jodi took the second of a slightly clearer head and pulled Erin's shirt off. She pushed Erin back onto the bed and palmed her breasts. She was so captivated that she almost didn't catch Erin's look that called back her feelings of concern when it was her shirt newly off. She looked right into Erin's eyes and told her the truth: "You're beautiful."

Erin shook her head. "There've been three kids…"

Jodi leaned down and kissed her. "You're stunning. I love everything about these." She gently lifted Erin's breasts. "And this." She let her hands roam down Erin's abdomen, much flatter than her own. "And…" She trailed off as she grazed the top of Erin's pajama pants. "Everything."

"Everything," Erin said nonsensically.

Jodi lay on top again, relishing the skin to skin contact and the interplay of their breasts. She kissed Erin deeply, infusing her desire into it, not wanting her to doubt at all. She worked her way down Erin's body, trailing kisses and licks, exploring all of the curves and dips. Erin's hips moved in response, drawing Jodi's attention lower and lower. When she reached the top of Erin's pajama pants with her mouth, she looked up, seeking permission before taking this last step.

Erin, who had been arched back, eyes closed, opened her eyes and looked down.

"Ready?" Jodi asked.

Erin nodded. She bit her lower lip, then let it go to say, "But, um, I...don't get as wet as I used to."

Jodi paused, propping herself up on her elbows. "Don't worry. Neither do I. And I've stayed in my age group, so I've, um, had experience."

Erin nodded again. She took a deep breath. "I'm very ready, then."

That was all Jodi needed. She pulled the pants off, removing the last layer between her and Erin's glorious center. She kissed her way back up Erin's long legs, paying attention to her inner thighs before finally giving Erin what she was looking for with every thrust of her hips. She ran her tongue up the length of her, causing her to gasp and cry out, "Jodi."

Jodi delighted in the sound, but a part of her remembered the situation they were in, and she reached up with one hand to touch Erin's lips. "We have to be quiet, remember?"

Erin kissed her fingertips, then took her lip into her mouth. Jodi went back to work exploring Erin's folds with her tongue as the tempo of Erin's thrusts increased.

"I'm close." Erin gasped out, clearly trying to be quiet.

Jodi shifted her attention to Erin's clit. She sucked it gently as she slipped a finger inside, checking for ease of entry. Erin's muscles clenched around her, and she moaned softly in pleasure, so Jody pulled it out only to add a second as Erin hitched her hips upward, searching for the contact.

Jodi met her thrust for thrust. When Erin grabbed her head and whimpered, she curled her fingers and flattened her tongue against Erin's most sensitive spot. Erin bucked and pulled a hand back, presumably to cover her mouth. Jodi stayed with her, drawing out the pleasure as much as she could, easing Erin down.

"Come here," Erin finally said, pulling on Jodi's arm. Jodi kissed up her body as she complied until she was kissing Erin's welcoming lips. Erin cupped her ass, still clad in her sleep shorts. She hooked her thumbs in the waistband. "Off."

"My, my, you have gotten demanding."

"I've been dreaming about this for a long time. I need you naked, Jodi."

Jodi shucked her shorts in record time. She eased back on top, shifting to find the friction she needed. Erin slipped a hand between them and cupped Jodi, causing her to moan.

"Shh," Erin whispered in her ear. "Remember, we have to be quiet."

Jodi nodded and closed her eyes.

"Can you…"

When Erin trailed off, Jodi opened her eyes again and searched Erin's for clues about what she wanted.

Erin bit her lip. "Can you look at me?"

Jodi kissed her chin, which was about what she could reach, given their current position, and nodded, looking into Erin's eyes. Erin slipped a finger inside her, and she had to fight to keep her eyes open. She rocked her hips, knowing it would not take long.

Erin nodded at her. "I want to see you come." She ground the heel of her hand into Jodi's center while thrusting with her finger, and Jodi came undone. She grimaced with the effort of not crying out or closing her eyes and drifted away on the waves of pleasure rolling through her.

"This, this is what I've been missing this whole time," Erin said. "You're amazing."

Jodi managed to whimper her agreement about having missed this the whole time they'd been apart. She hadn't felt this good, this connected, in a long time. But as she collapsed onto Erin's chest, a sliver of anxiety invaded her postcoital haze.

What if this was all they were going to have? She had to guard her heart, and it wasn't going to be easy.

CHAPTER THIRTEEN

When Erin woke in the morning, she was delighted to find herself curled around a naked Jodi. She was less excited to realize she'd fallen asleep right after they'd made love the night before. She should have expected it. She hadn't gotten that much sleep the prior night, and she was pleasantly sore from just the one go, but it still felt like a missed opportunity. Last night had been a reawakening, and she wanted more.

The sun was up, and she could hear sounds from the kitchen, indicating that the others were awake and precluding a second round this morning. She wondered if she should sneak out of bed while Jodi was still sleeping so they wouldn't emerge together like a couple.

Was that necessary if she was going to come out? Would Jodi want to share that they were exploring a relationship? Were they? Or had they ended that discussion prematurely by having sex?

The thought that maybe it had been a one-off slammed into Erin. Her predominant feeling was one of loss. Again. That was not what she wanted, but there were still so many obstacles to face. She sighed.

Jodi stirred in her arms. "Good morning."

Erin smoothed her short wild hair and smiled back at her. "Good morning to you."

"Have you been awake long?"

"Just long enough to worry," she said, trying to sound flippant.

Jodi rolled over to face her. "What are you worried about?"

"Oh, plenty. Coming out. If this was just…one night of amazing sex."

Jodi grinned. "It was amazing. On that, we can agree."

"Yes, and I hope we can agree on more."

"I think we can agree that we care about each other a great deal."

Erin nodded slowly. "Is it bad that I want more? Should I be, I don't know, playing the field and seeing what appeals to me instead of just running back to something I wanted years and years ago?" Playing the field wasn't what she wanted, but she did want to give Jodi a way to bow out gracefully. She still wasn't clear where they'd landed last night.

Jodi's face fell. "I…I mean, you should figure out what you want if you're not sure."

"It's not that I'm not sure," Erin said to reassure her, undoing the work of trying to seem casual about the whole situation. "I want to see if we can make this work. I'm just…not sure if that's what you want or how to get past the issues we face."

Jodi threaded her fingers through Erin's hair and worked them through to the ends, finding tangles—of which there were plenty because Erin hadn't put her hair back in a braid last night—and gently undoing them. It felt wonderful. Erin had never felt as pampered or as treasured as she had with Jodi, then and now.

"How about this?" Jodi said. "We enjoy this weekend together without worrying too much about the future. I know that's a tall order, but we just enjoy. We've got today, tonight, and tomorrow morning."

"That we have to share with the others," Erin interjected. She wished they could just walk away and be together, exploring and connecting, seeing if they should try.

Jodi cocked her head in acknowledgement. "It's not ideal. As for coming out, that's something you should do in your own time. I don't want to pressure you there." She paused and looked away, then back. "However, I…have a request."

"Yes?" Did she want some sort of gesture to show that Erin was serious about not living in the closet?

"I'd like to have someone to talk to about everything. Sal is my person for that sort of thing. Can I tell them? I won't do it this weekend if it makes you uncomfortable. I'll wait until everyone has gone home. And only if you say it's okay."

"You never told them about us?"

Jodi shook her head. "No. I only ever told a therapist I saw for a while. You didn't want anyone to know, so I didn't tell."

Erin was touched that Jodi had so carefully guarded her privacy, even after so long. It would have been so easy for her to tell Sal. "Yes. I think that's fair. Thank you."

Jodi cocked an eyebrow. "For telling Sal?"

"For not telling them, or anyone, all this time. I'm ready to take some steps to rectify that situation. You having to keep secrets, I mean. I want to tell Meredith and Sal that I'm a lesbian." It was easier to say the second time.

"That is a huge step. Can I support you in any particular way?"

Erin took a deep breath, thinking. "Just being there. I saw how you supported Sal, and I'm not worried about being out there alone. I think it'll be okay. Well. Actually, I think Meredith is going to feel really outnumbered, but I still want to do it."

Jodi nodded. "Okay. And how are we feeling about talking about this?" She touched first Erin's chest, then her own.

"I think…" Erin trailed off, not entirely sure what she did think about discussing this new-old thing with anyone yet. She wanted to shout to the world that she was into Jodi, to hold her hand and make heart eyes at her, but she also wasn't ready for the consequences of holding hands with a woman in public. She had seen same-sex couples holding hands. She was aware that things had changed since they were young, at least in some places.

However, this was all new for her. She had a lifetime of conditioning to overcome. She wanted to get there, but it wasn't going to happen today. "It's maybe too new?" She had trouble reading Jodi's expression. Resignation? Maybe a little relief? She decided to just ask. "Is that okay?"

"Yeah, it's fine. We don't even…we're…I think it's too new, too, but I have to admit that it brings up a little insecurity from last time."

"I get that. I promise, if we give this a chance, I'll take steps to show it'll be different this time."

"I believe you."

But Erin wasn't completely sure Jodi had that faith. And she didn't blame her for that, either. She couldn't admit, even to herself, what their relationship had meant back then. She could now. She just needed to do it at her own pace. Coming out to their friends today would be a hard enough first step without telling them she'd had sex with Jodi last night. And while Erin wanted to come out so she could be true to herself, she didn't want to get too invested in the idea of Jodi wanting a long-term relationship.

"Maybe we should get up? They might start wondering what we're up to in here," Jodi said.

Erin pulled her close and held her for one more moment before saying, "I guess we've got to go out there sometime."

"At the very least, I need the bathroom." Jodi's voice held some amusement, so Erin figured they were okay.

"Well, then, I'd better let you go. You can have the bathroom first."

❖

When Jodi was done in the shower, she stopped back by the bed and kissed Erin one more time. "Before I have to go all day without doing this," she said.

Erin kissed her back with enthusiasm, making it hard to stick to the plan of leaving the bedroom, but Jodi stayed firm.

She squeezed Erin's hand and said, "See you out there."

Erin held on as she stood. "Jodi?"

"Yes?"

Erin hesitated, then said, "See you out there."

Jodi squeezed one more time, then let go. The kitchen was empty, but there was a pot of coffee that she helped herself to. As she did, she thought about the events of the night. It had been some of the best sex she'd had in a long time. As she'd told Erin, she really did think sex could be separate from feelings, but she didn't fool herself into believing that last night was just sex. No, indeed. That superglue analogy Erin had mentioned last night was not wrong. When she already had feelings for someone and then slept with them? Well, she had some concerns about the future. What would trying look like? Weekends back and forth? Erin probably couldn't come to Portland often with a teenager at home, so Jodi would have to go to St. Louis. What if Erin didn't want to tell anyone for a long time? How would they make weekends work?

It wouldn't be far to go from where she was to love. If she let that happen, there might be nothing but heartache when Erin realized it would be hard to fit Jodi into her life. At the same time, they were going to be together for thirty-six more hours, and Jodi wouldn't be able to keep her distance with Erin right there in front of her. Not when Erin was interested in others, considerate, sexy, caring, adventurous, and smiling that special for-Jodi smile. But she absolutely could not fall for her, not without knowing Erin's true intentions.

Jodi realized she'd been standing with her mug in her hands for a few minutes, spacing out. She needed to get her act together and find one of the others before Erin showed up, or she'd mess up the whole staggered exit from the bedroom thing. She went outside and found Meredith sipping coffee and looking at her phone.

"Good morning," Jodi said, taking a seat.

Meredith looked up. "Hey. How'd you sleep?"

That was a nice enough greeting. Maybe Meredith had slept on the revelations of the night before and was going to be reasonable about her attitude. "Well. And you? Enjoy the bed to yourself?"

"I think I stayed up a little too late reading since I didn't need to turn the light off for anyone."

"Ah. Must be a good book. What is it?" Jodi took a sip, enjoying the warmth the coffee brought to her chest and the promise of caffeine.

"Oh, something I don't think you'd like."

"That is the wonderful thing about books, the diversity. There's something out there for everyone."

They sipped in silence for a while.

"Have you seen Sal?" Jodi asked.

"No. She was up and gone when I got up."

"Have you been up long?"

"Less than a half an hour, I'd say."

Jodi searched for something else to say. This stilted exchange made her think that Meredith wasn't coping well after all. Jodi wasn't sure what to say to change the mood. Or maybe that wasn't her job. If Meredith wanted to be withdrawn, that was up to her.

They went back to sipping.

"Is Erin getting up?" Meredith asked after a few minutes.

"She was stirring when I left. I think I heard the shower in the kitchen."

Jodi was thinking about going to get her book to entertain herself while she finished her coffee when Sal came around the corner in their running clothes.

"Hey, good morning." Jodi was maybe a little overboard with her enthusiasm because of seeing someone who might actually answer questions beyond the bare minimum.

"Hey," Sal said back.

"Did you sleep better last night? How was the couch?"

"Not bad, as couches go. I think I slept better out of sheer exhaustion if nothing else." They stood just to the side and started stretching. "How did you sleep?"

The deadpan delivery made her think it was possible Sal had overheard something. She glanced to see if Meredith had reacted, but she was resolutely staring at the grass. "Fine. Pretty well."

"Hmm." Sal bent to touch their toes.

Erin came through the sliding glass door, hair still damp from the shower. It made her look very different with her hair soft and loose around her shoulders, bangs covering her forehead. Jodi soaked her in for a few moments too long before looking away in an attempt to not be obvious. She caught Sal looking at her, speculation writ large. She made a quick sour face.

"Good morning, all," Erin said.

Meredith looked animated for the first time that morning. "Hey, sleepyhead. Did you catch up on your sleep in the non-snoring room?"

Erin nodded. "It was a good night."

Jodi grinned into her mug. She couldn't help herself. It had been a good night. They'd gotten a fair amount of sleep, too, as they'd both passed out. The grin faded when she noticed Sal looking at her again. They definitely knew. They wouldn't say anything, she was sure.

Erin took a seat on the other side of Meredith. Sal went back to stretching while everyone else sipped coffee.

"I was thinking of having a shopping day," Meredith said to Erin. Then to the others, "I imagine you two wouldn't be interested." She didn't wait for them to answer before she asked Erin, "But are you?"

Erin took a sip, no doubt to buy some time. Jodi exchanged a look with Sal at the outright disinvitation they'd received. Meredith was done with spending time with them in any meaningful way. Jodi felt mixed about that. On the one hand, if Meredith wanted to be so narrow-minded about Sal's gender that she was letting her I-don't-like-gays flag fly, well, Jodi didn't want to be in her life, either. Meredith had been friendly and an interesting conversational partner, but they hadn't been close friends since high school. It wasn't a huge loss.

Also, Jodi would one hundred percent choose Sal over Meredith anytime. It was rather awkward that they all had another day to spend together and then ride home tomorrow, though.

And Jodi worried for Erin. Meredith had seemingly been a real support to Erin these last nine months. Would she feel like she couldn't come out, given the way Meredith was acting? If she did, she was likely to lose Meredith as a friend, a much greater loss for Erin than Jodi. At the same time, it hurt to think that Erin would mask herself and choose to stay friends with Meredith over aligning herself with Jodi and Sal.

"I'm always up for shopping," Erin smiled. "Maybe half the day? I'd enjoy a walk on the beach, too, if people would be up for that." She smiled at everyone, inclusive. "There is something I'd like to say while we're all here together first." She set her mug on the wide arm of her chair, looking nervous.

Jodi's jaw dropped. Was she going to come out right here and now? She'd said she was going to, and Jodi had wanted to believe her, but a good part of her hadn't. Erin had lived so much of her life not just in the closet but hiding from herself that Jodi worried she would never want to be out and proud.

She closed her mouth. Maybe this was about something completely different.

"I've been doing a lot of thinking over the last year about who I am and what I believe to be right." She straightened her shoulders. "I'm a lesbian. I repressed that side of me because I'd been taught it was wrong. I married Grant, and I don't regret it because I have three wonderful children, but I was never very attracted to him. In fact, there is someone I'm extremely attracted to."

Jodi's mouth hung open again. Not only was Erin coming out, she was also going to tell everyone about the two of them. They'd just talked about *not* doing that because they didn't know what was between them for sure.

Jodi couldn't be unhappy about it. This was what she wanted, right? As Erin continued to speak, Jodi's emotions shifted from surprised to pleased and proud.

"She's sitting right here." Erin smiled at Jodi, who beamed back at her. "I don't know what's in the future for us, but Jodi and I…" She paused and looked at Jodi for permission, as if realizing she was doing something different from what they'd discussed. Jodi nodded. "Jodi and I were lovers during the end of our senior year of high school. I ended it because I was scared and indoctrinated, but this weekend, we've reconnected, and I hope Jodi will give me a chance to prove that I've changed."

Jodi nodded, smiling big.

Meredith looked between them. "Wait. You're saying…fuck. Am I the only straight one here?" She folded her arms and glared at Jodi. "Or are you taking advantage of a vulnerable woman?"

Jodi went back to jaw-dropped shock. "Seriously? That's your go-to? Predatory lesbian? What the fuck, Meredith? You need to get over yourself right now. You've been withdrawn and kind of shitty to both Sal and I ever since dinner last night."

Erin put a hand on Meredith's arm, drawing her attention. She withdrew it after the speed with which Meredith whipped her head around. "That is in no way what happened. In high school, it was me who first kissed Jodi. Neither of us knew we were attracted to women before her birthday party. Remember the kissing practice in the hot tub? Well, it was more for us. But Jodi was brave about who she was from the start, whereas it took me way too long to get there."

Meredith stood. "None of you are who I thought you were. Except maybe you." She gestured toward Jodi. "I was willing to be your friend even though you're gay. But it's clear that there's no place for me in this group. I'm going to pack and figure out a ride to the airport." She went inside.

Everyone was left staring after her. Jodi only wasted a couple of seconds on that before she got up and moved to the seat Meredith had just vacated, gathering Erin's hand. "Are you okay?"

Erin smiled. She looked a little proud, a little sad, and there was a good dose of affection in her smile, too. "I am, I think. It was hard, and I knew not everyone would take it well, but I'd hoped Meredith would come around. I guess not." She looked after her for a moment. "I am still proud I said it and proud that I'm…that we're…"

"Trying this," Jodi said decisively.

Erin's face lit up. "Trying this," she echoed.

"Oh, you guys." Sal stood in front of them looking like they might cry. "You're making me so happy right now." They pulled them into a hug.

Jodi giggled, which caused Erin to join in. Sal pushed them back and swatted them on the arms. "And you kept this from me all this time! I'm going to need details."

CHAPTER FOURTEEN

It was very awkward while Meredith prepared to leave. The other three stayed out back after Jodi made a quick foray into the house for a blanket they spread across all of their laps.

"I feel like I should, I don't know. Go talk to her or something. Offer to help?" Erin said, glancing over her shoulder uncomfortably.

"I mean, I won't stop you." Jodi sounded distracted. She was looking at her phone. "But do you really think she wants to talk to any of us right now?"

"What are you doing on your phone?" Erin asked.

Jodi looked up guiltily. "Looking up options for how Meredith can get back to the city."

Sal laughed. "Nice speech about her not wanting to hear from any of us."

Jodi sighed. "The thing is, what if she can come around? Like, what if she goes home, sits with this for a while, and realizes we're not monsters? We should be the gracious ones and make space, right?"

"Or we write her off as a lost cause," Sal said.

Erin supposed that Sal had had the most to deal with in terms of people judging them and was so worried about being disowned by their family that they'd kept themselves hidden in profound ways. They had the most reason to not want to make space in their lives for someone who didn't support them.

"Did you find anything?" Sal asked.

"Well, it's possible to Uber, but that would be really expensive. However, there is a bus to Portland out of Seaside, which is just up the coast. I'm going to go offer her a ride up there. If we leave in the next ten minutes, she'd make that bus." Jodi was sitting in the middle, so she eased her legs out from under the blanket and climbed awkwardly over it to get out.

"You could have just taken the blanket off and then put it back on us, you know." Sal had a note of fondness in her voice.

"But that would have been disruptive to your comfort. Not to mention the less interesting way to go," Jodi said over her shoulder at the door.

After she went in, Erin said to Sal, "Do you mind that she's helping her?"

Sal shook their head. "No. It's sweet. I just also don't know if it'll result in what Jodi hopes it will. Do you mind? This is sort of stomping all over your big moment."

Erin shook her head. "I should probably be upset, but I kind of expected it. Maybe not storming out, but that's better than if she stayed, and it was awkward for the rest of the time. I expect I'll lose some people over this." Erin looked sadly at her lap. "But it's worth it to have a chance at real happiness."

"With Jodi, right?" There was a note of glee that made Erin look up. Sal's eyes were sparkling.

"You're happy about us? You're not worried I'll break her heart or something?"

"Well, that is a possibility. But I've known for years that something happened that made it difficult for Jodi to be in relationships. She's been a little closed off, I guess. I've also felt like she was, I don't know, comparing everyone to someone. I wasn't sure who. She had a college girlfriend..." Sal trailed off.

"Yes?" Erin was very interested in where that was going.

"It's probably not my place to talk about. I'll just say that I was pretty sure Amber wasn't who she was comparing everyone to, but I couldn't quite figure it out. This solves a lot of mysteries."

"She really never told you?" While Erin did believe it, it was also hard to imagine that Jodi had kept this from her best friend this whole time.

"Really, really," Sal said comfortably. "Guess that means you can trust her, right?"

Erin nodded.

"Okay," Jodi said as she came back outside. "We're out of here. I should be back in about a half an hour, maybe a little more. I wouldn't be sad if there were breakfast plans when I returned." Jodi grinned and walked toward the door. Seemingly thinking better of it, she turned, gave Erin a quick kiss, then left again.

Erin was left grinning madly.

"So, *yeah*." Sal looked thoughtful. "I do worry about her getting hurt. You guys have a lot to figure out. You have to make choices about your family. I don't think she'll be happy being your dirty little secret." When Erin opened her mouth to reply, Sal held their hand up to stop her. "I see you've made great strides this morning. It was a huge thing, telling Meredith. I just have to wonder how it'll go down with your family, and if it doesn't go well, what your choices will be."

Erin wondered that herself. "Well, can you hang on for a minute? I need to check something before I say what I was going to say."

Sal nodded, looking curious.

Erin went to the room she was sharing with Jodi and picked her phone up. She'd texted Darcy that morning asking permission to tell her friends that Darcy was a lesbian. She'd explained that Jodi was a lesbian and what Sal had told them all. Darcy hadn't replied right away, and Erin had assumed she was busy with her team but hoped she'd replied by now. While Erin had outed her to Jodi without clearing it, she didn't want to take it any further without Darcy's buy-in. There was a reply.

Mom, that's soooo cool sure u can tell them

There were a few emojis, too, indicating enthusiasm for how cool her friends were. It warmed Erin's heart. When she got back home, she and Darcy were going to need to have a talk. It was time Erin told her about her own sexuality.

She sent back a quick note of love, support, and good-luck wishes for the game today. She set her phone down and returned outside. She settled herself in her chair and picked her cooling coffee up to take a sip.

"My youngest, Darcy, is gay. It was partially because of that that I divorced Grant. I was worried about how he'd take it and I wanted—want—her to have a safe home base. I feel a little like it's my job to test the waters for her. I can come out to her siblings and see how that goes so she can make an informed choice about coming out herself."

Instead of an encouraging smile or something of the sort, Sal looked worried.

"What?" Erin asked. "Why is that a bad plan?"

Slowly, Sal said, "What I would worry about here is, surely in the circles you've been a part of, you've heard the idea of grooming?"

Erin was shocked. It was clear what Sal was getting at, and she was surprised she hadn't thought of it. If Erin went first, telling her family that she was gay and trying out a relationship with a woman, then Darcy came out next, of course people would think that Erin had made Darcy gay. That was not remotely how it worked, but it was highly likely that people would believe it anyway.

Clearly, Erin's thoughts on the matter were showing clearly on her face because Sal nodded. "Something to think about, right?"

Erin nodded back.

They sat quietly for a while, each involved in their own thoughts. When Erin realized she'd gotten to the bottom of her mug, she went inside for a refill. When she came back out, she said, "I want to make this work with Jodi. I don't know how to do that if I don't come out, at least to my children. But I also don't want to hurt Darcy. I feel a little stuck."

Sal nodded. "I get it. I'm not out to my family. Of course, I don't have kids, and I only see them a couple of times a year, so it's different, but I get where you're coming from."

"If you see all this, why do you think that Jodi and I are a good idea?"

Sal sighed. "I don't mean to be negative. I love love, and I hope you two kids can make this happen." They grinned a little. "But I also think that it's high time Jodi got a chance to see if things can work if you're really in it, too. If it doesn't work out, maybe she'll be able to move on finally."

That was like a lance through Erin's heart. The idea that by trying, they'd just be making a clean break hurt so much that Erin pushed the pain away. She wasn't ready to examine what all that meant.

After taking a moment to gather herself, she said, "So about breakfast…"

CHAPTER FIFTEEN

The drive to Seaside was uncomfortable. Neither Jodi nor Meredith talked at all. When they got to the bus stop, Jodi got out and helped get Meredith's bag out of the trunk. Meredith stiffly said, "Thank you," and went to stand at the bus stop.

Jodi looked helplessly after her, but the thought of returning to both Erin and Sal took over. As she drove down the coast, she felt her excitement grow. She was going to get to spend the day with her lover and her best friend. They'd be able to talk openly about whatever. She'd be able to hold Erin's hand, at least at the rental, but maybe Erin would be open to holding hands out in town, too. After all, she wouldn't ever see these people again.

Jodi turned on her favorite sing-along playlist and did just that.

Entering the rental, she heard the sounds of a shower from one side and a hair dryer from the other. Clearly, Sal was in the shower, and Erin was creating her hair sculpture. Jodi went left, smiling already about watching Erin do her hair. She used to love to watch her work her magic in high school. Sadly, Erin turned off the dryer and walked out of the bathroom just as Jodi walked into the bedroom. Happily, that meant that Jodi could walk right to her, pull her into her a hug, and kiss her. She let her hands roam north as far as Erin's neck but restrained herself from tangling them in Erin's hair.

"Hi." Erin smiled against her lips.

"Hi, yourself."

"How was it?" Erin asked.

"Awkward. But it's done. She's on her way, presumably. I didn't wait for the bus to show up. And now it's just the three of us. I'm looking forward to it. How are you doing?"

A shadow of something crossed Erin's face, but it was quickly replaced with a smile. "Good. I'm glad you're back. I'm glad I came out. I'm looking forward to breakfast."

"Oh, man. Me too. Sounds like the shower stopped. Let's go see if Sal is ready."

❖

Over breakfast, they chatted like the old friends they were but also like new friends discovering each other's stories. Warm fuzzies abounded.

"Who's your type, then?" Sal put their chin on their hands in a classic "do tell" pose. Erin's head angled toward Jodi, which made her smile. Sal waved that away. "Aside from that one."

"Um, well, I like—"

"Wait. Do you not know? This is something you should figure out." Sal sat back and tapped their fingers together as if hatching a plan.

"What are you thinking?" Jodi asked her suspiciously.

"Nothing bad," Sal protested. "I'm thinking we figure it out. We share our types and maybe spend some time looking at YouTube clips."

"Okay, that could be fun." Jodi looked at Erin speculatively. "I'm very curious."

"You are?" Erin asked.

"Yeah, sure, why not?"

"It's just that, well, Grant would never have wanted to know if I found someone else attractive."

Jodi and Sal both burst out laughing.

"What?" Erin looked puzzled and maybe a little hurt.

"Welcome to the queer world. I mean, it's not universal, but we talk about these things," Jodi said. "It's fun. It doesn't mean you're going to act on them or anything. Oh, unless you're polyamorous or otherwise nonmonogamous, I suppose."

Erin looked startled.

"Don't worry. I'm monogamous," Jodi assured her. "I've just been one of those serial monogamists, I suppose."

Erin regarded Sal. "And you?"

"Very monogamous. Although, Brit and I are good friends with a thruple, so it's not like I have a problem with people who aren't."

Jodi pulled up an image on her phone. She held it out to Erin.

"Who is this?" Erin asked, taking it.

"Sue Bird." Jodi put her hands over her heart dramatically.

"You know…things are making some sense here," Sal said, examining Erin.

"What?" Erin asked.

"If you were a few inches taller, a couple of shades darker, and slicked your hair back…"

Erin looked at Jodi's phone again. "Nah. She's much prettier."

"Nah," Jodi said, taking the phone back.

"What about you, Sal? Show me a picture of Brit."

Sal complied with a small, pleased smile.

"She's lovely."

Sal looked proud. "I know, right?"

Jodi watched them, heads bent together over more pictures. Her heart swelled. It was a lovely scene, two of the people who meant the most to her in the world sharing a moment.

The thought brought her up short. She hadn't seen Erin in decades and had spent only a couple of days with her, and she was that important? It seemed she was. It scared her because she didn't know what lay beyond this weekend. She wasn't sure she was up for having her heart broken by Erin again.

Breakfast gave way to a stroll on the beach, which led to sitting in the living room with Sal showing them how up with the tech they were by casting their phone to the TV. They whiled away hours showing different clips and images to each other.

They discovered that Erin's type was, well, it was a little hard for her to define. Physically, she was into blondes but not as a hard and fast rule. Height didn't matter. She favored a butch style, but that wasn't exclusive, either. What did seem to be true was that it wasn't only about looks; she liked women who were confident, smart, and had something to say.

She checked Jodi out, realizing she fit the bill in every way.

"What? Have you decided I'm not up to your standards?" Jodi was teasing, but Erin detected a hint of worry.

Erin leaned into her. "No, I was thinking you make perfect sense."

Jodi's cheeks turned pink. "I'm flattered."

Erin was conflicted. She wanted to be sincere, but she also wanted to guard her heart a little. What if Jodi went home and decided a long-distance relationship with a single mom wasn't what she really wanted? She went with teasing. "As you should be."

They went to a late lunch or as Jodi quipped, "An old person dinner. Which, let's face it, we're closer to than to high school."

Erin mock wept at that. While they were debating on if they should have dessert or pick up dessert to take back to their rental, Erin got a text saying Darcy's team had made the semifinals, which would happen in the morning. They all cheered. Erin was happy for her. She wished she could be two places at once so she could watch the Stingers' triumph. But she got to see Darcy play a lot, and she wouldn't trade this weekend for anything.

Jodi bumped her shoulder. "Are you sad you're not at the tournament?"

Erin bumped her in return. "I'm right where I want to be."

Jodi grinned. "This calls for a celebration. Let's get stuff to make margaritas, some chips, and of course, some chocolaty dessert. Or it could be martinis." She said the last bit into her water cup.

Sal started laughing.

"What?" Erin asked, looking between them.

When Jodi gave Erin her full attention, their gazes locked before she explained, "When Sal first decided to give alcohol a try, Brit and I took them out for a margarita. It's a good beginner drink, right?" Erin nodded. "Well, then, they went out for drinks with coworkers a few weeks later, and they sent a text saying that they'd tried to order the same thing, but it wasn't the same at all. After some back and forth, I finally figured out they had gotten a martini instead."

Sal rolled their eyes. "In my defense, they both start with an M."

Erin's eyes sparkled with mirth. "Did you drink it?"

"Yes. I was embarrassed not to. But I've never gotten one again. Turns out, I'm not a fan of gin."

"So definitely martinis tonight, then," Erin said, deadpan.

They walked to the liquor store to pick up triple sec and tequila. When they exited, they realized the sun was about to set, so they detoured to the beach to watch. Jodi took Erin's hand and gave it a brief squeeze before dropping it. Erin was pleased by both the gesture and the recognition that she might not want to participate in PDA yet. The thoughtfulness and the circumstance—being far from home—made her brave. She upped the ante by wrapping an arm around Jodi's shoulders. Jodi slipped an arm around her waist. They stood, leaning into each other, watching the setting sun paint the clouds.

The warmth of Jodi seeped into her. The contact was also electrifying. Erin felt alive. Like she could fly. Here she was, on the beach, watching a beautiful sunset with a woman in her arms. Not just any woman. Jodi. It was too much, not enough, and just right all in the same moment. Too much because she felt like she might burst. Not enough because she was already thinking about going to bed that night. And just right because they fit in a way that made her feel truly herself.

When they decided to move on, Erin caught Sal looking at them with heart eyes. Erin just smiled back. She felt like she was floating.

They made a quick stop at the small store by their rental to supplement the snacks they already had. Then, it was back to eat, drink, and be merry.

In short, it was a truly excellent day. Aside from Meredith showing her true colors that morning. Erin felt a pang at the loss of the friend Meredith had been. She didn't regret anything. If Meredith couldn't accept her for who she was, then it wasn't much of a loss. That did make Erin worry about telling more people. She wanted to, but there were people in her life she couldn't stand to lose. Her children primary among them.

That was a worry for later. Right now, she was going to revel in this impromptu party with two of her oldest friends, one of whom she had plans for later.

Jodi held up her margarita glass. "Cheers to old friends and new beginnings."

Sal and Erin clinked their glasses to hers. Jodi winked at her, and she melted.

CHAPTER SIXTEEN

It might have been high school since the last time Erin had hung out with her friends all day without having to worry about what her kids or Grant might be doing. Only, this was even better because now they had the funds to eat good food, the age to buy alcohol, and no need to report back to parents. Also, she could wrap an arm around Jodi in front of other people. She'd wanted to do that back in their senior year more times than she could count, but it was never a possibility. Now, the world seemed to open in front of her. She was determined to live in the moment.

The current one involved getting ready for bed. With Jodi. They brushed their teeth side by side, a little giggly from the drinks. They'd only had two each, as no one had wanted to deal with a hangover, but it was enough to be a little silly. Enough to give Erin the courage to grab Jodi's fine butt as she passed on the way to dry her mouth. When Jodi winked, Erin spat her mouthwash out in the sink, grabbed Jodi's hand, and dragged her to the bed.

"Why, Erin. Whatever are you trying to tell me?" Jodi batted her eyelashes. She took off her glasses so it was clear she was in on the plan, despite her words.

"I'm trying to tell you that I want you in bed right now." Erin was surprised at her forwardness. She'd been a willing participant in their high school explorations, certainly. But words like that had never left her mouth before.

Jodi's expression went from amused to serious in the blink
of an eye, and she lay back on the bed with what Erin could only
describe as a come-hither look. Erin set her own glasses aside and
crawled up the bed, lowering herself on top of Jodi, who sunk her
hands into Erin's hair and pulled her head down so their lips met.
Erin had always loved that move, the hands in the hair, particularly
when she upped the ante with a little tug. It was that move in the
practice kiss they'd shared in the hot tub all those years ago that had
gotten Erin so hot and bothered that she'd suggested they practice
without hands. Grant had never messed with her hair. She'd never
asked him to. Jodi just did it unbidden, and Erin felt it in her core.

Erin dipped her tongue into Jodi's mouth and delighted in the
taste of her. A bit minty from brushing her teeth but also a taste that
was all Jodi. Erin felt like she could explore her mouth all night.
Again, she'd never felt that with Grant. She'd found kissing him
rather boring. That had seemed fine with him. He'd always been
anxious to get to the main event.

Erin slid her hand under Jodi's shirt and felt her soft skin.
All thoughts of comparing her to Grant fell away as her mind was
consumed by the feel of a woman. Her soft skin, the curve of her
waist giving way to the swell of the side of her breast. How could
Erin have ever convinced herself that she wasn't into women? And
into this woman particularly?

They shifted about until their clothes were no longer in the way,
and then Erin set about to showing Jodi just how into her she was.

❖

Erin's first thought upon waking the next morning was pleasure
at being pinned down by the leg Jodi had thrown over her own. She
was right on the edge of the bed, apparently having been shifted
in that direction by Jodi over the course of the night. She had a
memory of cuddling in the middle as they'd fallen asleep. She rested
a hand on Jodi's thigh with fondness. She couldn't help but stroke
her soft skin, moving upward.

Jodi murmured and stirred, shifting even closer.

"Careful or we'll both end up on the floor," Erin warned.

Jodi opened an eye. "Ah. Sorry about my bed hog ways." She scooted back toward the center, and Erin missed her immediately.

"I didn't want you to go away."

"Well, come join me in the middle." Jodi smiled a sleepy but seductive smile.

Erin went. Their kisses started out slow and sleepy, but it wasn't long until their passion built again. As they cuddled after, Jodi the little spoon and Erin's hand cupping her breast, Erin said, "I hope Sal is out for their morning run."

"Because you are worried about, what? Them drinking coffee all alone out there?"

"Because I think I might not have been as quiet as one might want to be when there is another person home."

"Ah. Well, I wasn't going to say anything…"

Jodi sounded way too pleased with herself. Erin shifted her hand so she could rub Jodi's nipple. "And you were quiet, were you?"

"Mmm, well, someone made me feel really good."

Erin couldn't help the pride that filled her, but it gave way fairly quickly to uncertainty. "When can we…"

"Do this again?" Jodi asked.

"Yes." Erin bit her lip, hoping they were still on the same page about trying. Hoping Jodi hadn't gotten it out of her system or something.

"Hey," Jodi said softly.

"Yes?"

"I want this. I want to give us a try. Sure, we have things to work out, but I want to see if we can."

The knot that had been tightening in Erin's chest loosened. It was still there. She still had to figure out how to talk to her family, *if* she should talk to them. They were going to have to navigate their relationship at a distance. She still wasn't completely convinced that Jodi wouldn't want to just move on. That was the pattern she'd built up her entire adult life. There wasn't an easy road ahead, but right now, Jodi was in her arms. Right now, Jodi wanted to try.

"We should probably get going," Jodi said. "We do have a timeline today."

Erin knew it was true, but she also didn't want to leave this bed where it was easy to be together and trade it in for the march toward distance that the day would bring.

They got up and showered together, just enjoying being together and the contact sliding by one another brought. Erin had had more sex in the last two days than she'd had in a long time before and didn't think she was up for more, but she craved Jodi's touch. She delighted in watching Jodi's naked body move. She looked up from watching her soap her breasts to see Jodi's knowing smile.

Erin grinned at her. "You're beautiful."

"Not as beautiful as you."

As they dried off, dressed, and packed their bags, they discussed when they might next see each other. One weekend, Erin was going to be chaperoning a tournament; another weekend, Jodi was going to a convention. There were plenty of things in their already busy lives conspiring to keep them apart, but they finally settled on a weekend in early November. It was only five weeks away. Erin told herself that was fine.

CHAPTER SEVENTEEN

H ow's the long-distance thing going?" Sal asked.
"Fine?" Jodi shot a look at the overcast sky, hoping it wouldn't rain on her before her walk was over.

"That sounds convincing."

"She's great. I'm enjoying having her in my life again, even at a distance, but I do miss touching her and…"

"And?"

"I don't know what we're doing."

There was silence on the other end of the phone.

"I know, I know. We said we were trying, whatever that means. We picked a weekend to get together. I guess I'm going there? But I haven't bought tickets. She hasn't mentioned it again. I don't think she's even told Darcy. We text all the time, talk sometimes. I just… think it may have just been a weekend fling, at least in terms of being in a relationship. I think we might just be friends now?"

It was crazy to think that because they'd gotten so close over the reunion weekend. Erin had made such strides, coming out, wrapping her arm around Jodi on the beach. Jodi had felt like with another few weeks like that, she'd have to bite her tongue to keep the words "I love you" in. Instead, Erin was putting her firmly in the friend zone. A good friend, sure. A friend she'd slept with a couple of times, yeah. But a friend.

"Have you brought up the weekend?"

"Well, no. I haven't wanted to pressure her." Jodi felt a raindrop. Shoot.

"Maybe she's waiting for you."

"Did you hear the part about her not coming out to anyone? I think she's just gone back to her life and decided this was a blip, and that's that." More raindrops were falling now. Jodi considered turning back toward home. She was nearly halfway through her loop. She could cut for home and be back in about ten minutes instead of twenty.

"Or she's scared, needs support, and is thinking you're the one pulling back."

Sal might have a point, but Jodi wasn't completely sure she wanted to admit that. She'd been initiating some of the contact and had been responsive every time Erin had reached out, but she also hadn't brought up seeing each other again or really invited closeness beyond friendship. In the week and a half since she'd seen Erin, she'd treated her as a friend just as much as Erin had treated Jodi as a friend. Jodi could admit that as long as their romantic relationship stayed in the box of the weekend at the beach, she was protecting her heart. But if one of them didn't make a move to shift the romantic relationship into real life, they might let a great thing pass them by.

"Fine. I'll bring up planning for the weekend," Jodi grumbled. "Listen, it's starting to really rain here, and I'm going to make a dash for home. Talk later?"

"Wimpy. How long have you lived in the Pacific Northwest?"

"Okay, pot, kettle. I've been outside with you when it's started to rain."

Sal laughed. "Yeah, yeah. Go get yourself some shelter."

Jodi hung up and started a fast walk home. Nothing made her break into a run.

"So, um, I was looking at flights?" Jodi hated the hesitancy in her voice. She was a confident full adult. She was fifty-one, for crying out loud. There was something about Erin, though, that made her feel like she was in high school again. Not something about her. Jodi knew what it was. Their patterns of behavior with one another had been etched in when they were teenagers with a secret relationship that had been harder on Erin than on Jodi. Jodi was used to being the one pushing for time together, not that Erin hadn't wanted it. She'd just thought she shouldn't want it. It had seemed, over the weekend, that they'd started charting a new course, but now, well, now that they felt more like friends than lovers, some of the old patterns seemed to be rearing their heads.

Jodi cleared her throat and went to try again, more confident this time.

Erin spoke before she could. "Oh, good. I was hoping you were looking. How long can you stay?"

Okay, so maybe Erin had been waiting for Jodi to make the first move. But why? Jodi needed her to be as invested. She needed to know Erin wanted a real relationship, which would only happen if they were out with the people closest to them, and that included Erin's family.

However, this was also one-step-at-a-time territory, and Erin had been brave on the reunion weekend. Jodi shoved her misgivings aside, and they talked schedules for a while. They decided that Jodi would fly in Wednesday. She'd have some work to do before the end of the week, but she'd be able to record what she needed in her makeshift studio before she went. She just needed to take her laptop for editing and publishing, and she'd be set. Erin would also have some work to do, so that would be fine.

Jodi was relieved to have plans. Not only because she wanted to see Erin, but because having plans for a visit made it seem like Erin wasn't friend zoning her after all. The conversation flowed much more smoothly after that.

They chatted awhile longer while Jodi loaded her dishwasher and wiped down her kitchen. Jodi mentioned a book she was reading for one of her podcasts, and Erin said, "I feel like I'm getting an insider sneak peek about what will be on future podcasts. Do you always review the books you pick?"

"Nah. I try to keep the podcasts mostly positive, so if I feel eh about a book, I usually won't discuss it. If I really hate a book, I might mention it in passing but try not to give time to it."

"Seems like you have to read a ton. How do you decide what books to read?"

Jodi squeezed out her sponge and set it in its designated spot. Some of her short-term girlfriends had left sponges sopping wet in the middle of the sink, which had bothered her no end. Jodi wondered if Erin was a sponge in its spot sort of woman. A memory of her carefully hanging up a washcloth during the reunion weekend flashed in her head. She warmed at the thought. "I get sent books by publishers and authors who want publicity, mostly. I usually get ARCs, advanced reader copies. I'm on BookTok, Instagram, and Twitter, also. Sometimes, there will be a book that I see there that I want to read, so I'll go get it for myself. To save time, if I'm not into a book, I don't finish it. I have a robust DNF policy."

"DNF? BookTok?"

Jodi washed and dried her hands. She was pleased at Erin's asking follow-up questions rather than just uh-huhing her way through the conversation. And a little embarrassed that she'd slipped into jargon. "Oh, sorry. DNF means did not finish, and BookTok is the book corner of TikTok."

"I'm mostly on Facebook, although I do have an Instagram. I, um, have looked around your accounts, and you don't follow a lot of people, so how are you keyed into all these book corners?" Jodi could hear dishes clattering on the other end. Erin was also doing the after dinner cleanup.

Jodi liked that Erin had checked out her accounts. She'd certainly checked out Erin's. This reminded her that the situation wasn't exactly balanced. "Ah, yeah, so I have my official accounts and my personal ones. I've been meaning to rectify the fact that you follow my official accounts, and I follow your personal ones. I use 'notthatjodi' everywhere. Jodi spelled my way." She pulled out a mug, filled it with water, and put it in the microwave for tea.

Erin laughed. "I've always said you look like Jodie Foster."

"I take that as a high compliment."

"You should. She's hot. And gay. I've learned this recently."

She was such a cute baby gay. "Yup, another one for our team." Jodi stood and watched the microwave go around and worried in the split second before Erin answered that she'd disavow being on their team.

"Indeed. Along with JoJo Siwa. Whom I heard about from Darcy. I'm very out of the loop."

Jodi laughed and stopped the microwave before it started beeping. "We've gotta get you more in the loop, for sure." She was excited to explore all sort of things with Erin. LGBTQIA+ culture was only part of it.

"I look forward to it." The background sounds at the other end had grown quieter.

"Done with dishes?"

"I am. Sounds like you are, too?"

"Yeah, just making a cup of tea. Do you have evening plans?" Jodi dipped her tea bag in and out of the hot water. She hoped Erin didn't. She wanted to spend more time with her, even if at a distance.

"Not really. Darcy's team does a weekly group study after practice where they have tutors to help the girls. That's tonight, so I don't expect her until ten."

Jodi looked at the clock. It was seven fifteen, which meant nine fifteen for Erin. "I was thinking we could start a series together. Start introducing you to gay culture beyond *A League of Their Own*."

"Hey," Erin said, mock affronted. "I have also watched *Glee*."

Jodi rolled her eyes for her own amusement. "Okay, I stand corrected. You're well versed."

Erin laughed. "Okay, what do you have in mind?"

"Have you watched *Orange is the New Black*? I find the main character, Piper, kind of annoying, but a lot of the other characters are great." Jodi squeezed out her tea bag and threw it away before moving to the living room, still shaking the heat off her fingers.

"No, I haven't. Where can I find it?"

Jodi set her tea on her coffee table and settled on the couch. They worked through where and how to watch together. They had to pause frequently to discuss what was happening, exactly as Jodi had hoped for. Erin paused once more in a spot that surprised Jodi, but she was willing to go along with it.

"Hang on a sec. Darcy is home."

That explained it. Jodi could hear the conversation in a muffled sort of way.

"Are you watching…"

"Yes. I'm…with Jodi."

Erin muted the microphone, and Jodi was left to wonder what she'd told Darcy about them and what she was telling her now. Jodi knew that Erin had tried to keep her kids away from anything too explicit as they were growing up, so if she was feeling defensive about watching *Orange is the New Black*, it could be because of that, not because of the queer content. Jodi tried to tell herself that was the reason and not that Erin was embarrassed by what she was watching or who with.

Erin came back on the line. "Sorry about that. Darcy is off to her room. Apparently with more homework to do."

"It's no problem for you to say hi to your kid." Jodi meant it, too, but she also was feeling a little bummed that Erin didn't seem to be telling Darcy about…anything. Still, she'd noticed a hint of worry in Erin's voice. "Are you concerned about how much homework she has?"

"Kind of. I mean, I remember hardly sleeping as a teenager. There was school, cheer, working at Target, and then homework."

"I got more sleep than you did because I didn't care as much about homework. And I didn't have cheer. But I definitely remember. There was one night when I slept over at your house, and when we woke up in the morning, you said, 'Isn't it nice to get eight hours of sleep? I feel so refreshed.' I agreed because it seemed like the thing to do, but in reality, I was thinking, 'Eight isn't nearly enough to catch up on the weekend.'"

Erin laughed. "I don't remember that day specifically, but that is something I remember, delighting in eight hours of sleep but functioning fine with just a few hours when I couldn't get it."

"Now I'm glad when I get more than seven."

"Really? Are you that busy?"

"No. I just don't sleep as well as I used to. And if I sleep in, the not sleeping is worse the next night, so I usually make myself get up at seven."

"Ah yes. I wake up in the middle of the night to pee all the time and sometimes have a hard time falling back asleep. It's a crime what aging does to us."

"I didn't notice you getting up when we were in Cannon Beach." Jodi took the last glug of her now cold tea.

"I guess you really tired me out. Didn't we also wake up around eight?" Erin's voice was a mixture of affectionate and playful, music to Jodi's ears. It was further confirmation that they were more than friends.

"Clearly, sleeping with each other is good for our health, and we should do it more often."

"Clearly. How many more weeks until you get here?" Erin groaned a little in frustration.

While Jodi shared the sentiment, she was also amused and flattered. "Too many, I think."

"You sound far too amused," Erin said.

"You're just cute is all."

"Flatterer."

"You're right. You're not cute at all."

"Well." Erin sounded surprised but also laughed a little.

"You're beautiful."

"Aw. I mean, I like to think cute, too, but beautiful is nice."

"And modest."

"Obviously."

Jodi looked at the clock on the microwave. "Do you want to finish watching or…"

"Let's finish the episode. Then, I should probably get to bed, even though I won't sleep as well since you're not here."

Jodi groaned and let her head fall back to bump the couch. "I really, really wish I was." She also really, really wished that Erin would tell Darcy. Everything would feel more real then. Were they going to have to pretend to be friends when she went to visit?

At the same time, this evening had felt more like they were a couple than Jodi had felt since Cannon Beach. She could be patient. Erin was worth it.

CHAPTER EIGHTEEN

Erin waited excitedly but also a little nervously just outside security at the airport. She wanted to be right there to hug Jodi and to show she was excited about her being there. She was, too, so excited. The last five weeks had seemed endless. Well, four and a half, really, because it was Wednesday.

These last couple of days had snuck up on her. She'd been putting off having the conversation with Darcy for reasons she wasn't entirely sure about. Finally, she'd sat Darcy down Monday night. She'd have put it off until last night if she wasn't thinking that Darcy might need a little time to adjust:

"There's something I need to tell you." Erin sat on the edge of Darcy's bed.

Darcy looked up from her math homework and seemed to chew her cheek.

"It's not bad, don't worry." Erin took a deep breath. "You've been so brave about telling me who you really are, and you deserve the same from me."

"What? You're queer, too?" Darcy teased, then, no doubt seeing something in Erin's face, she said in a much different tone, "Wait. You're queer, too?"

Erin nodded. She could do this. It was only the third time she'd said it aloud, but she could do this. "I'm a lesbian."

"Mom! Seriously? Like, how? I mean, what about Dad? Does he know? Do Brad and Lindsey? Who knows? Mom, seriously, since when?" She pushed her homework to the side and knelt on her bed.

Erin held her hands up to stop the onslaught of questions while a corner of her mind envied her daughter's young knees. "Other than my high school friends, the ones I just had the reunion weekend with, only you know. And since always, really, even though I suppressed it for many years. I did love your dad. He was a good friend when we got together. I fooled myself into thinking it would be enough because I was told I was supposed to grow up, marry a man, and have kids. It was a different time, and well, you're familiar with the church I grew up in and your grandparents. I thought it was what I had to do."

Darcy opened her mouth to say something, then closed it again.

"I don't regret it. I have you kids, and there's no change I'd make that would mean I didn't."

"But you knew back then?" Darcy sat back on her heels.

Erin nodded. "I did, yes. Well, sort of. I mean, I had a girlfriend in high school for a while."

Darcy's jaw dropped. "Seriously? Who? I don't even have a girlfriend, but you did back in the eighties?"

"We kept it a secret, but yes. After a few months, I couldn't take the stress of lying about it. Also, I believe differently now, but I thought I was sinning then. It was a really hard situation. We were seniors, and she was leaving for college anyway. I couldn't see a life for us, so I'm the one who ended it."

"Wow. Then, you met Dad and married him, but you knew you were a lesbian the whole time?"

Erin shook her head slightly. "Yes and no. I mean, I really suppressed it for a long time. Do you know when I faced the fact that I was? Or at least that I liked women in that way more than men?" In her head, she added, *Or at least one woman a lot more than who I was married to?*

Darcy looked fascinated. "No, when?"

"When we first watched *A League of Their Own*."

"Whoa. Is that really why you and Dad divorced?" She moved to sit next to Erin, one foot tucked under her thigh.

"No. Well, maybe. I mean, I didn't tell him or even have a chance to tell him I was unhappy. As soon as I said we should talk, he fessed up about Teri and asked if I wanted a divorce. I said yes. There were lots of reasons at that point."

"Was I one of them?" Darcy pulled the corner of her mouth between her teeth.

Erin put an arm around her. "I wanted your home to be a safe space, so that was a part of the consideration, I won't lie. However, I think it's abundantly clear that your dad and I had our own reasons for not staying married. The divorce was in no way your fault."

Darcy sighed. "I know that, I guess. It's been better without him." The corner of her mouth pulled in again. "Is that a bad thing?"

Erin shook her head. "It's just what it is. You have seemed happier. And more confident about talking to me. I've felt it, and I'm glad."

Darcy slumped a little to rest her head on Erin's shoulder. As tall as Erin was, Darcy had more than an inch or two on her. Of course, she was nowhere near as tall as Brad, so Erin was familiar with having a person who used to be inside her body now be bigger than she was, but it was a little bittersweet that it was her baby girl who now looked her in the eye, plus a bit.

They sat quietly for a few moments. Then, Erin said, "There's more."

Darcy straightened. "Oh my gosh, Mom, do you have a girlfriend?"

"Yes."

Darcy threw her hands up. "Argh. Why do you have a girlfriend, and I don't? Who is it? Is it Ms. Holder?"

Rhoda Holder was one of the new friends Erin played tennis with at the community center. She'd come over for lunch after playing one Saturday, so Darcy had met her.

"No. You know how Jodi is coming to visit this weekend?"

"Your high school friend? Oh my gosh, was she your high school girlfriend? Is this a second chance romance?" Darcy's mouth gaped.

Erin's cheeks felt a little warm, but she nodded. "Yes."

Darcy flopped back on her bed, arms splayed. "Wow. Okay. And she's still staying with us?"

"Yes."

"In your room?"

"Yes."

"I don't even know what to say, Mom. Just…make good choices."

Erin laughed and tickled her belly. "Yes, Mom."

Darcy curled protectively around her stomach, shrieking. "Do I get to have sleepovers with my hypothetical future girlfriend?"

"You're sixteen, so I'm going to have to go with, probably not."

"Hypocritical much?" There was no heat behind it.

"Parental privilege."

"What about when I'm seventeen?"

"Get a girlfriend, and we'll talk."

"Wow, Mom, way to kick a girl when she's down."

"I imagine you'll survive." Erin patted her arm. "How's the homework going?"

Darcy rolled her eyes. "Fine. All I have left is math, which is easy enough."

"Well, I'll leave you to it." Erin patted her arm one more time and stood.

"Can I tell your girlfriend embarrassing stories?"

Erin paused at the doorway. "I've never done anything embarrassing in my life, so you'd be making stuff up."

Darcy looked sly. "We'll see about that."

Erin shaded her eyes with one hand and shook her head. "This is going to be an interesting weekend."

Erin watched passengers streaming out of security, wondering if they'd been on Jodi's flight. Darcy had wanted to come to the airport, too. She was dying of curiosity, but she had practice. They were going to meet at home after practice and go to dinner together. Erin was a little nervous about how that would go. She really wanted them to get along.

Finally, Jodi emerged from behind two taller people. She was looking around, and Erin saw the very moment she spotted her. Her step gained a little bounce, her eyes lit up, and a smile lifted the corners of her mouth.

Erin felt her entire body come awake. She had a quick stab of concern about how far gone she was, considering the circumstances of their relationship, but it was overwhelmed by her excitement.

She moved up through the waiting people to meet Jodi, who dropped her backpack next to her roller bag and wrapped her arms around Erin's waist. Erin pulled her even closer. She wanted very much to kiss her but held back. They were in public in the city where Erin lived. She needed to be careful not to be outed before she was ready. Jodi hugged her back tightly. When they separated, Erin took the handle of Jodi's suitcase.

"You don't have to do that," Jodi said. She seemed amused for some reason.

"I know, but you've got the backpack, too. I can help. Unless you don't want me to."

"No, it's fine. I mean, thank you. It's just funny because Sal has this thing about always carrying heavy stuff."

"Well, you'll note that I didn't pick up that backpack. I took the easy way out with the roller bag."

Jodi laughed. It was a good sound. Erin was very pleased to hear it in person.

Chapter Nineteen

A fter Erin started the car, she seemed to be looking around. Jodi presumed it was to ensure the area was clear before backing out, even though this car was new enough that it had a camera. When Erin instead leaned over the center console and pulled her in for a scorching kiss, Jodi was a little surprised but more than willing to go with it.

"I've missed you," Erin said when she pulled back.

"I can see that." Jodi let her amusement show. More seriously, she said, "Me too. I mean, I missed you."

Once they were out of the airport, Erin dropped a hand on Jodi's thigh. She covered it with her own, delighted. "Darcy will meet us at the apartment. She might be there already. It depends on traffic and how long she lingers with her friends. Then, we'll go out to dinner, all three of us, if that's okay."

"Sure. I'm excited to meet her. And a little nervous. Teenagers can be cruel." Jodi was only partially kidding. She wasn't generally an anxious person, but teenagers weren't her forte. She did okay with her cohost's kids, but they hadn't even hit the preteens yet.

Erin laughed. "Darcy is a good kid. You'll be fine."

"*Okay*, if you say so. What if she doesn't approve? In some ways, this is more stressful than meeting the parents."

"Is that something you've done?" Erin studiously faced the road. "Meet the parents?"

"Oh, yeah, sure. I've met a few parents, but other than Amber, none of it was because we were serious. More just incidental. And of course, I've met your parents." Jodi chuckled.

Erin laughed. "That's true. Amber was your college girlfriend, right?"

"Also my longest relationship. That lasted just under a year."

"Wow."

"It doesn't mean I'm not willing to commit long-term. I know it's very player-y to say that I'd settle down for the right person. But I would." She squeezed Erin's hand, willing her to believe.

"That does make it sound like it was all those other women's fault for not being the right person."

"It's not their collective fault that they aren't you." Jodi couldn't help grin at the cheesy line.

"Oh, wow. Really, wow. Now you sound like a huge player."

Jodi laughed. "I know. Way over-the-top, right?"

"Just a little." Erin moved her hand down Jodi's thigh and squeezed her knee.

Jodi about jumped out of her skin.

"Still a ticklish spot?" Erin asked innocently.

Jodi glared. "Not at all."

"Okay." She squeezed again.

Jodi's knee hit the underside of the glove box. "Hey! Concentrate on your driving, woman."

"Maybe a little ticklish?"

"Fine. It's ticklish. Now will you leave it alone?"

In answer, Erin slid her hand back up Jodi's thigh. That was much better.

Her apartment was in a nondescript complex. She led Jodi to a first-floor unit near where they parked and let them in. "It's nothing special. I needed something inexpensive, available, and not too far from Darcy's school."

"It's great." She could have lived pretty much anywhere, and Jodi would have thought it was great. She was so glad to share space with Erin again.

It was a standard-looking, modern apartment outfitted with typical middle-class furniture. There was a sectional couch that looked just a little bit too big for the living room. It had probably fit great in Erin's last house. Jodi wondered if she missed the larger space. Instead of a coffee table, there was a square ottoman that matched the couch. There was a low dresser thing with a TV on top. It was a nice-looking piece of furniture. There was art on the walls. They added some visual interest. It was interesting to see what Erin choose to bring with her into her new life. Jodi wanted to see pictures of her old house to see what she left behind. She wanted to know everything about the new Erin.

Erin snorted. "Sure, great. It's boring and a little cramped."

Jodi shrugged. She slid her backpack off and set it next to her suitcase. "Looks comfortable."

"It is that," Erin said. "I sold the couches that looked nice but were like sitting on cement and kept the comfortable ones. Plural because there's one in my office, too. Come on. I'll give you the grand tour before Darcy gets home."

Jodi wasn't sure how Erin knew Darcy wasn't home yet. Maybe she usually left stuff in the living room or something. She was nervous about meeting Darcy and kind of wanted it over with, but it was nice to have Erin to herself for a little longer, too.

The living room was spotless, with nothing out of place aside from Jodi's things. Jodi wondered if Erin had cleaned up for her or if it was always spotless. Jodi had a few things that had to be just so, her kitchen sponge for one, but she did have a tendency to leave some items where they landed, sometimes for days. Things like hoodies, for example. She wondered if that would be a problem for Erin. She must be used to a little mess from the kids, but Jodi was a grown woman. She could make an effort to put things away if it made Erin happy.

Making Erin happy was one of her goals in life, particularly this weekend.

On one side of the living room, close to the front door, an opening led down a hall, presumably to the bedrooms. A jolt of excitement went through Jodi at the idea of Erin's bedroom. On the other side, there was an arch about the size of two doors that led to a kitchen and dining room that were open to each other. The kitchen was a little bigger than Jodi's, but the appliances looked older. The dining room was surprisingly spacious and held a large table.

"Wow. Didn't expect that." Jodi pointed to the table.

"I know. A lot for two, right? But it's one of the things I liked about the apartment, that the dining area was big enough to hold that table because I love it."

Jodi could see why it. It was a dark walnut with character. She traced a finger over it. "It's lovely."

Erin took her arm and pulled her in. "You're lovely." She lowered her head, and Jodi met her lips in a kiss. Her hand crept up to Erin's neck as their lips and tongues moved together. She was dying to sink her hands into Erin's hair, but that wouldn't be welcome when Darcy was about to come home. It would be an indication of what they'd been up to.

"The back's okay," Erin said against Jodi's lips. "There's no product back there."

Jodi chuckled a little at how well Erin knew her. She pushed her hands into Erin's hair, parting her fingers around the silky strands. In high school, Erin had always used hair spray on her entire 'do, so apparently, there had been some subtle changes to her style.

Jodi sucked Erin's lower lip, pulling it into her mouth, then nipped it before caressing it with her tongue. Erin moaned and deepened the kiss. Jodi's center pulsed. She wanted to drag Erin to her room. Or this table would work just fine. Erin could sit on it and…

"Mom?"

They sprang apart. The call had come from the living room, so at least Darcy hadn't walked in on them. Jodi burned with mortification at the idea that the first time Darcy ever laid eyes on her might have been when she was passionately kissing Darcy's mom.

Erin fluffed her hair, but she looked amused, not alarmed. Darcy must have taken the talk really well. "In here, Darce. I was just giving Jodi the nickel tour."

Darcy came through the doorway smiling. She was at least as tall as her mom and had dark brown hair like her. By contrast, hers was in a messy ponytail, she was wearing softball practice clothes, and she was sporting a copious amount of dirt. "That's about what it's worth, yeah. Hi—you must be Jodi."

Jodi held out her hand, feeling foolish for offering to shake with a teenager. What did teenagers do in greeting anyway? Luckily, while Darcy's smile turned amused, she shook Jodi's hand. Jodi wasn't sure what she'd have done if Darcy had left her hanging and felt grateful. She smiled, feeling very short. "Nice to meet you, Darcy. Are you still practicing outside? It's cold out there."

Darcy laughed. "It is, but you warm up when you're running around. Only two more weeks, and we have the last tournament of the season. After that, we move indoors."

"How do you play softball indoors?"

"The team has a warehouse. Well, the org has a warehouse. We share it with the other teams, so we practice less often for scheduling reasons. But there's a whole infield in there and a batting cage and stuff."

"Wow. That sounds amazing."

Darcy shrugged. "It's good we get to keep playing, but I prefer outdoors. Well, maybe not in February."

"Go shower so we can eat," Erin said. "I thought we'd go to Ana's."

"Yum." Darcy walked away.

"So that was Darcy."

"She seems great."

"She is." Erin looked after her fondly.

"Whew."

"Whew?"

"Yeah. I wasn't sure, you know, with a teenager. What if she wouldn't talk to me or something? One hears things." Jodi was only partially exaggerating her relief.

Erin laughed. "They're not a different species." She looked thoughtful for a moment. "Maybe they are." She chuckled. "Come on, let me show you the rest."

They went back through the living room, collecting the roller bag and backpack, and went down the hall. At the first door on the left, Erin said, "That's my office. It could be a bedroom, but it's pretty small."

Jodi stuck her head in and saw a tidy desk, a file cabinet, a shelving unit, and a loveseat. The furniture pretty much filled the room. There were some pictures of Erin's kids on the walls. Jodi walked over to look more closely. She wanted to see all she could of the people who were so important to Erin. They were all candid and included ages from babyhood to what must be a recent shot of all three of them, considering their apparent ages. "I love these pictures."

Erin joined her. Their arms brushed. Jodi wanted to notice all the little moments of being together to store away for their next stretch apart. Erin touched the three kids creating a pyramid, all grinning wildly for the camera. Darcy was on top and had a gap in her smile, clearly in the tooth shedding period of childhood. "I took a ton when they were little."

"I mean, they are all very photogenic."

Erin smiled at her. "Thanks."

Jodi glanced at the door to make sure they were alone, then pushed to her tiptoes to kiss Erin. "They take after their mom. It's a cozy little office. And I'm glad to see there's a place for me so we can work in the same room, if that won't be disruptive for you."

"Not at all. I was hoping the couch would work for you."

They'd planned to work a full day on Thursday and hopefully half days at most on Friday. Both had too much work to do to completely take the time off.

Opposite the office was a door that was ajar and unlit, a bathroom. "Both Darcy's room and mine have ensuites, but there's also this one." Erin indicated it with a hand.

The hall ended with two doors opposite each other. Erin pointed at the closed door. "That's Darcy's room." She went in the other, and Jodi followed. "And this is mine."

There was a queen-sized bed, nightstands, a couple of dressers, again the typical. The bed had a collection of decorative pillows. That wasn't Jodi's thing, but she had to admit, it looked nice.

Erin pulled the door closed behind her.

"I don't think we have time for what I want to do behind a closed door." Jodi touched the bed.

Erin pulled her lower lip between her teeth. "Why is there always someone else in the house?" She dipped her head, slowly approaching.

"Life, I guess," Jodi murmured against Erin's mouth. She threaded Erin's long hair between her fingers and pulled her closer. Erin walked her backward toward the bed until her legs hit the side. "That's a step too far for needing to stop," Jodi protested.

Erin groaned and pulled away, clearly agreeing. Instead, she showed Jodi where she could put her things while they waited for Darcy to get cleaned up.

Dipping a chip into the salsa, Darcy said, "So you guys are girlfriends, then."

Erin spat out a little bit of water, then dabbed her chin, giving Darcy a look.

While they hadn't exactly clarified their position as girlfriends, Jodi was happy with the moniker. She laid a hand on Erin's thigh under the table and said, "Yes." She paused. "Do you, um, have any questions about that?"

Erin placed a hand over Jodi's. She wasn't sure if she was supporting or warning.

Darcy looked serious. "Yes. What are your intentions toward my mom?"

"Darcy," Erin said. "That's between us."

"I don't mind, I mean, if you don't," Jodi said. Erin looked curious, so Jodi said, "I have every intention of doing all I can to make this relationship work. She's very important to me. I will, of course, never pressure her into anything she isn't comfortable with. I plan on being by her side as she navigates this next chapter. If she'll allow me, of course."

Darcy nodded, still serious. Then, she broke into a grin when she looked at her mom. "Mom, seriously?"

Erin ran a finger under her eye, trying to catch a tear, likely before it ruined her makeup. She squeezed Jodi's hand. "Thank you."

"I guess if it's good enough for Mom, it's good enough for me." Darcy dug into the salsa with another chip.

"So," Jodi started, feeling awkward, "what do you like to do other than softball?"

Darcy swallowed her bite, shrugging. "Not much. It takes up a lot of time. I'm looking forward to catching up on some streaming over the break. What do you like to do other than date my mom?"

Jodi grinned. There'd been a brief moment where she'd thought the question was going to be a little different. "My job is in podcasting. I host a couple and produce and edit many more."

"Really? What kinds?"

"Podcasts about books."

Erin cleared her throat, drawing Jodi's attention. Was she not supposed to talk about her podcasts? That would be weird. "She actually has a podcast about books with sapphic characters."

Whew. It seemed she was just clarifying.

"Really? Are there a lot of those?" Darcy asked.

Jodi nodded. "Tons. Are you a reader?"

"Maybe I would be if I could read about girls like me."

"Well, do I ever have some suggestions for you," Jodi said in her salesman's voice. Relief made her a bit giddy. She modulated her tone as she launched into some suggestions.

Meeting Darcy was going as well as she could have possibly hoped. Erin was sitting next to her, brushing knees under the table. She tried to put a stamp on the moment to refer to later. It was one of her new happy places.

CHAPTER TWENTY

Erin thought that dinner couldn't have gone much better. Jodi and Darcy had found things to talk about. Darcy might even read a few books. Erin hoped she stuck with the YA books Jodi had mentioned. She'd been careful not to talk about steamy ones, but once Darcy started looking, she might find them on her own. Erin knew teenagers had to chart their own way on these things, but it still made her a little uncomfortable to think about.

When they walked in the door, Darcy said, "I have homework," and disappeared down the hall.

"Is she normally this conscientious about homework?" Jodi asked looking after her. "Or is she giving us space?"

"She's pretty conscientious about homework, but she also sometimes claims homework when she wants to hang out online." Erin cocked her head. "And it's possible she's giving us space. You seem to have the Darcy stamp of approval."

"Well, let's not ruin that by doing anything rash. Maybe we should just watch a movie or something."

Erin sighed. "You may be right. What do you want to watch?"

They cozied up on the couch and settled on a rom-com. Erin put her arm around Jodi and spread a blanket over both their laps. It was nice having Jodi in her arms, but it was hard not to let her hands roam, not to turn Jodi's face toward her and kiss those soft lips.

And it turned out they could have pushed the boundaries a little because when Darcy came out to say good night, she called from the hall, "I'm coming into the living room now." It was a little obnoxious, but Erin would have appreciated it had she been sucking face with her girlfriend, as the kids said.

Jodi straightened from resting her head on Erin's shoulder. Erin squeezed her shoulder.

Darcy came into the living room, making a show of covering her eyes and peeking through her fingers. "Are we all decent out here?"

"For goodness sake's, Darcy. Do you take us for a couple of hormonal teenagers?"

Darcy dropped her hands to her hips, jutting one out to the side. "How do I know what you might be getting up to?"

Jodi put a hand to her face. "Darcy, I'm going to commit right here and now that I will do my level best never to put you in a situation where you see me doing something indecent with your mom. The very idea of it is mortifying to all, I can assure you." Her cheeks were pink.

"Okay, you've embarrassed my girlfriend. Are you happy now?"

Darcy looked somewhat pleased with herself and somewhat mortified. "Well, I was just coming out to say good night."

Erin squeezed Jodi's shoulder again, then got up to hug Darcy. "Good night."

"It was nice meeting you, Jodi. See you tomorrow."

Jodi returned the sentiment with a little wave.

"Maybe we should go to bed, too?" Erin asked hopefully. She had no desire to finish watching the movie. At the moment, she couldn't have even said what it was they were watching.

Jodi grinned and stood. "Yes. Your door locks, right?"

Erin grabbed the remote to turn off the TV before taking Jodi's hand. "It does."

In the bedroom, Erin closed and locked the door behind them. She leaned against it for a moment, feeling amazed at her own audacity in dragging Jodi to her room to have her way with her. She'd never been the instigator in her relationship with Grant. For what were now obvious reasons.

Jodi pressed her up against the door. "Hi," she breathed more than said.

"Hi, yourself." Erin's gaze zeroed in on Jodi's lips.

Jodi's lips hovered millimeters away. When she spoke, the air moved between them. "I've been dying to do this all evening."

Erin could wait no longer. She closed the gap, sealing their lips together. She lost minutes to the sensations created from the slide of lips and tongues. Her desire pulsed and spread through her entire body as their mouths moved together.

Eventually, her attention was diverted from Jodi's mouth to the feel of her body pressed along hers. Erin was standing with her legs spread so that their mouths were level, which also meant that their breasts were pushing together in a most enjoyable way.

Erin felt the need generated by their kissing, by the press of Jodi's breasts, and by all the time they'd been apart when Erin dreamed of this moment settle in her center. She ran her hand down Jodi's back to the curve of her butt. She lingered there for a long moment, squeezing a cheek and eliciting a moan, before she journeyed a little farther south, pulling in on the back of Jodi's thigh, needing pressure against her middle.

Jodi took the hint, nestling her leg between Erin's and pushing up. Erin gasped and moved both hands to Jodi's butt, pulling her in even closer. Jodi wrenched her mouth away, causing Erin to open her eyes.

Jodi gave her a cocky grin and pinned her hands against the door above her head. Erin whimpered in protest at the break in contact, not only of her hands but of Jodi's thigh from her center.

"Leave these here, yeah?" Jodi said, tapping Erin's palms.

Erin nodded. She wanted her hands all over Jodi, but also found the take-control attitude sexy as hell.

Jodi unbuttoned her blouse, following each button with kisses from chest to belly. Erin's stomach tightened incrementally with each touch of her lips. She ached for more. She squirmed when Jodi licked her way back up from belly to bra. Jodi pulled back slightly, a wry grin playing about her mouth. She touched Erin's mouth with her finger.

"Someday, I want to have my way with you when we can both be as loud as we want, but remember…shh."

Erin hadn't realized she'd been making noise, but it didn't surprise her, either. She nodded. She parted her lips and pulled Jodi's finger into her mouth. She bit down gently and sucked, watching Jodi for her reaction.

Jodi rewarded her by dropping the wry grin, her eyes fluttering closed. She opened them again, pulling her finger away and replacing it with her mouth. As they kissed, she pulled Erin's shirt up, leaving it on her arms, furthering the feeling of restraint. Erin's knees felt weak.

Jodi kissed her way down Erin's neck to the top of her bra. She licked across the skin just above the cup on each side before reaching around to undo the clasp. Erin arched in assistance. Jodi pushed the bra out of the way and lavished attention on each of Erin's breasts while she writhed against the door.

"Please." Erin was desperate for more.

"Please what?" Jodi said, not moving away from Erin's breast. She blew a little on the damp breast, and Erin stifled a moan.

"I need you."

"Where?" Jodi trailed her hand to the button on Erin's jeans. "Here?"

Erin nodded. Jodi stood back. Erin went to pull her back in.

Jodi shook her head and tapped Erin's hand. "Leave them there, and I'll give you what you want."

Erin nodded a little too long, putting her hands back in place.

Jodi grinned. "Good." She kissed her.

Then finally, finally, she undid the button of Erin's jeans. Erin pulled her legs together so Jodi could pull her jeans down, which she did incredibly slowly. Erin wanted to kick them down quickly, but when she lifted her foot, Jodi stopped. Erin subsided, getting the message that Jodi was in charge. She loved it. And she needed more.

"Please," Erin said again.

"Since you asked so nicely." Jodi finished pulling the jeans down and tossed them to the side. She trailed her fingers up the inside of Erin's legs, making her squirm again. When she reached the apex, she paused. Erin thrust, looking for contact. Jodi held the tops of Erin's thighs in her palms and brushed Erin's center over her panties with her thumbs. Erin jolted at the contact.

Jodi hooked her fingers into the waistband of Erin's panties. "Would you like these off, too?"

"Yes. Please."

Jodi pulled them down in one quick motion, a contrast to the slow tease of the jeans. Then her mouth was on Erin's center and Erin pulled her lip between her teeth to keep herself from calling out her shock and need.

The long wait, followed by the long evening of proximity without acting on their desires, followed by this long buildup, and culminating in Jodi's sudden warm mouth on her unraveled Erin. She came nearly at once. Jodi pulled additional waves out of her with her clever mouth. It was all Erin could do to not drop her hands onto Jodi's head and scream. Instead, she clenched her fists and bit her lip as she rode out her pleasure.

At the end, she sank to the floor. Jodi eased the transition. Erin sat, legs spread, arms still bound up in her shirt, back against the door and looked at Jodi in amazement.

Jodi sat before her, spider style. She pulled Erin's shirt off, freed her from her lopsided bra. She looked into Erin's eyes. Erin pulled her in and kissed her, tasting herself on Jodi's lips.

"I had no idea I could come so hard or so fast," she said, resting her forehead against Jodi's.

Jodi sounded a little proud when she replied, "Glad I could be of service."

"Oh, you were. But now…"

"Yes?"

"Now you'd better get out of those clothes and into my bed."

"Yes, ma'am." Jodi undressed quickly. She was under orders, after all.

CHAPTER TWENTY-ONE

When Erin's alarm went off, Jodi felt like she'd been woken up in the middle of the night. When she cracked her eyes open, she was proven wrong as there was sunlight peeking through the gap in the curtain, so it was clearly morning. She closed her eyes again and groaned a little.

Jodi felt Erin shift and presumably shut off her alarm because the noise stopped. She shifted some more, and her hand went over Jodi's that was wrapped around her middle. Erin liked to sleep with a pillow between her legs to protect her back, which made it easier for Jodi to be the big spoon, even though she was by far the shorter one.

"I've got to get up, but you should sleep more. It's really early for you." Erin pulled Jodi's hand up and kissed it.

"I should get up and shift, or we'll be on different schedules the whole visit. But I may just take a few more minutes."

Jodi had fallen asleep easily last night after sex, even though it should have been early for her. She'd gotten up early for her flight, and then there'd been the excellent sex, which in Jodi's experience, often led to good sleep. So she shouldn't have been tired. It was just that her body was telling her it was not time to wake up yet.

"Take all the time you want." Erin kissed her hand again, then slid out from under the covers.

Jodi missed her immediately, which woke her up a little more. Still, she didn't get up. She knew Erin got up with Darcy to get her off to school. Darcy drove herself, and Erin had said that she was more than capable of getting herself up. However, getting going at the same time gave them time together in the morning, sometimes all they got in a day. Darcy had a busy school and softball schedule. Knowing all that, Jodi figured she'd give them their morning alone without her intruding.

When Erin emerged from the bathroom, she was dressed for the day in jeans and a flowy blouse. She stopped by the bed on her way out and smiled down at Jodi. "You look good in my bed."

Jodi took her hand. "I'm a fan of this bed, particularly when you're in it." She tugged a little, pulling Erin in for a brief kiss. "Go see Darcy off, and I'll see you after."

"You can join us, you know. It's fine."

"It's okay. I'm going to lie here for a few more minutes, then take a shower. I'll let you two have your time."

Erin kissed her again, then squeezed her hand. "See you in a bit, then."

Jodi did stay in bed a little longer. She checked her phone. There was a text from Sal, checking in, which she answered. There wasn't anything else she needed to deal with at the moment, so she set her phone aside and listened to the sounds of Erin and Darcy preparing for their day. She couldn't hear what they were saying, but she did pick up on their tone. They clearly enjoyed each other's company. Between the sounds of dishes clanking and cupboard doors opening and closing, their voices wove together, accented by occasional laughter. Jodi had never had a particularly strong maternal instinct. She had once thought she'd have kids if she found a woman she wanted to spend her life with who wanted them, but it had never been a driving factor in her life. However, listening to Erin and Darcy, she felt a complicated mix of affection for Erin and nostalgia at what could have been.

Perhaps she dozed a little because it felt like she'd only listened for five or ten minutes when all of a sudden, there was a called good-bye, and the front door closed.

She yawned, stretched, and padded to the bathroom to prepare for the day. She was in the shower when she saw movement through the frosted glass door. She hoped what she thought was happening really was and was rewarded when the shower door opened, and Erin stepped in.

Jodi grinned at her. "Don't you have work to do?"

"It can wait. I couldn't stand the thought of you in here naked while I sat at my desk."

Jodi pulled her into her arms. "I'm a fan of this, to be clear."

"And we're home alone."

"No need to be quiet, then."

And they were not. If any of the immediate neighbors were home, they likely got an earful.

During the activities, they'd moved from the shower to the bed. They lay there, tangled together. Jodi rested half on top of Erin. She ran her fingers through Erin's damp hair.

"Now you're going to have to do your hair again."

Erin chuckled. "Worth it."

"I mean, it did sound like it." Jodi was a little smug about the sounds she'd elicited.

"You were not exactly quiet yourself, my dear."

"True enough." Jodi propped herself up so she could look at Erin. "I'm really glad I'm here."

"Me too." Erin pulled her in for a kiss.

When they parted, Jodi said, "As lovely a wake up as this has been, I haven't had any coffee yet."

"Goodness. That is a situation that needs to be rectified immediately, obviously."

"Despite your teasing tone, yes. Yes, it does."

Erin laughed a little. "Despite my teasing tones, I do understand the pressing need for coffee. There's a pot made in the kitchen."

Jodi kissed her briefly. "You're the best."

"You may be the first person to tell me that."

"Really? Not even your kids?"

"Well, sure. I mean, I did get a few 'Best Mom' cards or mugs or whatnot over the years. But just plain best?" Erin looked thoughtful. "No. I really don't think so."

Jodi was amazed at the way Grant had apparently taken Erin for granted all those years. Had he really not seen what he had with her? Apparently not, as he'd been cheating on her and left without a backward glance when the opportunity arose.

"Well, you are the best. I think you're amazing."

Erin rewarded her with a kiss. "I think you're the best, too. I've never felt about anyone else the way I feel about you."

It felt so good with her. Jodi felt herself falling for her again. It was dangerous to let herself. She needed to wait and see if Erin was really in this or if she was going to opt out again. If she was going to once more decide that, actually, being gay wasn't godly or wasn't compatible with her family life. Things were off to a much better start for them than when they'd been teenagers. Erin had come out to Sal, Meredith, and Darcy. However, that was only a start. It was a start that Jodi loved to see, but time would tell if Erin was really, truly willing to make a serious try with Jodi or if this was just some try it on for size thing.

Jodi tried to push the what-ifs to the side and concentrate on the here and now, where life was good.

After exchanging a few more kisses, they got up and set about preparing for the day a second time. Dressed and with a mug of coffee each, the first of the day for Jodi and second for Erin, they settled in Erin's office. Jodi pulled her laptop onto her lap and set her headphones next to her.

"Are you sure you'll be okay over there on the couch? I like having you in here, but there's also the table," Erin said.

"I'm fine." She was better than fine. She liked the idea of working side by side with Erin. Having her here to look up at was a pleasure. "Unless I'm recording, I usually work sitting on my couch at home."

Erin swiveled to face her. "How much time do you spend recording as opposed to other stuff?"

Jodi had work to do, but she'd much rather talk. She liked that Erin was interested in her work. "Much more time not. I record for *Lesbians on Books* on Mondays and for *Books in Space* on Tuesdays. We generally record for about three hours, which I cut down to about an hour of material per episode. I listen in on two of the weekly podcasts I produce, feeding information to the hosts and keeping them on track. That's another three or so hours a week each. The rest of the time is editing, marketing, and planning and preparing for new episodes."

"That sounds like a lot to manage."

"Probably not more managing to do than you have. You're running your own business, too. You've got your different clients, finding new clients, all of that." It was so impressive how Erin had set up a new life for herself, building a new business from the ground when she hadn't been in the workforce for so long.

"Eh." Erin waved a hand. "Most of my new clients have been word of mouth. Once I got the ball rolling, things just kind of happened. I haven't had to do any real marketing beyond hustling for those first few. Besides, I think the marketing you're talking about isn't finding new clients, right? It's social media and stuff." Erin shuddered. "I barely remember to post on my personal Facebook. I'd have a hard time putting myself out there like that."

"I get that. I don't do a lot of personal social media, as you've seen. I mean, I do on occasion, but I'm more of a lurker. I spend time on there to hear about new books, trends, and the like, but I don't really post unless it's for one of the professional accounts."

Erin looked surprised. "You have more than one professional account?"

"Yup. There's the one you follow for *Lesbians on Books*, one for *Books in Space*, and one for *Podcast Central*."

"Is Podcast Central the name of your company? I don't think I knew that."

"It is. I put out regular posts about my services for podcasters. I'm nearly full up on what I can handle at the moment with that work, but there's a decent turnover. Not every podcast idea is a winner."

Erin scooted closer. "I get how you make money producing. I'm sure you charge people for that. But how do you make money on the podcasts themselves? Advertisements? Does that pay enough?"

Jodi wobbled a hand back and forth. She explained how some income came from advertisements but more from associated merch.

"That all sounds like so many different things dividing your attention. How do you know what to work on at any given point?"

"I have a schedule for both recording and producing." Jodi pulled up her calendar and turned her computer around. "The different colors are the different podcasts. Recording and producing are top priorities. The other stuff, I just kind of work in here and there as I have time in my day. Or evening. Or weekend."

Erin frowned. "Do you usually do a lot of work outside of traditional office hours?"

Jodi wanted to smooth a thumb across Erin's forehead. She didn't like seeing her looking troubled. She put her laptop aside, not wanting it between them. "Honestly, it depends on what else I've got going on in my life, but, yeah. I kind of flow between work and nonwork with working from home and not having a lot of reason not to." She put a hand on Erin's knee. "Are you worried about my work-life balance?"

"Maybe a little, but it feels presumptuous. I was just thinking about…"

When she didn't go on, Jodi took her courage in her hands and asked, "About what my work schedule might look like if we someday lived together?"

Erin looked relieved and pleased. "Yes. But I realize I'm jumping several steps ahead here," she hastened to add.

"I don't think there's anything wrong with thinking about the future. And it makes me feel good that you're considering what it would be like if we were to live together. Someday." Jodi really did feel a wave of pleasure at that idea and the idea that Erin was considering it. That also seemed like a good sign. But she couldn't let herself pin her hopes on what was likely a passing thought of Erin's. She took a breath. "Well, like I said, I haven't had much reason to concern myself with a lot of hard boundaries between work and the rest of my life. And when I first made the leap to doing this full-time, I really did feel like I needed to hustle to make it work. These days, I think it'd just be a matter of calling the day done at a reasonable hour."

Erin smiled. "That's good to hear."

Erin's smile had Jodi feeling gooey inside. She lost some time looking into Erin's beautiful brown eyes. Erin's computer chimed, breaking the spell. "I suppose we should get to work."

"I suppose so."

Erin started to roll away, but Jodi pulled her back for a quick kiss before pushing her chair toward her desk. "Stop distracting me."

Erin mock glared as she adjusted her chair under her desk. "Excuse me. You kissed me."

"But you were looking so kissable, so it's really your fault."

Erin didn't say anything, but the little smile on her face was answer enough.

CHAPTER TWENTY-TWO

They had a productive morning once they settled in. Or at least, Erin's morning was productive, and Jodi reported the same when they took a break for lunch. Sitting across the table from Jodi with her blue eyes and teasing smile, it had crossed Erin's mind to drag her to the bedroom rather than go back to work. But she did have work she needed to get done. And if she really knuckled down, she could be done for the week between this afternoon and a couple of hours in the morning. Plus, she had to admit that she was a little sore from the night before and this morning's activities. She should probably give her lady bits a bit of a break.

She hadn't realized she'd sighed until Jodi asked, "Something wrong?"

"Not at all. Except that I was thinking about dragging you to the bedroom, but then I remembered that I'm old and have responsibilities."

Jodi's pupils dilated. "I mean...work could wait."

Erin was surprised to feel herself responding. "It would be nice to take advantage of still having the place to ourselves."

Jodi stood, came around the table and pulled Erin up after her. "Decided, then."

As quickly as they'd abandoned the dregs of lunch and run to the bedroom like schoolgirls—where Jodi had pushed Erin playfully onto the bed—once they were together, they were slow and gentle.

After having sex twice in the last sixteen hours or so, Erin was there more for the physical connection than the reward of a quick orgasm. Not that she'd have been sad to have one.

Jodi positioned herself on top and gave her a slow, lingering kiss. She pulled back to gaze into Erin's eyes. Erin cupped her face and stroked the curve of her cheek with her thumb before pulling her down for more kissing. They made out like lovestruck teenagers, just as they had been all those years ago. Kisses and exploring hands interspersed with long, lingering looks into one another's eyes.

Erin was torn between thinking this was enough, this was everything, and wanting to undress Jodi so she could feel her skin unencumbered. They had traded positions, and Erin was on top when Jodi finally made a move to remove her shirt. She stopped with a hand holding each side of Erin's shirt and raised an eyebrow. "Do you want this off?"

That was when the seesaw tipped from happy with connection to wanting more. Erin sat up and removed her shirt herself. Jodi's adoring look turned hooded as she ran her hands up Erin's bare sides. "You're so beautiful."

Erin reached back and undid her bra, flinging it to the side.

Jodi bit her lip. "So beautiful." Sincerity was written all over her.

It made Erin believe she was beautiful, something she hadn't truly felt since, well, since high school, when Jodi had made her feel that way.

She scooted down, lying flat on Jodi once more. They continued their slow exploration, even with their clothes off. When Erin's climax came, it was a lovely cherry on top, but what had been the best part was definitely the long, slow caresses, lingering eye contact, and kisses she'd gotten lost in.

Erin spooned Jodi for a change and languidly trailed her fingertips across Jodi's breasts.

Jodi shifted her head a little. "What time does Darcy come home?"

Erin looked at the alarm clock. "Soon," she said with a tinge of regret.

Jodi reached back and cupped her butt. "We should get up, then."

"We should have just enough time to shower if we don't linger."

"Take all the fun out of it, why don't you?"

"Yeah, yeah. I, for one, need a break anyway."

Jodi stood and gave Erin a hand. "Me too. We're not seventeen and eighteen anymore, are we?"

"No, but I was so confused at eighteen that I can't wish we were."

They walked hand in hand to the shower.

"I'm home, everyone."

Jodi and Erin were back at in their respective spots in Erin's office when Darcy's call reached them from the front door.

"Does she always announce herself, or is she being extra careful not to walk in on us in a compromising position?" Jodi asked.

"The latter, for sure. The child takes delight in just appearing in my doorway like a wraith."

"Hey," Darcy said from the door. "Are you calling me a wraith?"

Erin beamed at her. "Maybe a little."

It warmed Jodi's heart to see how she clearly adored her kid.

"Just a little wraith? I don't think I've been accused of being little in a decade or so," Darcy said.

She was very tall. Jodi had realized the night before that she had a couple of inches on Erin. She felt like a Lilliputian next to the two of them. "Hi, Darcy. How was school?"

"Eh. Fine."

Jodi didn't know if Darcy gave that typical high schooler answer because she was there or if it was normal. Sometimes stereotypes existed for a reason.

Darcy pushed off the door frame. "I need to go get ready for practice." She was off.

"It's Thursday, so she has her study thing after practice tonight, right?" Jodi asked.

"You remember her schedule?"

"Sure. I pay attention."

Erin gave her a huge smile. "That means a lot."

Jodi gave an answering smile. She couldn't look at Erin smiling and not. "So…can I take you out to dinner tonight? Just the two of us?"

"Like, on a date?" Erin raised both eyebrows.

"Exactly like a date. So like a date that it is a date."

"That would be lovely."

"Great. It's a date." She paused. "But since we're in your town, do you have a favorite place? Maybe someplace a little…special?" Jodi felt a little mixed about asking. She could do some research and pick a place, but it was Erin's town, and she had insider information. It would be silly not to ask, right?

Erin smiled. "I've got just the place in mind."

Jodi considered asking for details but let it go. Erin looked happy. So what if she was picking the place and driving? Jodi had suggested it and would pay. It was like they were taking each other on a date, sharing the responsibilities. Like partners. Jodi liked the sound of that.

"Do I at least get to know what type of food we'll be eating?"

Jodi's teasing tone let Erin know she could get away with stringing her along a bit. "Mum's the word."

"General region of the cuisine, perhaps?"

Erin took a hand off the steering wheel to mime zipping her lips shut before placing her hand over Jodi's hand on her thigh. She took a moment to admire how handsome Jodi was before turning her eyes back to the road. When Jodi had produced a suit while they were getting ready, Erin had been a little surprised. As a teenager, Jodi had worn dresses for special occasions like school dances. When she'd put on the slacks and jacket over a low top, Erin had considered leading her to bed for the third time that day. It was partially the date and partially the fact that she really did need a break that stopped her.

"Speaking of regions of the world," Jodi said, "you lived overseas for a while, right? And I know you've lived various places in the States. But where have you traveled? Do you like to travel?"

"Yes, we were stationed in Germany for three years. It was fun because the officers and their spouses, nearly all wives at the time, were pretty tight because we didn't have other family around. We did some exploring around Europe. Lindsey was little, and dragging a preschooler around to historical sites is not exactly a good time. Or it wasn't for me. Grant enjoyed the trips. That was why we kept taking them. And it seemed like we should take advantage when we could. To be honest, I'm not very into travel. Is that a problem?"

"Not even a little bit. I usually spent my vacation time going back home to visit Mom until she passed."

Erin squeezed her hand. "I was so sorry to hear about that. She was pretty young, wasn't she?"

Jodi sighed. "She was seventy-one. I miss her all the time."

"Sorry to bring the mood down."

"No, no. I...I like talking about her. When people avoid the topic, it feels like, I don't know, like she wasn't important or something. I do prefer talking about the good parts, though."

"Sure, that makes sense. Did she work as a nurse until she retired?"

"She did. Labor and delivery the whole time. Because of their pension program, she was able to retire early. She had a lot of good years of hiking and taking pottery classes before the stroke."

Erin squeezed her hand again. "I'm glad she got time to do what she loved."

"Yeah, me too."

Erin took her hand back to signal and turn into the restaurant's parking lot.

Jodi sucked in a breath. "Is this what I think it is?"

Erin laughed. "It's not exactly fancy, but I couldn't help myself."

"It's extremely fitting."

The building was done in a Victorian style with "Fargo's Pizzaria" written in lightbulbs across the top. "Apparently, our Fargo's was opened by two brothers after one of them married Italian royalty. The brothers were from Missouri. One of them, the one not married to Sophie, came back some years later and opened a replica here."

Inside, the Victorian theme continued both architecturally and with the servers decked out in costumes. When they were teenagers, Erin, Jodi, Meredith, and Sal had gone to Fargo's regularly. It was their celebration place, their post-SAT place, and their end of the school year place. Because of the theme that included wax replicas of Sophia and her husband at a balcony table on the second floor, they felt like they were doing something special. And yet, the pizza was cheaper than at a lot of places.

When they'd started their teenage relationship, Jodi had said more than once that she'd wished they could go there on a date. But it wasn't possible. While they could pass as friends in a lot of situations, they'd never gone to Fargo's in any combination other than all four of them. And, sure, Meredith and Sal would not go on their own and see them there, but it was a popular hangout for their entire school. Chances were high that someone would see the two of them and mention it to the others. They'd never come up with a good excuse to have gone alone.

When Jodi had asked to go someplace special, Fargo's had popped into Erin's head. It was silly, but it was a chance to fulfill a dream.

Jodi bounced a little in her seat. "So exciting. Although, I feel a little overdressed."

Erin waved her off. "We're overdressed together." She was wearing a sweaterdress that she'd ordered from Title Nine after Jodi had confirmed some of her basic items were from there and that she loved them. "Besides, we'll fit right in with the staff."

"Except we're modern dressy, and they're Victorian dressy." Jodi leaned over the console as if she wanted a kiss. Erin put a hand on her shoulder with what she hoped was both affection and warning. A disappointed look crossed Jodi's face before she settled back and smiled. "I forgot."

"It's just that…it's possible I'll know people here."

"I understand. I really don't mean to push. I don't want you to be forced into any conversations before you're ready."

Erin felt bad. Why should she be embarrassed to claim Jodi as hers? She wanted to. But there was too much at stake.

Sal's words about people thinking she was a groomer had burrowed into her head and made themselves at home. When she'd returned home, she'd spent some time researching if it was possible for Grant to gain custody of Darcy simply because Erin was gay. The answer was no. Even if Darcy were also queer, it was still no. It was unlikely a lawyer would even take the case. Still, the conversation had popped Erin's happy bubble of a dream about coming out to everyone right away. It made her think seriously about how her family would take the news and how that might affect Darcy's own coming out. She knew her parents would be appalled but had already decided she didn't care about that. They weren't close.

The big problem was Lindsey and Brad. They'd been raised nearly as conservatively as Erin had. She had no one to blame but herself. Well, and Grant. Erin had tried to instill in her children a belief that people were people and to be accepted for who they were. However, many people in their lives had told them that being gay was wrong. When Erin came out to them, she might lose them. She wasn't ready for that. She needed time to prepare.

Fargo's here was like Fargo's in Colorado Springs, popular with teenagers. It was quite likely there were people there who went to school with Darcy or were on her softball team. There was a clear line between one of those kids and Grant. He would delight in making Erin look bad to the kids. Not to mention the possibility of Air Force families. No, it was too dangerous.

"I'm sorry."

Jodi gave her a smile filled with what might be slightly forced cheer. "Truly no worries. Let's go have some pizza."

"Don't forget the salad bar."

"How could I forget all that iceberg lettuce and pasta salad?"

Jodi opened her door. Erin hastened to open her own before Jodi could get any ideas about opening her door for her. She pulled her coat around her when the cold hit.

Jodi zipped her down jacket up all the way. "Yeah, cold, right?"

"It is. Let's get inside."

Erin had been here a few times over the years with her kids: post season celebrations for sports, end of the year class parties, that sort of thing. She wasn't exactly overwhelmed with the charm of the place. But Jodi's eyes lit up with recognition and excitement that brought back Erin's tender feelings for Fargo's. "Pretty cool, right?" Erin grinned.

"So cool." Jodi shoulder bumped her.

They moved into the line to be seated. It wasn't long, but there were a couple of families in front of them. Erin wished she could wrap an arm around Jodi and pull her close. She considered doing it anyway. Who would know it wasn't a friendly gesture? She was lifting her hand when she heard her name.

"Erin?"

She lowered her hand as she took in the woman standing to her left. It was Shelby Tanner, an officer's wife. Behind her, looking bored, were her two kids. One of them was wearing a hockey jersey. A few other kids in the same jersey were heading out the door.

"Oh my goodness, Erin, it is you. How are you? It's been so long. What are you doing here?" Shelby looked around as if expecting Darcy to materialize.

Once the shock cleared, Erin felt a huge wave of relief that she had not put her arm around Jodi. The thought of Grant hearing from Shelby's husband that Erin had her arm around a woman at Fargo's was terrifying. Maybe Grant's first thought wouldn't be that Erin was gay, but it was best not to go there. He would absolutely pass the information on to Lindsey and Brad if for no other reason than to try to turn them against her. She needed that coming out to be on her own timeline so she didn't lose them.

Erin smiled big. "Shelby. Wow. It's so good to see you. Hi, Chris and Natalie. How are you two?"

The kids waved without any real enthusiasm.

"Hockey event?" Erin directed her question at Shelby, knowing she wouldn't get much of a reply out of Chris.

"Yes." Shelby rolled her eyes. "It's always Fargo's, right? What about you? Is Darcy here?"

"No, it's just Jodi and me tonight." Erin gestured to Jodi, who was watching this exchange politely. "Jodi, this is Shelby Tanner. Her husband serves with Grant. Shelby, this is an old childhood friend of mine in town for a visit, Jodi. We had a Fargo's in Colorado Springs we went to when we were growing up, so we thought it would be fun to come for nostalgia's sake."

"Oh, Erin. I hope I'm more than your husband's coworker's wife." She turned to Jodi, clearly appraising her haircut and clothes. Shelby didn't look like she approved, but she said, "It's nice to meet you. Erin and I used to play tennis together all the time, and we go to the same church. Although, I haven't seen you there lately." The last was directed back at Erin and was delivered with tones of disapproval.

"With the move and all, Darcy and I started attending a different church, one that's closer to our new home."

Shelby grasped Erin's arm. "I was just so sorry to hear about you and Grant. I should have reached out, really. But you know how busy life gets. And when you stopped attending church..."

Erin wanted to rip this woman's hand off her arm. Instead, she smiled sweetly. "I do know. It's been a lot with going back to work, the move, the divorce, and settling into the new church."

Natalie pulled on her mom's jacket. "Mom. You said I could go to Taylor's after this."

"Okay, just a minute, Natalie." Shelby sounded impatient. "Kids. You know how it is. I should go. But it was so nice running into you. Give me a call. We should play sometime." Shelby turned to Jodi. "Nice to meet you. Enjoy your visit." She left, chivying her kids in front of her.

Erin took a breath and realized they'd lost their place in line. "Sorry about that."

"No problem. Are you okay?" Jodi was regarding her warmth and concern.

"I'm fine. It was just…I really am sorry about that."

"It's really okay. We could go someplace else or get takeout if you'd rather."

"I'm okay to stay if you are."

Jodi shrugged. "Sure. Shall we get back in line?"

Once they'd checked in, been led to a table, and taken their seats, Erin ignored the menu. She put her elbows on the table and leaned toward Jodi. She'd been thinking about what to say next and was still a little unsure if she should bring up what had just happened or try to get the playfulness they'd been sharing back. She decided on the latter.

"See how much pull I have in this town?" She spread her arms to indicate the table where they sat.

She was sure she'd made the right move when Jodi's eyes twinkled at her. "I do see. We're at the table of honor."

Mostly likely, the reason they'd been sat there was that there were only the two of them, and this was a two-seater. But it was also the double of the balcony table the waxed couple sat at. They could see nearly the entire restaurant. The downside was that they were on display as well, but it wasn't like they were going to be holding hands even if they'd been in one of the dark corner booths.

Erin lowered her voice. "It's likely because the hostess took one look at your outfit and decided we should be showcased."

Jodi made a show of buffing her nails. "I do look good. But…" She looked Erin up and down. "I'm not the looker in this c—um, pairing."

Erin shoved aside the niggle of worry that they might appear too caught up in one another. She grinned, reminding herself that friends could banter like this. She picked up her menu. "What shall we get on our pizza?"

Jodi eyed Erin over her iced tea. They'd both opted not to drink this evening: Jodi simply because all Fargo's had was wine and beer, and while she occasionally drank wine, she preferred mixed drinks most of the time. Erin not getting a drink was more notable. She enjoyed a glass of wine nearly every evening. To not get one on a date seemed odd. However, this pretending-not-to-be-on-a-date date was odd already. Jodi had not had to deal with pretending to be the friend instead of more since, well, since she'd last dated Erin.

It wasn't that she didn't understand. Erin needed to take coming out at her own pace, and there was certainly no need to tell her personal business to a woman she clearly hadn't spoken to in over a year and had no interest in resuming a friendship with. Yet, for Jodi, it was weird to have to remind herself not to take Erin's hand, much less kiss her.

What it all amounted to was that Jodi was pretty sure Erin had chosen not to drink because she felt the need to keep her wits about her. And that choice on top of everything else made this feel like it wasn't a date.

Jodi could live with that. She was still mostly enjoying herself. Fargo's was a kick in the nostalgia sweet spot, for sure. And she enjoyed Erin's company as a friend as well as a lover. She could do this.

But she also hoped Erin would decide she was ready to come out soon.

For now, she would follow Erin's lead. "So, I have not been to Fargo's in"—she paused to do the math—"thirty-two years, I think? That would have been sometime in college. But you are clearly still a loyal Fargo's customer. When were you last here?"

Erin looked like she was trying to scowl, but a smile broke through instead. "I take offence at being called a loyal Fargo's customer. And it was last year for a team event of Darcy's."

"So, yeah. Thirty-two years versus one. I'm gonna call a horse a horse here."

"It might have been more like ten months."

"Oh yeah, that makes it better."

Erin tipped her Diet Coke at Jodi. "It does."

Jodi cast about for something else to talk about. Usually, conversation flowed with Erin, but Jodi found herself policing topics in her head. She was still considering when Erin spoke.

"What shall we do after diner? What do you think about catching a movie?"

The mirror that displayed the number of the orders ready for pick up lit up with their number. Instead of answering, Jodi said, "Our pizza is ready. I'll be right back."

As she fetched the pizza, Jodi considered their evening. If Erin was so concerned about the way they presented in public, Jodi would rather go back home where Erin was open with her affections in ways that teenage Jodi could have only dreamed of. Erin was taking steps. She was showing Jodi mattered to her. Jodi reminded herself yet again to give her time. Still, she wanted to go to Erin's place and be in their own little bubble.

She returned and slid the pizza onto the table. "It looks the same as I remember."

"As far as I know, they've not changed the recipe."

"Gotta stick with a winner, I suppose."

They each took a slice and without any discussion, tapped them together like they were toasting. They laughed.

"Oh my God. I haven't done that with pizza since the summer before college," Jodi said. "And yet, there it was, just waiting to be done."

"Exactly. It's muscle memory or something."

"Do you do it with your kids?"

"No. It's been since then for me, too. I guess it's our thing."

"Well, ours and Meredith's and Sal's, to be fair."

Erin dipped her head in acknowledgement.

Jodi wondered if she was nodding with a little grief, too. She swallowed her bite and asked. "Do you miss Meredith?"

Erin met her gaze. "Some. But then I remember her reaction to my coming out, and, no. Before you ask, I don't regret it. Contrary to what tonight might indicate, I really do want to live true to myself. I just…"

When she didn't continue, Jodi finished the thought for her. "Need a little time."

Erin looked like she was about to say something more, clarify or something, but Jodi was feeling raw about it. She had promised to focus on fun, and that was what she was going to do. "I was thinking about what we should do after pizza. A movie sounds good, but I think we should just go back to your place where we can be alone."

Erin looked around as if to see if anyone could overhear. "That sounds nice, but I should tell you that I...think I need a break."

Jodi laughed. "That's fine. Me too." She had gotten loud with the laughing and made a point to lower her voice when she continued. "We can just snuggle and watch a movie. That's all I meant."

"Sounds perfect."

CHAPTER TWENTY-THREE

The rest of Jodi's visit passed in a blur of cuddles and conversation punctuated by sex that only seemed to get better, to Erin's astonishment. They did also go to a game of Darcy's where Erin carefully and shamefully introduced Jodi as her high school friend in town for a visit. Jodi had seemed to take it in stride. She'd chatted amicably with the other parents and cheered for the team.

Erin had driven her to the airport, kissing her in the car in the dim light of the parking garage. She'd tried to infuse into the kiss how much she cared for Jodi, how much she was going to miss her. They'd parted with a hug when Jodi got into the line for security.

Erin had gone back to the car and cried before driving home. She'd had such a good weekend. She hadn't wanted Jodi to go. But she was also crying because she had wanted to tell everyone Jodi was her person, and she knew she'd hurt Jodi by not doing so.

Maybe she needed to just tell people. Maybe Sal was wrong when she'd said the thing about how people might think she was a groomer. A, she wasn't. Obviously. B, the people who would judge her were people she was better off without having in her life. Except that C, Lindsey and Brad might fall into the judging category. And D, it was difficult to fully put to the side the possibility that Grant would be able to use this as a way to get custody of Darcy. He clearly wanted to be out living his life rather than caring for their teenage daughter, but he would also certainly think that Erin was an unfit mother. She might find herself back in court. Worse, what if the judge actually agreed with him, and Darcy had to go live with him for her last two years at home? That would be the worst possible outcome.

But no. No judge would come to that conclusion. Besides, as Erin had learned when she'd looked into all of this, teenagers voted with their feet. It was a saying in the legal system. The judge could say where they should go, but they simply moved in with the parent they wanted to live with, and that was generally that.

No, the worst possible realistic outcome was that Erin would lose her relationships with her older kids. She couldn't bear it. Not now that Lindsey was calling her every Sunday just to chat. They'd gotten closer than they'd ever been after Lindsey had gotten married and even closer after the divorce. When Lindsey had heard about Grant's infidelity, he'd lost a lot of his shine in her eyes. But Erin had every reason to believe that learning her mother was a lesbian would be worse. Plus, she was thinking about starting a family and Erin could soon be a grandparent.

While Darcy was clearly accepting and Brad seemed to be slipping away from religion—if his lack of wanting to talk about it was any indication—Lindsey was very religious. She and her husband attended a conservative church and regularly visited Erin's parents, who were also very conservative.

Her parents. She'd lose them for sure. Was it bad that she didn't feel that bad about that? Her relationship with her parents was perfunctory at best. They doted on the grandchildren, even learned how to text to stay close. They sent gifts. But with Erin, it seemed they didn't much care. After she'd married Grant, they'd cared more about him than her. After the divorce, they'd made their displeasure clear and made it clear they thought it was Erin's fault. As far as Erin knew, no one had bothered to tell them about Tami, the new girlfriend. Erin hadn't bothered because she figured they'd just say that it was ultimately Erin's fault for driving him to cheat. Erin found she didn't miss the weekly phone calls. They still spoke occasionally, but Erin would be just as happy if they let those drop, too.

It probably did make her a bad person.

As for Brad, well, he'd always been closer to her than Grant. The dynamics weren't the same. But he did have a strong sense of right and wrong. Erin didn't know where he stood in regard to his thinking about people in the LGBTQ community. And he was getting busier and busier with his move into adulthood. She couldn't push him away more.

As for issue B, who cared about the Shelby Tanners of the world? Not Erin. She'd happily kiss Jodi in front of her just to see her squirm. But losing her kids? That was the terror that kept her quiet.

When Erin parked in the apartment lot, she pulled out her phone and looked at her text chain with Lindsey. She scrolled up through, seeing all the minutia she and Lindsey shared, little GIFs they sent one another. Her gut clenched at the idea that Lindsey might drop her if she knew the truth.

Erin: *Just thinking about you. Hope your Sunday is a lovely one.*

There was no immediate response, which Erin expected. Lindsey and her husband usually stayed for the after-service luncheon that Lindsey helped serve. She'd be busy until midafternoon at least, and it was only noon in Colorado.

Erin sighed, sent a similar text to Brad, and went inside. Darcy was gone for another softball game. Erin had considered driving there to catch the second half instead of home, but she had wanted some time to herself to miss Jodi and to think. Now she regretted it a little. Maybe the distraction would have been better than moping around, thoughts running circles in her head. She regarded the apartment, trying to decide what to do with herself. If she'd been in the old house, she'd have gone out back and used the rebounder. It was cold but not wet. She could go to the park and hit against a wall? Or maybe she should just clean the apartment.

Her phone chirped.

Brad: *Trying to find some time to chill. Got a couple big projects due this week. Can we look at flights for Xmas break?*

Erin: *Of course. It might be easier on the phone. Call me?*

She hadn't been sure he was planning on coming home for Christmas. He was still responsive—his quick text back was a recent example—but he was pulling away from family life more and more. There had been the internship that had kept him away for all but a week of summer. He'd opted not to come home for Thanksgiving that was coming up in a couple weeks. Erin had wanted to see him but wasn't too upset. Thanksgiving was a short and expensive time to come home. She'd hoped he would come for Christmas but had decided not to press about it and just see what developed.

She went to her office, sat at her computer, and started searching flights. She hadn't gotten very far when her phone rang. She answered with her work headset so her hands would be free. "Hey-o, boy-o."

"Hey, Mom."

"Busy at school, are you?" It was a basic question, and she wouldn't blame him if he blew through it. However, he was the kid who'd talked the most growing up but only if she asked questions. Lindsey would have been annoyed by the question. Darcy said more when given the space to express herself. Brad likely wouldn't mind the stupid question and would use it as a jumping-off point.

"Yup. Senior year is no joke. All my classes got hard." He laughed. He was a smart kid, and school had been pretty easy for him, even when he made the transition to college.

"Hard for real or just more work?"

"Both. Seriously. But this term is almost over, then just one more semester and done."

"Are you still thinking you want to try for a job with the company in Austin you interned with?"

"Yup. I really like it down there. You'll have to come visit and see it."

"If you move there, I will. I promise. Now, about the plane tickets. What dates are you thinking?"

"Well, Lindsey said she'd be there on the twenty-second, but I can't leave until the twenty-third because I have a final at the very end of final's week, so—"

"Wait. Back up. Lindsey is coming here for Christmas?"

"Oops. I guess she hasn't told you yet. I thought she was going to today. Surprise."

Erin laughed. "Maybe she was meaning to do it after she got home from church. I'm excited. All my kiddos together. I assume she's bringing Steve." Erin laughed again at the idea that Lindsey wouldn't bring her husband. "I thought it was his parents' turn for Christmas."

"Apparently, his parents decided to take a cruise for Christmas, so you're up."

"Their loss is my good fortune." A terrible thought occurred to her. "Um, are you going to only be at my house for Christmas, or are you planning on time with your dad?"

"I barely talk to him. I'm not going to spend Christmas there. I suppose Lindsey and Steve might go to service with him if anything."

"I'm pretty sure he stopped going to church. Or at least, to the old church. I ran into Mrs. Tanner—remember her?—this weekend, and she hasn't seen him since the divorce."

"Really? I always thought he was the religious one."

"Me too." Erin wanted to say more about her ex-husband and his actions versus his stated beliefs, but her son wasn't the audience for that. "Anyway, let's look at tickets."

They sorted out tickets, mostly her approving of the ones he had found, and went on to chat about school for a while. "And you, Mom? What have you been up to?"

Her stomach flipped at the sanitized version of the weekend she was about to share. She really hated lying to him. Well, she wasn't going to lie. She was just going to leave out some key points. "Do you remember me telling you about Jodi, the high school friend I reconnected with on that reunion weekend?"

"Sure. It was with...I'm remembering Meredith and some other people?"

Of course he'd remember Meredith. She was the one she'd talked about being in touch with before that weekend. "Right. There were four of us, Meredith, Sal, Jodi, and me. I ended up really connecting with Jodi again." That was an understatement. "And Sal to a lesser extent." True enough. "And Meredith, well, we didn't get along as well in person, unfortunately."

"Aw, Mom. Sorry to hear that."

"It's fine. Well, Jodi came out for a visit this weekend. It was nice." Huge understatement.

"That's great, Mom." Erin heard voices in the background, then Brad's muffled voice. After a moment, he said clearly, "Mom? Sorry. I've gotta go. My group project people are here."

They said a quick good-bye, after which Erin sat and stared at the wall for a while. How would Brad have taken it if she'd told him the truth? She honestly had no idea. She was still brooding when her phone rang again. She didn't look before answering.

"Hello?"

"Um, hi. Bad time?" It was Jodi. She must be on her layover in Denver.

Erin spoke hastily to reassure her. "No, of course not. Are you in Denver?"

"I am, waving at the hometown now."

Colorado Springs, where they'd grown up, was about sixty miles south of Denver, but the drive from the airport out on the eastern side of the city took about an hour and a half when traffic wasn't bad. It was a long wave.

"You should wave at Lindsey. She's much closer. She's in Glendale."

"That's on the east side of Denver, right? I've never been that familiar with the suburbs."

Erin could hear some sort of airport announcement and waited it out before replying. "That's right. Conveniently located for airport runs."

"Nice, but I doubt she really wants to be waved at. I mean, she'd have no idea who I am, right?"

The casual assumption that Erin wouldn't mention Jodi to her kids hit her like a dagger to her heart. "She knows you're a high school friend."

"Ah." There was an awkward pause while another announcement played, then Jodi continued. "Well, that's my flight boarding.

It's a short layover, which is nice since I made it. Just wanted to call and say I miss you already."

"Me too. Let me know when you make it home."

"Will do."

The line went dead. Well, that could have gone better. Erin went back to staring at the wall, thinking about her life choices. She was once again interrupted by her ringing phone. This time, she looked first. It was Lindsey.

"Hey, Linds."

"Hi, Mom. I hear that my surprise is no longer a surprise." She sounded a little annoyed.

"Yeah. Your brother spilled the beans. But I'm really excited you and Steve are coming for Christmas."

"Honestly, so am I." Her voice dropped to conspiratorial levels. "Don't tell Steve I said so, but I prefer our family's Christmas traditions."

Erin laughed. "My lips are sealed. If you and Steve want to stay with me, you two can have my room. I'll take the fold-out in the office, and Brad can take the living room. It'll be snug but fun to all stay together, if you want."

"That'd be great. We're trying to save up for a down payment, so it'd be nice not to pay for a hotel, and I don't want to stay with Dad's girlfriend. Anyway, we're talking about buying a house."

"Are you? That's exciting. In Denver, I take it?"

They discussed Lindsey's life for a much shorter time than Erin had spoken with Brad before Lindsey changed the subject. "You had your high school friend visiting this weekend, right? Jodi? How was that?"

"It was really nice," Erin said truthfully.

"What did you guys do? Anything fun?"

"We went to Fargo's, so that was pretty fun." Erin injected a wry note into her words.

Lindsey laughed. "Fargo's? Seriously?"

"Yes. Remember how I told you I went there with my friends in high school? It was nostalgic."

"I can see that, I guess. Please tell me you did something more interesting, too."

"Not really," Erin lied. "We talked a lot. Still catching up, I guess." The talking a lot part wasn't a lie.

"I can see that. I'm looking forward to catching up with my high school friends when I come for Christmas. Oh, Mom." Excitement surged in her tone. "We should do the friends open house like we used to do when we were kids."

Erin had started a tradition for her kids when Lindsey was little that on Christmas Eve Eve, she hosted an open house for her kids' friends, as well as any parents who wanted to stay, but it was focused on the kids. People were welcome after noon, and particularly as the kids got older, many ended up spending the night. It had been a popular tradition when they were stationed overseas, where people were living away from their extended family. "I've continued to do them for Darcy's friends. We usually do it the weekend before you come home."

"Oh, yeah. Darcy did say. That's not quite the same as on Christmas Eve Eve."

"True enough. But Brad doesn't get in until two that afternoon."

"All the better. We'll welcome him home with a party."

"And who will pick him up?"

"Oh, we can send Steve," she said cavalierly. "He'll be thankful for a break from socializing with people he doesn't know."

Erin started to feel excited about the idea. It was always fun to have Darcy's friends over, and it would be even more fun to see Brad and Lindsey's old friends. How many of them were still around? Presumably, a lot of Brad's friends would be home for Christmas, at least. And Lindsey must be tracking her old friends enough to know that some of them would be there. Erin had always loved a full house. It happened so rarely these days. "Okay, then. It's a plan."

"Really?" Lindsey squealed. Actually squealed. "That's great, Mom. I'm going to go text the old crew. I'll send you our flight information."

Erin smiled as she pushed disconnect on her phone. She did so love making her kids happy. She'd always gone out of her way to do what she could to ensure their happiness. Just because they were grown didn't mean she was going to stop. The delight in Lindsey's voice made it worth it.

The only thing that would make this Christmas better would be if Jodi could be there, too. Her heart sank. How had Erin not thought of that sooner? She wanted to invite Jodi to join her and the kids, but they'd have to spend the whole time pretending to be friends. That was unfair to Jodi. But so was not including her for Christmas.

Thinking about it filled Erin with anxious energy. Without really thinking about it, she got up and started cleaning. She was vacuuming and didn't notice Darcy had come home until she stepped in front of her. Erin leapt into the air with a shout.

Darcy held her hands up. "Whoa. Sorry. Are you okay? Did something happen? You're stress cleaning."

Erin stood with one hand on the vacuum and one over her heart. She gave a small smile to show she was amused by her over-the-top reaction. "What makes you think I'm stress cleaning? This could be just cleaning, cleaning. You took me by surprise."

Darcy was still in her game clothes. She was her usual postgame dirty as she pointedly looked up and down the hall. "You finished vacuuming the hall, then reversed to vacuum the hall again. Stress cleaning."

"You're probably right." Erin tried to change the subject. "How was the game?"

She grimaced. "Not our best. We had too many errors and fell behind in the fifth inning. Never recovered."

"Ah, Darce. I'm sorry."

"You win some, you lose some. We'll get them next time. We'll have plenty to work out in drills this week."

Darcy was competitive, yes. She didn't like to lose. But she'd had an early coach who'd worked hard to get her athletes to adopt exactly this attitude. Even with all that, some of the kids still took loses hard. Erin had done her best to reinforce the win some, lose some attitude at home, but Brad had still been one of those kids with tennis. When he'd lost a match, he'd withdrawn and pouted for a while. Darcy didn't let it get her down. Erin admired that about her. She gave her a wry grin. "Sounds fun."

"Oh, you know it." Darcy grinned back. "But, seriously. What's the stress cleaning about?"

"Nothing, really. I'm a little sad about Jodi leaving."

"She's pretty awesome, Mom. I'm glad you reconnected with her."

"Me too." Erin's gut churned with the stresses of balancing how much she wanted Jodi in her life versus protecting her relationship with her kids. Darcy didn't need to know all that. "Brad, Lindsey, and Steve are all coming home for Christmas. We'll have a full house."

Darcy grinned. "Cool."

"And we're going to have a Christmas Eve Eve open house. So let your friends know."

Darcy pumped a fist. "Excellent. Can people sleep over?"

"Sure, why not? It's going to be a packed house, but we'll figure it out." Erin's stomach clenched again because it would not be quite as full as she wanted it to be. It would still feel empty without Jodi by her side.

CHAPTER TWENTY-FOUR

Jodi dropped her backpack to the floor just inside her condo. She regarded the lifeless space. She didn't even have plants. Aside from the likelihood of a few ants—the building always seemed to have an ant problem—there was nothing living in her condo aside from herself. Was this what she wanted?

"It was a good weekend." She said it aloud experimentally to see how the words landed. They rang mostly true. It had been a good weekend. She was tired from sitting on airplanes today, but she'd enjoyed her time with Erin. She'd even enjoyed getting to know Darcy a little. She'd been fun. It was easy to imagine herself fitting into that life. She could make a tiny studio in the closet of the den. They'd go to all of Darcy's games. She'd hold Erin in her arms every night. It would be a good life.

When they'd woken up together this morning, Jodi had felt at home. It was as if she had fallen in love as a seventeen-year-old and was still in love now. It just took being with Erin to realize it.

But that couldn't be. She couldn't let it be. Erin had shown her that she wasn't ready to take the steps she needed to take before Jodi could stop guarding her heart. Remembering that was like being doused with a bucket of ice water.

Had it been a good weekend? Yes. And a little no. Mostly yes. But the no was enough that she needed to be more careful. She was finding it difficult to do when her condo seemed so empty. She turned around and left again. It was raining, but she felt like a walk.

❖

It was a busy week. Jodi had put off a few tasks when she'd been at Erin's that were now pressing. There was a mix-up when she was recording for *Lesbians on Books* that had resulted in Val's side of the conversation not being recorded. After listening to her own side, which included Val but through the video chat, they'd decided to rerecord. That was a fiasco.

Jodi of, course, texted with Erin, and they managed to have one short video chat during the week, but it was a far cry from how much Jodi wanted to talk and a striking contrast to actually being with Erin.

They finally found a pocket of time where they were both free on Saturday. It was afternoon for Jodi, evening for Erin. Jodi settled on the couch with a mug of tea, wanting to get the most out of the time they had.

Erin's beautiful face appeared on her screen. She was smiling with a softness to her eyes that showed how pleased she was. Jodi wanted to reach through the screen and stroke her face. Instead, she tried to put everything she was feeling into her expression. "Hi there. What a sight for sore eyes."

"Oh my gosh, same. You have no idea how empty things feel around here without you."

The thought that she was missing Jodi warmed her heart. "It can't come close to how empty this place felt when I came home. At least you've got Darcy."

Erin half nodded, half waved dismissively. "That child is as busy as can be. Always off at school, softball, or with friends."

Jodi smiled, thinking of the mornings Erin and Darcy had spent together as they'd prepared for their days. Erin had no idea what living alone was like. Not that Jodi minded or hadn't so far. She liked being able to set her own schedule, follow her whims. She liked not having to consider what someone else wanted for dinner, streaming what she wanted. This feeling of emptiness in her own home was a very new thing.

They caught each other up on their weeks, sharing the little stories that made up life. Jodi was flowing along, smiling and laughing, commiserating about the things that had gone wrong, when Erin's tone shifted. She sounded like she was trying for light but not quite succeeding when she said, "I got calls from both Brad and Lindsey on Sunday after you left."

Jodi wasn't sure what to make of the tone. "Are they both okay?"

"Oh yes. They're both doing well. It was nice talking to them." She paused and looked to the side. Jodi once again tried to puzzle out what was going on. Erin looked back at the camera. "They're both coming home for Christmas."

"Oh." Christmas. They hadn't discussed that at all. Jodi's standing plan was spending it in Seattle with Brit and Sal. She always drove up on Christmas Eve in time for a movie with all the good snacks. Then, on Christmas Day, Brit and Sal hosted an orphan's Christmas for any and all. People trickled in and out all day. Jodi loved it.

But now she wanted to spend Christmas with Erin. She just hadn't considered it before. That didn't seem to be a possibility. Jodi felt a little hurt but pushed it away. Of course Erin would have plans with her family. "That's a good thing, right?"

"It is," Erin said slowly. She looked away, then back again. "What do you usually do for Christmas?"

Jodi explained, and Erin looked lighter.

"That sounds like fun."

"It is." Jodi considered her next words. She didn't want to put pressure on Erin, but she also wanted to let her know that she was taking them seriously, and part of that meant holidays together, at least eventually. She hoped. "It would have been lovely to spend Christmas together. Maybe next year?"

Erin bit her lip. "I would love to spend Christmas with you. I hope we can make that work sometime." Jodi didn't love the vagueness of sometime. "What if we do an early Christmas? Maybe you could come out the weekend before, and we can have a little Christmas for you, me, and Darcy."

That sounded like a reasonable compromise. They'd only just gotten together. Jodi's feelings were probably out of proportion to the amount of time they'd dated. She wasn't going to act like one of the women she'd dated who'd tried to move too fast, causing Jodi to pull away. "That sounds fun. What will we do for our mini-pre-Christmas Christmas?"

Erin rubbed her hands together. "The beauty of it is that we can create our own traditions. This is the fun part. What do you like best about the holidays?"

"Cookies." Jodi grinned.

Erin laughed. "Any particular type? Is it making them or eating them that's the best?"

"Both, of course. My mom and I used to make cookies together." Jodi smiled sadly at the memory. "I haven't made Christmas cookies since she died."

Erin's expression turned compassionate. "Oh, honey. Will it be good to do it again or too sad?"

"I'm sure it'll be bittersweet, but let's bake. We did a bunch of different cookies, but my favorites were sugar cookies. She'd cut them out, and I'd decorate them." Jodi hesitated. "Do you think Darcy would want to decorate cookies with us?"

Erin's eyes sparkled. "I'm sure she'd be delighted."

They talked about other Christmas memories and traditions, including what they'd done with their friends when they were teenagers. They built a plan for a Christmas weekend that Jodi was very much looking forward to.

When they got hungry, neither wanted to say good-bye, so they moved to their respective kitchens and cooked, then ate together. They talked until Erin, who'd gotten up early for a pancake breakfast fundraiser for Darcy's team, was nearly falling asleep.

"You should go to bed, legs." The endearment slipped out.

Erin looked more awake than she had in minutes. "I haven't heard that since, well, you know."

Jodi did know. It was an endearment she'd used when they were teenagers. She'd wanted something special to call Erin but had worried that the usual things—babe, sweetheart, etc.—would be too obvious if one slipped out in front of other people. She'd always been attracted to Erin's long legs. So there it was.

Erin yawned. "You're right. I should go to bed. I just wish you could come with me, tot."

Jodi laughed. Erin had come up with a name for Jodi, too, based both on her stature and on her love of tater tots. "I wish I could, too."

"Do you think we can find a weekend before our Christmas? That's a month away. It feels too long."

"I agree. Next weekend is Thanksgiving, which will make travel horrible." Jodi also didn't know if Erin wanted her there for Thanksgiving. Maybe it was going to be another family event Jodi wasn't invited to.

"But with a lot of built-in time off. It'd be quick to pull together, but it would be nice to have you here. It's just going to be Darcy and me." She looked more awake. "Seriously, you should come if you can swing it. But what do vegetarians eat at Thanksgiving?" Her tone took on a teasing note.

"Pretty much everything except turkey. And gravy made from turkey. And stuffing if you're mean and put it in the bird." Jodi was getting excited. She pulled up a search window and started looking at flights.

"Seems like a problem we can work around. Are you looking at flights now?"

"I am. No time like the present. Hmm." Jodi clicked back to the call. "It looks like the best pricing would involve either flying out on Monday or waiting until Thanksgiving Day and staying until Tuesday. That's over a week if I went with Monday." She tried to keep a neutral look. She wanted to go on Monday, and she wanted Erin to want her to, also. But she didn't want to look needy.

"If you can make it work to come out the day after tomorrow, please do. Oh my gosh, I'm so excited I get to see you. Why didn't we think of this earlier?"

Jodi smiled a relieved smile. "I have no idea. Booking now." She clicked back over and did it.

The excitement carried them through another half an hour before Erin started yawning again. "I think I'd really better go, tot. I l—can't wait to see you."

Jodi's heart gave a lurch at what she thought Erin had been about to say. She told herself to settle down. Erin had likely been half-asleep and about to just give a typical family good-bye. She didn't mean it.

"'Night, legs. Sleep well."

CHAPTER TWENTY-FIVE

It had been less than two weeks since Erin had last picked Jodi up at the airport, but she was no less excited this time. She might have even been more excited. Last time, she'd also been a little nervous. This time, she had experience to draw on of having Jodi there, and that experience had been good, so very good. Not just the sex, although that had been literally the best she'd ever had, but the cuddles and the company. She enjoyed talking to Jodi maybe more than any other person in her life. Even just having Jodi sit in the same room and work while she worked had made her workday that much better.

Erin eagerly watched people stream from the secured area. Would Jodi come in this group, or was this a different flight? Finally, she caught sight of Jodi's blond pixie between two other passengers. She waited until Jodi stepped out of the flow before wrapping her in a hug.

"I'm so glad you're back. I missed you," Erin said.

"I missed you, too."

Erin could hear the smile in her voice, and it warmed her. She took Jodi's roller bag and headed for the exit. She wanted to take Jodi's hand as well, but she'd learned her lesson regarding not knowing when she was being observed. Once they were in the car, though, Erin pulled Jodi into a kiss.

Against her lips, Jodi said, "Maybe we should get back to your place before Darcy is home from school."

Erin smiled at the thought but had to dash the hope. "Sadly, there's no school all week, so she is home. There are parent-teacher conferences today and tomorrow. Sorry, I'll have to go into the school tomorrow for mine. And then a planning day on Wednesday, all of which amounts to no school all week."

Jodi sat back and let her head fall against the headrest. She groaned. "I was hoping for a little empty apartment time." She straightened and looked at Erin. "Not that I mind having Darcy around generally. She's great."

Erin put a hand over hers. "I know you like her. Don't worry." She infused some playfulness into her voice for the next part. "Also, I'm happy to report that she has sleepover plans tonight and will be taking off for that in just a couple of hours."

"Sweet." Jodi smiled.

Erin laughed at her. "What are you, a Millennial?"

"Nope. Hella Gen X."

Erin adopted a look of horror. "Seriously, stop talking like a Millennial. It's freaking me out."

"Wouldn't want to freak you out, legs. At least, not in that way."

Jodi leaned back over the console and kissed her lightly. She deepened the kiss, making promises about their evening to come.

While Erin was away for her parent-teacher conferences and Darcy still hadn't returned from her sleepover, the apartment was as quiet as it was going to get. Jodi closed herself in Erin's closet and opened her laptop. She put on her headphones, set up her microphone, and rang Val.

"Nice closet you're in there, Jodi," Val said by way of greeting, with just enough slyness to her tone that Jodi knew she meant it in more ways than one.

"Ha ha. Very funny."

"In all seriousness, how's it going?"

"Good. Great. Erin is…she's great."

Val looked skeptical. "I'm mostly convinced. You looked dreamy for a minute there, but then it's like reality set in. Having problems with pretending in public again?"

"Nope. We haven't gone out. And Darcy was away on a sleepover last night, so, yeah. It's been dreamy."

"Oh my God. How many times?"

Jodi grinned. "Only twice. We're old."

Val, who was only in her late thirties to Jodi's fifty-one, scoffed. "Twice in less than twenty-four hours is a lot even now, what with work and the kids and everything. I dream of weekends away." She did look dreamily into the distance at the idea.

"Okay, okay. Dream of sex weekends on your own time. We've got a podcast to record."

"We do. And it needs to be as fast as possible. I still have to pack, and our flight is in six hours."

"A lack of planning on your part does not constitute an emergency on mine," Jodi teased.

"Listen, you're the one who up and flew to see your girlfriend at the last minute. Otherwise, we'd have done this yesterday."

"And you're the one who put off packing until the last minute. Otherwise, we'd have plenty of time."

They grinned at each other. They liked to tease, and the banter warmed them up. Plus, they tended to operate well under pressure conditions, unlike Jodi's other cohost for *Books in Space*. Luckily, they'd been able to record for that one on Sunday, so there hadn't been much of a time pressure.

"Ready to do this?" Val asked.

"Let's get 'er done."

They rolled on through, and despite the setting—surrounded by Erin's clothes rather than in Jodi's spare room that she'd turned into a makeshift recording studio—Jodi was feeling good about it. They'd been clicking along. It would need editing, of course, but it should be pretty fast. She was just saying her good-byes when she heard Erin come home.

"I hear your girl over there. You should go get it while you can." Val pumped her eyebrows up and down a few times.

"Go pack and mind your business."

Val stuck out her tongue. "You're no fun, but you are right. I've really got to get that done." With a quick wave, she disconnected.

Jodi emerged from the closet feeling creaky. She'd stiffened up sitting on the floor for so long. She heard a gasp and looked up. Erin was standing in her room, hand over chest.

"Sorry. Didn't mean to surprise you," Jodi said.

"I thought I was expecting it because you mentioned needing to record, but you still took me off guard. I guess I'm just not used to people in my closet."

Jodi put her hands on Erin's hips. "I think that's generally a good thing? But it's good acoustics in there."

"That worked out? Good. Then you can just stay." Her tone was mostly joking, but Jodi wanted it to be true. She fancied Erin meant it a little bit.

"Are you kidnapping me?" Jodi grinned, trying to show she wouldn't mind.

"Maybe just trapping you here in the bedroom for a little while." Erin began to back her toward the bed.

"I'm home." It was Darcy calling from the living room.

Erin groaned, gave Jodi a quick kiss, and stepped away. "Welcome home,"

Darcy showed up at the bedroom door. She crossed her arms. "Am I interrupting anything?"

"Not at all," Jodi lied. "I just finished recording my podcast in your mom's closet."

"And I just got home from the parent-teacher conferences," Erin said in a foreboding tone.

Jodi wondered if Darcy really was doing poorly or Erin was joking. She'd gotten the impression Darcy was a good student.

Darcy rolled her eyes. "Yeah, yeah. I'm sure they had nothing but complaints." Then, her tone changed from flippant to mildly concerned. "Did they?"

Erin smiled and pulled her into a hug. "No. Mostly all compliments. Although, your English teacher thinks there's room for improvement."

Darcy huffed. "We can't all be experts in everything."

"True enough," Erin said lightly.

"What kind of problems do you have with English?" Jodi asked. When both of them looked at her, she held her hands up. "If you don't mind me asking. None of my business, really."

"No, it's fine," Darcy said. "I'm not the fastest reader in the world, so when we have tests where we have to read a passage and then answer questions about it, I don't always finish."

"Ah. Can I ask…have you read any of the books we talked about?"

Darcy looked down and mumbled, "No."

"It's okay." Jodi held her hands up again, trying to show she wasn't pressuring. "No worries at all. It's just that everything I've read about reading says that if you read for pleasure, it really helps boost reading skills overall. But it's completely up to you."

"I mean, there were some you mentioned that sounded interesting."

"Maybe we should hit up a bookstore, and you can pick one out. I can find out if it's in a local bookstore or if we'd need to order it online."

Erin squeezed Jodi's shoulder. She wasn't sure if it was in warning or in thanks. Was Jodi being too enthusiastic? If they were at home, she'd have a bunch of books Darcy could choose from. She was sent review copies all the time. Maybe she should just pick out a few to bring next time rather than trying to talk Darcy into a book here and now.

Darcy kicked the carpet. She was a little shy when she said, "There was one you mentioned about a basketball player?"

"Oh, yeah. I bet we can get that at any bookstore, but let me dig a little." Jodi didn't want to waste the moment of buy-in from Darcy. Going to a bookstore where it wasn't available might be enough of a stumbling block that she would lose interest. Jodi considered the time. It had been a little after two p.m. when she'd wrapped up the call. There would be plenty of time to shop before dinner. Unless Darcy was going out with friends again. "If you want, we could go in a couple of hours, and then I could take you both out to dinner?

Unless you have other plans." She looked back and forth between them.

"My only plan was a nap," Darcy said.

"I had an idea of something to cook for dinner, but we can have it tomorrow instead. Dinner out sounds good."

"Great, it's a plan." Jodi clapped and immediately felt uncool. She wouldn't be surprised to see Darcy looking at her with pity, but when she peeked, she just looked amused.

"Okay, well, I'm going to sleep for a while. Leave at four?" Darcy threw the question over her shoulder, not waiting for an answer, and disappeared into her room.

"Whew," Jodi said softly. "That was harrowing."

Erin hugged her. "You did great."

"I think I was a little too enthusiastic?"

"No, you were fine."

Erin moved away and Jodi missed her. But Erin just closed the door, turned the lock, and came back. "We'll have to be quiet."

Jodi nodded quickly a few too many times. "I can work with that."

CHAPTER TWENTY-SIX

W hat does the CWE stand for?"
Jodi muttered the question, so Erin wasn't sure if she actually wanted an answer or was looking it up herself. "Central West End?"

After the fun and games in the bedroom, they'd gone into the office to work. Ostensibly. Apparently, Jodi was doing something else.

"That makes sense," Jodi said, mostly to her laptop screen. She looked up at Erin. "Would it be a problem to go there? For the bookstore, I mean."

"No, aside from parking being a challenge." Erin wasn't a fan of parallel parking. She'd never lived anywhere it was strictly necessary and had never developed the skill. It was fine. They could always pay to park in a garage. "But we should be able to make it work."

"Cool. Have you been to Left Bank Books?"

"No, never have."

"It looks pretty cool. Like, I mean, the building is cool."

"Excellent. It'll be an experience for all of us." Erin considered for a minute. She swiveled back to her screen to look up what she'd just thought about. "We should eat there, too. In the CWE. I know a place."

"Sounds like a plan. Man. I really need to get some work done." Jodi chuckled a little. "It's sure easy to get distracted around here."

At the low chuckle, Erin turned to find Jodi looking at her with a crooked smile. "Okay, now I'm not the one being distracting."

"You're always distracting."

Erin quirked an eyebrow. "You could always go back to the closet."

Jodi's face fell. "I don't think that's where I want to be."

Erin realized her mistake. What with the way she was making them stay in the closet metaphorically, she understood why Jodi would react that way. She scooted her chair over and put her hand on Jodi's knee. "I didn't mean it that way. I just meant…"

"No, I know. I shouldn't have taken it like that. I knew what you meant."

Jodi smiled, but it looked strained. Erin wished she hadn't been the one to put that look on her face. She cast about for some way to fix the problem. Aside from coming out and endangering the home she'd built for Darcy and her relationship with her other kids. Finally, she settled on, "Maybe I should come visit you in January. What do you think?"

Jodi looked interested. "Do you think you could get away? What about Darcy?"

"She could stay with a friend for a weekend. You could show me all around Portland. I'd love to see your city."

Jodi smiled a true smile. "That would be excellent. How do you feel about dancing?"

"Um, I mean, I haven't danced a lot since high school, so my dancing hasn't exactly progressed since you last saw it." Was Jodi thinking of hitting up a club? Erin wasn't sure how she felt about that. She liked her early evenings.

"You never had to go to, I don't know, officer balls or whatever?"

"Well, yes. But Grant isn't much of a dancer, so we generally stayed off the dance floor. What exactly do you have in mind?"

"I was thinking of taking you to a queer club if you want. Don't worry, the dancing starts early. I can have you home and in bed by ten. I just want to slow dance with you like we couldn't do at prom."

That did sound really nice. They'd gone to prom together in the sense that their male dates were friends and wanted to double. Rusty had been Erin's date. Patrick was Jodi's. When Jodi and Patrick had danced, Erin had been hot with jealously she couldn't show. It wasn't that she thought Jodi had any feelings for him. It was that he got to dance with her, and Erin didn't. "Are you still in contact with Rusty or Patrick?"

"Yeah, actually. Rusty plays in the San Francisco philharmonic, and Patrick is a programmer for one of the tech companies in Silicon Valley."

"Wait. Are you saying they're…"

"Gay and a couple? I am." Jodi nodded.

"But how…I mean, Patrick went to college in the Springs like me."

"I'd almost forgotten about that. He moved to California after he graduated to be with Rusty."

"That's…awesome." Erin wasn't sure of the feelings coursing through her. She was happy for the boys. Men, now, she supposed. They were her age. But she was also jealous again. This time of their acceptance of themselves at such a young age. Why couldn't she have figured it out sooner? Then, again, she hit the wall of not wanting to wish her kids away. Things happened like they happened. She was here now, with Jodi.

"There seems to be a lot happening behind here." Jodi smoothed a thumb over Erin's forehead.

"Just processing. I'm really happy for them. Together all this time. That's impressive, especially considering how things were when we were growing up. Also, Rusty went to my church, remember?"

"He stopped going in our sophomore year, when he started playing *Dungeons and Dragons*. He said that it made him realize they were probably wrong about a few things. And then he and Patrick started dating just before junior year."

Erin's mouth dropped open. "Seriously? Did you know?"

Jodi shook her head, eyes sparkling. "No. They kept it well hidden. Can you imagine how useful we'd have been as beards for each other had we only known?"

Erin slapped her knee. "Opportunity missed. When did you find out?"

"I ran into Patrick when I was home on break from college at some point. I was all into coming out to people, so I mentioned my girlfriend. He lit right up and told me all about him and Rusty. We stayed in touch after that."

"Did you tell him about us?"

"No, of course not. I didn't tell Sal, why would I tell him?"

"I still can't believe you kept it a secret all these years from everyone, even when they were telling you all these things about themselves."

Jodi looked Erin in the eye. "I would never betray you. You said you didn't want me to tell anyone ever, so I didn't. Well, again, except that one therapist."

Erin felt like Jodi was wrapping her in a hug with her words. She moved to the couch so she could actually hug the woman who made her feel so…she wasn't ready to finish that thought. "I'm sorry it messed you up so much you needed therapy."

Jodi leaned her head on Erin's shoulder. "Listen, therapy is a good thing. You don't have to be messed up to benefit from it. That said, being a lesbian in the early 90s, at least once I was out of college, was a thing I had to navigate. It wasn't so much about us, but I was happy to have the chance to talk to someone about it. But I'm a proponent of therapy. Have you never done any?"

Erin buried her nose in Jodi's hair. Her voice was a little muffled when she answered, "No. It's never really come up."

"Hmm."

Erin kissed her head. "Well, back to work for both of us. We only have an hour before Darcy is up and we're supposed to go."

"Noses to the grindstone. There's work to do."

"This place is cool," Darcy said.

Jodi was relieved. She'd thought even this bookstore, with its corner location in this ornate brick building, might be boring for Darcy since she wasn't much of a reader. Yet. She waved an arm expansively. "Let's look around some. Feel free to pick up a few books. My treat."

"Really? Cool."

"If you can't find that one you were looking for or need any recommendations, I'm here."

Darcy was already wandering away.

"You don't have to do that, you know."

"What? Bribe your daughter so she'll like me? I mean, I think I do." Jodi accompanied the words with a little grin to show Erin she was mostly joking. Mostly. "Besides, books are my jam. I like sharing my jam."

"Okay, okay."

"Speaking of sharing, let's pick you out a book, too."

"Are you buying it for me?" Erin asked with a tilt of her head and a cute smile.

"Absolutely. This book shopping trip brought to you by your friendly book peddler." Jodi wanted to grab Erin's hand and drag her to the LGBTQIA+ section. She had a good idea of a book about a tennis player who fell in love with her much younger doubles partner's mother to suggest. Instead, she just smiled and led the way.

It was about an hour later that they left the store with Darcy carrying a bag of books. There were three young adult books featuring lesbians for Darcy and the tennis one for Erin.

"Why didn't you get any for yourself?" Erin asked as they walked to the restaurant.

"I get enough sent to me. Plus I do a lot of reading on my e-reader."

"Why?" Darcy asked. "I mean, they're always telling us to have less screen time. That seems like more."

"That's true. Although my e-reader is a fancy one designed to be easy on the eyes and to change light when it's close to bedtime and all that jazz, so I don't worry about it too much. As for why, well, I read so much that I like to be able to easily carry a book with me and have another available at a moment's notice. And it's lighter, which I like for reading in bed."

"Maybe I need an e-reader, Mom."

Erin shoulder bumped Darcy. "Read what you've got there in the bag, and then we can talk about it."

"Fair enough."

Darcy looked pleased, which made Jodi feel good. If she was happy about the books, maybe it would be the start of creating a new reader in the world.

Over dinner, talk flowed from books to dramas in Darcy's world to their Thanksgiving plans.

"I only bake pies a few times a year, but Thanksgiving is the time to go wild on pies," Erin said. "At least, that's our tradition."

"That is a tradition I can get behind. What kind of pies are we talking? Aside from pumpkin, of course, which I assume is on the menu," Jodi said.

Darcy pulled a face. "You shouldn't assume. Pumpkin pie is gross. Like eating baby food."

Erin put her hand over her daughter's. "Not everyone thinks so." She looked at Jodi. "We'll do a pumpkin, certainly. But also an apple, a blueberry, and a chocolate cream."

Jodi felt her eyes go wide. "Are more people coming? I mean, aside from the three of us?" She'd been considering dessert, but it seemed she needed to hold off for all this pie coming her way soon.

Darcy laughed. "No, we just really do go crazy for pies. We'll be eating pie for days."

"Tomorrow is pie making day," Erin said. "They're good to do a day ahead, saving Thanksgiving proper for cooking the main meal."

"I've never made a pie. I don't think my mom ever made a pie. She worked a lot of Thanksgivings and never made a big deal out of the day." Jodi finished and pushed her plate away a little.

Erin gave her a soft look. "I remember. You came to Thanksgiving at my house a couple of years."

Jodi moved to touch Erin but pulled her hand back. Darcy looked between them. What was she thinking? Her eyes were narrowed just a smidge, as if she was thinking about something. Jodi wanted to be a role model for her, show her that love between two women was nothing to hide, but she had to respect Erin's wishes about not being out in public. It made her feel a little sick to her stomach. "I did, yeah. I also spent a couple of Thanksgivings at Meredith's."

"Not Sal's?" Erin asked.

"Nope, their family wasn't big on inviting extras to family days. I actually did some youth group stuff with Sal, though. Did you know? We painted fire hydrants at the zoo once."

"I had no idea. What else were you two hiding from the rest of us?" Erin looked like she was trying for an accusatory expression, but the smile at the corner of her lips ruined the look.

Jodi quirked up a corner of her mouth. "A lot, but mostly, that was just Sal hiding."

"True enough. Poor Sal. It must have been so rough for them."

"Sal is your nonbinary high school friend?" Darcy popped a fry in her mouth and chewed. She swallowed and said, "It's amazing they figured it out, considering the dark ages you guys were living in."

"It took a while. They knew something was different about them. It kept them from really committing to our friend group. They were always a bit of an observer. Even when they went to college and started dating a girl, they still didn't have words for how they felt about their gender. That came a lot later, as the world has gotten more comfortable talking about gender stuff." It was always a battle. Progress was made, then, rights were taken away. Jodi didn't want to bring the conversation down, so she simply said, "It's a much different world than when we were kids, and I'm grateful for many of the changes."

"But we have to fight still." Darcy pushed her plate back and put her elbows on the table, leaning in. "There are states where you can't say gay in schools and states that want to make it so trans kids can't live as themselves. It's better than then, but it's still bad in places."

Jodi should have known that Darcy wouldn't be blind about these issues. She had social media at her fingertips. Who knew what she and her friends talked about? Hadn't Erin said she had a friend who used they-them pronouns? "You're right. There's more to be done, and there are places where progress has gone backward, particularly lately. It's too bad that that's reality for us, but it is."

"Yeah. I can't even tell, like, my dad."

"I'm sorry. At least you have a mom who loves and supports you?" Jodi suggested.

"Yeah. Yes. I mean, yeah." Darcy fiddled with her fork.

What was that about? Did Darcy not feel like her mom was in her corner?

They were interrupted by their server collecting their plates. "Anything else for you ladies?"

They said no, paid the bill, and headed home. Well, to Erin and Darcy's home. Jodi would be well advised not to think of it as home herself. She was a guest. It was hard to remember that sometimes. Like when Darcy disappeared to her room with her new books, leaving Erin and Jodi to settle in on the couch to watch an episode of their current show. It felt nice, homey. Home. But it wasn't. And it couldn't possibly be, not until Erin was ready to live her truth outside of these walls.

CHAPTER TWENTY-SEVEN

I really liked the book," Darcy said after she'd taken her first few sips of coffee. She'd been drinking coffee since she was fourteen, and if it had stunted her growth, Erin had yet to see evidence of it.

"Wait, you finished it already?" Jodi held her sandwich halfway to her mouth. While Darcy had just gotten up, Erin and Jodi had been working all morning. Really working for a change. They both had plenty to do, and Erin was taking the afternoon off to make pies. Jodi had said she needed to work some more. Erin was a little bummed about it because pie making was a good time, but Darcy also enjoyed it, so they'd have some mother-daughter time.

Erin had the same question. This was a kid who'd read begrudgingly for school but had never read for pleasure. She had been more of an active player as a kid, and that inclination had grown into sports. Now she was either playing fast-pitch, at school, doing homework, or hanging out with her friends doing...

Honestly, Erin wasn't totally sure anymore. The kids used to hang out at their house frequently before they'd moved. They'd watch TV or sit around and talk. She supposed they were still doing those things, just at other people's houses. She hoped that wasn't because Darcy was embarrassed about where they lived now. Probably not. She was excited about the Christmas Eve Eve party.

"Yeah," Darcy said, pulling Erin out of her straying thoughts. "I started last night and...what can I say? It was good. I had to find out if they were going to get together or not."

Jodi looked pleased as punch. Erin was pleased herself. She hadn't been the best role model for reading, but she knew kids should. It helped develop all sorts of skills that would help them in life. To see Darcy reading was great.

"Spoiler alert, if it's a romance, they end up together," Jodi said. "It's just how it is."

Darcy set her mug down and regarded Jodi with judgment in her eyes. "And now you've ruined the other two."

Jodi held up her hands defensively. "I like romance. Not exclusively. I like to mix things up. But I read a bunch of romance, and knowing they'll get together in the end does not ruin them. It's the path to getting there. It's the characters, how they change and grow. It's watching the couple figure out how they fit together."

"Plus you watch rom-coms," Erin put in. "It's the same formula, yet you still watch them."

"The book was so much better," Darcy said with passion. "For one, they're both girls, which I've only seen a few times in movies, and for another, you get to know them so much better than in a movie."

Erin wondered what movies Darcy had been watching. Aside from *A League of Their Own*, they hadn't watched anything sapphic together. She hoped it wasn't too spicy, as Jodi and Val would say on their podcast.

Jodi said, "Exactly. That's part of what's awesome about books. Plus, there are so many of them to read, and sapphic stories in movies and TV shows is still sadly lacking."

"Or they kill them off," Darcy said darkly.

Again, what was she watching?

"To see sapphic joy, you mostly need to turn to books," Jodi said.

"Or TikTok," Darcy said.

They both laughed. Maybe Erin needed to check out TikTok. She'd resisted, but if they were both on there, maybe she needed to go see what Darcy was seeing. She'd ask Jodi to get her started.

"Do you have any book recommendations where they play softball?" Darcy asked, hope in her eyes.

"There's one I can think of, but…" Jodi cut her eyes to Erin; it was one of the spicy ones.

"Maybe finish what Jodi bought you before you press for more," Erin said. It did make her a little sad when Darcy looked disappointed, but that wasn't the sort of thing Darcy needed to be reading at her age.

"Which one are you going to start next?" Jodi asked, taking the hint.

"Oh, I already did."

And they were off talking more about books. Erin needed to get reading to keep up.

After Jodi was done eating, she put her plate in the dishwasher, kissed Erin on the head, and went back to the office.

"Ready to start baking?" Erin asked.

"You know it." Darcy put action to words and stood. "Chocolate cream pie first?" She picked the playlist, they divvied up the first tasks, and got to work.

A half an hour later, Darcy was well into the cookie crust for the chocolate cream pie while Erin was working on the filling. She took her pot of creamy chocolate goodness to the island and caught sight of Jodi lingering at the door. "Are we being too loud?"

Jodi stepped in. "No. Not at all. You just sound like you're having too much fun out here. I don't want to intrude, but could you use an extra hand?"

"Of course," Erin answered automatically, happy to have Jodi join them. But Darcy might not be so excited. No, Darcy smiled and waved Jodi in. *Whew. Okay.*

Jodi went to the sink to wash her hands. "I'm a little concerned that I'll be in your way."

"You'll be fine," Darcy said. "We'll give you the easy stuff."

"That is a fair assessment of my skills," Jodi said.

They had a great time. There was flour everywhere, the smell of baking pies in the air, dishes to do, spills to clean, talking, listening to the music, occasional dance parties, and laughter. It was by far one of the best pie-making days Erin had experienced. No, scratch that. There had been some good ones with the kids over the years, but this was the best.

Darcy was in a good mood, happy to be there, and old enough to be self-directed. What really made the day was Jodi's presence. She brought a light to the kitchen that kept pulling Erin's attention. They'd catch eyes, and Jodi's would sparkle at her. Erin would pass her, and Jodi would trail a flour-covered finger across her arm.

Plain and simple, it was magic. And there was no question that Jodi was the main reason why.

CHAPTER TWENTY-EIGHT

Erin woke slowly. Jodi was wrapped around her, hand draped over her stomach. She was still asleep. Erin could feel the rhythmic breath on her back. She hadn't set an alarm. Their turkey was as small as Erin had been able to find. She and Darcy both liked turkey but not so much they wanted to be eating it three meals a day for a week. Also, they'd decided the night before that no one cared when they ate, so if it didn't make it onto the table until late evening, so be it.

It was freeing. Grant had ideas about when Thanksgiving dinner should be, preferably at two p.m. They'd invited young officers without family in the area to join them, so Erin had always had to do a big turkey. Last year had been the first year that there had been no pressure from Grant, but with Brad home from college and Lindsey and Steve there to make sure she wasn't lonely on Thanksgiving after the divorce, there had still been a sizable gathering. Tradition had prevailed.

This year, she was waking up on her own wrapped in the arms of the woman she—

She cut the thought off. They weren't there yet. She sometimes saw the hesitation in Jodi's eyes. She clearly got tired of people and moved on. Erin wanted to believe she was different but didn't know for sure. It was part of why she couldn't come out to Lindsey and Brad. They might stop talking to her if she told them she was gay. Then, if Jodi decided to move on after that? No, it was impossible for now.

Still, waking up snuggled in bed with Jodi, a day of connection though cooking and food ahead of them? It was bliss. Erin lay there for a while, enjoying a slow morning. Eventually, her antsy-ness to get the cooking started took over. As much as she was glad of the more relaxed schedule, a part of her felt like she needed to get started.

She slid out of bed, trying not to wake Jodi. And sure enough, Jodi mumbled something but subsided back into sleep.

Entering the kitchen, Erin found she was enjoying the quiet. It was a special sort of quiet, containing the feel of people she lo— cared about sleeping nearby. First things first, she got the coffee going.

When she straightened from checking the monkey bread she'd made for breakfast after having gotten the turkey in the oven, arms slipped around her from behind.

"Good morning. How long have you been up?" Jodi asked. "It smells fantastic in here."

Erin put her hands over Jodi's. "Not too long."

"I think it's been pretty long to have gotten all this done. You could have woken me."

Erin turned in the circle of Jodi's arms and leaned down for a kiss. "But you were sleeping so peacefully, and I didn't want to disturb you."

"Well, I'm up now. What can I do?"

"Sit at the counter and have your first cup of coffee. This monkey bread is nearly done, so it's a perfect time to break for breakfast."

Jodi sunk her hands in Erin's hair and pulled her down for another kiss. Erin was happy to oblige. When they parted, Jodi said, "This is quite the holiday. Monkey bread for breakfast, the regular feast, and five pies. Will there be any more food surprises today? Perhaps it's tradition to have tacos for an evening snack? I need to know these things so I can plan my eating accordingly."

Erin laughed. "No, no more surprises. Go sit." She patted Jodi's butt as she went. Jodi looked over her shoulder and winked.

After breakfast, which they did not hold for Darcy, as it was likely they wouldn't see her until noon, Erin put Jodi to work. Now that there were two of them, she also put on music. If it woke Darcy up, well, there would be three sets of hands.

Exceeding Erin's expectations, it was eleven when Darcy stumbled into the kitchen and poured herself a mug of coffee. "You two have been busy. Will we be eating soon?"

"The turkey still has a couple of hours, I think. If you're hungry, there's monkey bread." Erin pointed her spoon at the remainder of breakfast.

Darcy fixed her coffee to her liking and took a sip before pulling a piece off the bread and eating it standing. "That should do me for now. Put me in, coach. I'm ready."

Erin set her to work peeling potatoes. The three of them settled into a similar rhythm to the day before, but if anything, with more familiarity. Darcy had stayed up late finishing the second of the books. Jodi was promising her another trip to the bookstore. Things burbled on the stove. Opening the oven to baste the turkey resulted in the kitchen being filled with better and better aromas.

They were in their own little world, and Erin loved it.

"Surprise!"

Erin jumped about three feet in the air and spun around. Lindsey was standing in the doorway to the kitchen. Steve was grinning over her shoulder. Erin was dumbfounded. How had they even gotten in? She didn't think they had keys. No, wait, she had given Lindsey keys when she'd last visited.

Why was her mind focusing on that right now?

Darcy ran over to her sister and hugged her. "You're here! Why are you here?"

"We didn't want you two to spend a sad little Thanksgiving all alone, so we decided to surprise you. Right, Steve?" Lindsey smiled over her shoulder at her husband.

"Right." He pushed Lindsey farther into the room and hugged Darcy as well. "Goodness, you're tall."

"No taller than last time," she said.

"So you say," he said.

Erin stood in the kitchen frozen, baster in her hand. She was glad to see Lindsey, of course, but how was she going to explain Jodi being there? She hadn't told Lindsey that Jodi was coming back. It seemed too quick a turnaround to be explained away easily.

"Mom? Are you in shock?" Lindsey, apparently giving up on Erin introducing them, addressed Jodi, "Um, hi. I'm Lindsey. And you are?"

That finally propelled Erin into movement but not fast enough.

Jodi stuck her hand out. "Jodi. How nice of you to surprise your mom for Thanksgiving." Her voice sounded strained.

"You remember me telling you about Jodi. My old high school friend. She came to have Thanksgiving with us." Where was Erin going to say Jodi was sleeping? There wasn't a bed made up for her in the spare room. Erin felt like she was trapped in a bad dream.

"Oh, right." Lindsey still looked perplexed.

Erin finally remembered to hug her. "Welcome. I'm so glad you're here." She never thought those words spoken to any of her children would be a lie. "And Steve. This is lovely." She hugged him, too.

"I hope we have enough turkey," Darcy said brightly, drawing attention.

"Oh, we'll be fine," Erin said absently. She was still trying to figure out how to behave and what to do about the fact that Jodi didn't have a bed. She snuck a glance at her. She was wearing a smile that looked painted on. Shit. Erin had introduced her as her high school friend. Again.

"I just happened to be in town for a work thing, and your mom was nice enough to invite me for Thanksgiving, but I don't want to get in the way of your family holiday. I'll just head back to the hotel."

Hotel? Oh, she was covering. "No," Erin said. "You should stay. You were invited."

Jodi shook her head, looking very sad behind her eyes. "I think I'll clear out. It's turned into a whole different thing than you expected."

"You should stay," Lindsey said, sounding like she mostly meant it. "We're the ones crashing."

"No, really. It was nice to meet you, and I hope you have a great Thanksgiving. I'm just going to go get my coat." Jodi hooked a thumb over her shoulder, indicating the hall.

Erin was frozen. She was supposed to stay until Monday. Was she really just going to walk out? Erin wanted her to stay but didn't know how to stop her. They couldn't make a scene in front of Lindsey and Steve.

"Mom, why don't you walk Jodi out?" Darcy took the baster from Erin's limp hand. "Lindsey and I will take over here for a while."

"Yes. Right. I'll be back." Erin walked stiffly out of the kitchen. What was she going to say? Maybe Jodi didn't want to meet Lindsey? Maybe she'd decided that more family was too much? Sure, Erin had introduced her as an old friend, but Jodi knew where Erin stood on coming out. She wasn't ready. If Jodi was going to be so delicate about it, she probably wasn't going to stay the distance anyway.

The reality of Jodi leaving hit when she got to her bedroom door and watched as Jodi shoved her laptop into her backpack. As much as Erin needed to let her go if that was her choice, the sight of her in her room where they'd shared so many intimate moments preparing to leave tore at Erin's chest.

"Jodi."

She looked up. The hurt in her eyes was so intense that Erin felt it like a physical push. "I can't do this again, Erin. I can't pretend to be your friend while wanting so much more. I can't wait, hoping you'll realize we're meant to be together, only to have you choose your family over me. Again."

Erin stood, frozen once again. She had done that in high school. It wasn't her plan now, but what was? She couldn't march out there with Jodi's hand in hers and declare herself. Could she?

She snapped out of it when Jodi brushed past her. "Bye, Erin. I hope you figure out what you want."

"Wait." Erin tried to say it loudly. She wanted Jodi to turn and say it was all okay. That Erin could take her time. That they'd figure it out together. It was what she'd been saying.

But maybe this was for the best. If Jodi would have gotten bored and left anyway... At least this way, Erin still had Lindsey. That thought strangled Erin's voice in her throat when she tried again to call after Jodi.

When the front door closed, it was too late. Jodi was gone.

Erin told herself that Jodi was always going to leave. This had just sped things up.

This? Lindsey. She needed to go back to the kitchen and pretend her heart wasn't breaking.

Later that evening, Lindsey tapped her glass to get everyone's attention—a theatrical move when there were only four of them—and said she had an announcement. Erin gave her full attention. This was what she'd chosen, her family. Lindsey was glowing in the candlelight. Her oldest daughter was a beautiful woman and had done a lovely thing by coming to surprise her mother.

"I'm pregnant. Mom, you're going to be a grandma!"

Erin jumped up and hugged her. "Oh, Linds. I'm so, so happy for you." And she was. She was also relieved. She wouldn't be getting this news if she'd claimed Jodi as her girlfriend when Lindsey had arrived. It was all working out for the best.

But as she lay in bed by herself that night, she gave in to the pain that she'd been shoving aside all day. Even the news of her impending grandmother-hood was tainted by the fact that the person she most longed to tell had walked out of her life this afternoon.

CHAPTER TWENTY-NINE

Jodi requested a Lyft, then opened the airline app. She didn't want to stay in St. Louis. Not that it wasn't a surprisingly nice city. She'd previously considered it to be…well, the truth was, she hadn't really considered it at all. But it had been lovely. Welcoming. A river through the center. Plenty of Pride flags, at least in certain parts of town. In some ways, it felt a little like Portland. That must have been part of why she'd experienced it as welcoming.

She stifled a sob as she pushed the other reason out of her mind.

Right now, she needed to focus on next steps. And the next step was to get out of St. Louis. She hoped not many people would be wanting to fly on Thanksgiving Day, particularly in the afternoon. She hoped she'd be able to get a flight.

But no. Most flights were full. Shouldn't people have already been where they were going for the holiday? Shit. She finally found an available seat in business class, so it cost her and arm and a leg. Figured. She was in the Lyft on her way to the airport when she tapped the final button, blowing a small fortune on her need to run away with her tail between her legs. It would be a little tight, but she'd get there. There was hardly any traffic, and she wasn't checking a bag.

She did her best to concentrate only on what needed to be done minute to minute until she made it onto her flight. It was then that she started sobbing, greatly alarming the middle-aged man sitting next to her. He didn't seem to want to actually deal with a crying woman because after one alarmed look, he put in his earbuds and started a movie on his tablet.

Jodi cried as quietly as she could all the way to Denver, where she had to pull it together to make her connection. She also sent a text to Sal: *Headed your way. I can take a Lyft to your place if you can't meet me at the airport. About to board my flight. Here are the deets.*

She had no concerns about being welcomed at this very last minute by Sal and Brit. They were the caretakers of their friends. She knew they had people over for Thanksgiving, which was why she didn't know if they'd be able to pick her up, but she did know they'd be waiting with open arms when she arrived.

"She just let you leave?" Sal asked. They were sitting on one side of Jodi, Brit on the other. Sal had met her at the airport, concern written all over their face. Jodi had asked to wait until they were back home before telling the story so she wouldn't have to repeat it for Brit. She'd also apologized for pulling Sal away from their guests.

"No problem," Sal had said. "People were starting to leave anyway. Brit is there for the stragglers, but they'll all be gone by the time we get back."

Now Sal had their arm around Jodi while Brit held her hand on the other side. Jodi had been right to come here. She needed love and support from people who weren't ashamed of her. "Yes. I should have known she'd choose her family over me again. It was stupid to think it would be different this time."

"I'm not sure I'd say it was stupid. It was hopeful. I had hopes from how she was at the reunion weekend," Sal said.

"What do you need?" Brit asked. "Or do you know?"

"Just to not be alone, I think. We can watch a movie or whatever. I just…didn't want to go home to my empty condo."

Sal and Brit exchanged a look over her head, but she wasn't in any sort of space to parse what it was about.

"Do you want to talk it out more?" Brit asked tentatively.

"No. I think it'll just make me cry more, and I've cried enough."

Apparently she hadn't actually cried enough. While she didn't cry during the movie, she did cry more once she was alone in the guest room. She cried again when she woke up on Friday at seven a.m., even though she hadn't gone to bed until after midnight and had cried for some indeterminate period.

Her eyes burned and felt gummy. She was so tired, she ached. She hurt physically and mentally. It was so much more hurt than she'd experienced the first time she and Erin had broken up. As much as she hadn't wanted that to happen, she'd seen the writing on the wall. Also, she'd had hopes that when she went to college, she'd find someone new. She'd been going to an all-girls school because she'd wanted to be out and proud, but the side effect was that it was a large pool for dating. Her preference had been that Erin go with her, but that was clearly not going to be. The result was that when Erin had pulled the plug on their being more than friends that hot night at the end of June, Jodi had hurt. It had been horrible. But it was nothing on this.

She thought she'd protected her heart. She'd thought she'd walled off parts so that she could see how it would be this time. She had clearly done a horrible job.

Not only that, but now she'd dated other women. Lots of other women. She knew that what her heart wanted was Erin. It had been stupid to try. She couldn't lie to herself so much as say that it wouldn't have hurt if she'd nipped this in the bud on the reunion weekend, but it would have hurt a lot less than this.

Plus, she was old now. These crying jags and lack of sleep hit her so much harder. Her whole body hurt. It was hard to parse what was old lady stuff and what was heartbreak, but the end result was pain.

She got up, dressed, and snuck out of the house. Maybe she hadn't needed to sneak. It was very possible that Sal, at least, was already up and out on a run. But she didn't want to talk to anyone this morning, so she snuck.

Brit and Sal lived in a neighborhood north of downtown. It was not quite as hilly as downtown notoriously was. It didn't matter. Jodi wasn't out for exercise. Well, maybe she was. If she wore herself out, she was more likely to sleep. Aside from the early wakefulness and occasional insomnia menopause had brought her, she usually didn't have trouble sleeping. But if last night was any indication, she'd have some trouble now. She just needed to move. So she walked.

It was cold, made colder by the slight drizzle that seemed ubiquitous in the Pacific Northwest through winter. It wasn't really there all the time, but the fact that it was today was suiting. It fit her mood.

She tried putting in her earbuds and listening to a podcast to distract her, but the voices sounded like so much nattering. She switched to music, but anything bright was grating, while anything sad annoyed her. She silenced all audio but left the earbuds in. They helped her feel separate from the world.

While she walked, her mind played scenes of Erin, both in their teenage years and from the last few months. That made her cry. Then, she angrily tried to banish all thoughts of Erin, only to get caught in a circle of thinking about how stupid she'd been and how Erin didn't want her. She got angry and power walked for a while. The scenes started again. This whole process repeated ad nauseum.

Sometimes, she thought of Darcy. She'd miss the girl. Then, her thoughts went to Erin's other children: Brad, whom she'd never met, and Lindsey, standing in the kitchen looking puzzled at Jodi's presence. Then, hurt and anger.

She wondered if she'd overreacted. Maybe she should have stayed, played the friend, gotten to know Lindsey. If Lindsey knew her and liked her, that would have made it easier for Erin to tell her the truth about them. But, no. She couldn't let herself get more attached. It would only hurt more when Erin still chose to not acknowledge their true relationship to most of the people in her life.

Over and over.

At some point, she'd come to the water and turned south. Now, she blurrily realized that her route was becoming increasingly busy. She was approaching Pike Market. Her stomach rumbled. It was annoying that her body still needed things when she was in crisis, but she hadn't had anything to eat or drink yet, and her body was making those needs known. What time was it anyway? She pulled out her phone and saw she had a bunch of texts from Sal. Nothing from Erin. Her heart squeezed again. Clearly, Erin really was fine with this being over. That was her choice. It was obvious.

Feeling guilty about just disappearing until—shit, it was afternoon—Jodi looked at the texts. They started off with: *Hey, I'm guessing you went for a walk. Just let me know if you need anything.* And escalated to: *It's been a long time now. Just text me back to let me know you're still alive.* And lastly: *Please. We're worried.*

Jodi was messing everything up. She fired off a quick: *I'm alive. Out on a long walk. Not sure when I'll be back. Sorry.* She tucked her phone away again.

She went up the stairs from the water to the market, where she got a coffee and a cinnamon roll. As much as she usually loved the rolls, she only managed half. It was just too hard to bother to chew. She did at least drink the coffee. Then, she kept walking.

Jodi returned to Sal's house late. She'd wandered so far that she'd taken a Lyft to get back. Sal would have come and picked her up, she knew, but she felt like she was already imposing too much. She'd showed up unannounced the night before, crashing their Thanksgiving, then had just disappeared today.

Brit paused the show they were watching, and Sal got up to pull Jodi into a hug. "I'm sorry you're going through this."

"Yeah. Listen, I'm sorry for crashing your long weekend. I'm going to take the train home in the morning."

Brit made a dismissive noise from the couch. Sal held Jodi at arms' length and said, "You listen. You're not a burden. You're our dear friend. No. Family. You're welcome anytime. And if you want to go home, that's also fine. I'm happy to drive you down."

"No, no. I'm not going to ask you to do a six hour drive. That's ridiculous. The train is fine."

"You're not asking. I'm offering." Sal relented. "But if what you need is time alone, then I respect that. Please, at least let me take you to the train station."

Jodi acquiesced. After discussing times, she retreated to her room where, thanks to a day of walking and a horrible night's sleep the night before, she fell gratefully into oblivion.

CHAPTER THIRTY

M om?"
Erin hated that Darcy sounded so tentative. Erin had really fallen down on her motherly duties if Darcy felt like she had to walk on eggshells around her. She tried to inject some play into her reply. "Yes, my darling child?" Even she could hear that it came out a little stilted.

Darcy came fully into Erin's bedroom. Erin had been spending a lot of time in bed these last couple of weeks. Too much time but she couldn't seem to help it.

Darcy sat on the edge of Erin's bed. She was still dressed for school. Did she have practice today? Erin didn't even know for sure. Before December, she would have had practice every day. Now it was only three days a week because the org only had one indoor practice space, and the teams had to share. But what day was it? She really needed to pull it together.

"Mom, I'm worried."

Erin knew that. She knew it in her gut. But still, she asked, "What about, sweetie?"

Darcy took a deep breath, apparently steeling herself for this intervention she was holding. "You, Mom. You're not okay."

Erin felt all the bluster she'd put on for her daughter rush out, leaving her slumping like a deflated balloon. "I'm so sorry." She put her hand over Darcy's. "You shouldn't have to worry about me. I'm going to pull it together."

Darcy looked angry. "I don't mind stepping up, Mom. It's okay if you need someone to lean on sometimes. It's not that. It's that you are sinking further and further into this pit of despair. I'm here to say it's time to start climbing out. Maybe you won't get back together with Jodi, and you have to find a way to be okay with that." Her voice hitched.

Erin felt like someone stabbed her in the chest. Darcy had, of course, gotten attached. This breakup was happening to them both. "Darcy, I—"

"No. Let me finish. Maybe you won't, although, I don't know why. Jodi is great. Maybe you think there's something wrong with being queer." Her voice hitched again.

"No," Erin interjected, sitting up. "No, Darcy. There's nothing wrong with it."

Darcy started crying. "Then why wouldn't you just tell Lindsey? Jodi wouldn't have left if you'd told Lindsey she was your girlfriend."

Erin gathered Darcy into her arms. "I was trying to protect you. And there's a large part of me that worries Lindsey won't take it well. You know your sister."

Darcy straightened, pulling away. "How is it protecting me to look like you're ashamed of being queer? I haven't told her for the same reason. I'm scared she'll be homophobic. But you acting like you are isn't helping."

Erin pulled her knees to her chest. Was that what she'd been doing? She could see how it could be interpreted that way, but she knew who she was, and she liked who she was for having admitted it to herself. She felt better in her own skin. She was proud of Darcy for realizing it so much sooner. She wanted to celebrate, not hide. But there were reasons for not telling people. Reasons she hadn't wanted to burden Darcy with. But if her actions were making Darcy think there was something wrong with both of them, maybe that was more harmful in the end?

She'd been so quick to want to keep her relationship with Lindsey that she was in the middle of destroying Darcy's trust in her.

"Darcy, I'm sorry it's made you feel this way. I'm sorry you're worried about me. I'm going to pull it together. I'm going to figure this out. I don't want you to have to worry anymore." She swung her feet out of bed and stood. "I'm going to take concrete steps. I'm going to start with a shower and then…" She thought for a moment and realized it was Wednesday and that Darcy didn't have practice tonight. "I'm going to set up a time to play tennis with Rhoda, work for an hour, then take us out for dinner. Okay?"

Darcy regarded her suspiciously. She opened her mouth, closed it, then opened it again, and with much hesitation, said, "Okay."

Erin marched to the shower. It wasn't that she hadn't gotten up at all today. She had. She'd gotten up with Darcy in the morning, but she hadn't showered. She'd worked for a few hours, then had gone back to bed. She was pretty sure she hadn't eaten lunch. Darcy was right. She needed to pull herself together. She also needed to take a good long look at her actions and decide if she needed to change course. What she'd been doing was not working for her. It had lost her Jodi and put Darcy into this tailspin.

Jodi. Erin prodded the wound. It still ached. It was going to continue to ache until she really dealt with it. Instead of really examining her feelings about Jodi crashing out of her life, Erin had gone through the motions over Thanksgiving weekend. Once Lindsey and Steve had gone back home, she'd basically gone to bed and had been barely functional since. She'd retreated into sleep rather than face the loss of the woman she—had come to care about so much.

It hurt that Jodi had left. Yes, Erin's actions had contributed to that, for sure. But it still seemed as if Jodi was likely to have left at some point anyway. She reminded herself that it was better this way.

She needed to be a good example for Darcy Jodi or no Jodi.

A wave of sorrow broke over her at the idea of no Jodi in her life. If it hurt this much now, it would have been even worse when Jodi had moved on to greener pastures later.

At least, that was what Erin told herself.

For now, she let herself cry in the shower. When the shower was over, she dried her tears as well as her body and went to her office. She needed to work, but she also needed to deal with her emotions. She emailed her minister and asked if she had time to meet. Before an hour passed, the pastor answered. If Erin wanted to come in right away, she had a slot open in the morning. Erin quickly accepted.

❖

Erin followed through on her promises to Darcy. She talked to the minister for a half an hour the next day. It was all the time she had available, but it was a start. The minister had asked probing questions Erin didn't have the answers to quite yet, but she spent a lot of time thinking about them.

Two days later, she was playing tennis at the indoor court at the community tennis center. She had to admit that it felt good to whack the ball. When they were done playing, Rhoda suggested getting smoothies. Erin had some work to catch up on—not as much as she would have at other times of the year, thankfully—but she also had a lot of socializing to catch up on, so she agreed.

Rhoda was about the same height as Erin. It was one of the things that had caught Erin's eye when she'd gone to the pickup game hour first looking for new people to play tennis with. She was younger by about ten years and blond to Erin's nearly black hair. As soon as they'd gotten their drinks and sat, she said, "It felt like you were working some things out on the court today. Everything okay?"

They were tennis friends more than real friends, but someone didn't move from situational friends to something more without opening up a little. Erin wasn't even sure what Rhoda's political beliefs were. However, she had no connection to Erin's kids or ex. She was safe to tell. If she reacted poorly to Erin coming out, that was good to know now rather than later.

"Not really. I recently had a breakup, and it's hitting me hard."

"I didn't even know you were dating again."

Erin had told Rhoda about the divorce, which was still in process when they'd started playing. "Yes, so…I think I mentioned the reunion weekend I was going to back in September?"

"Yeah, I remember. You and your three best high school friends, right?" She leaned over the table. "You met a guy that weekend?"

"No. I rekindled a high school romance. Her name is Jodi."

"But it didn't work out?" Rhoda asked with sympathy.

The fact that she didn't even bat an eye at the revelation was a balm. That should have been how it always went, but Erin had plenty of reason to believe that that was not how it would go with everyone. She took a moment to feel her relief before she told Rhoda the whole story. When she got to Thanksgiving, she faltered.

"It sounds like a dream second-chance romance. What went wrong?" Rhoda asked.

Their smoothies were long finished, but neither of them made a move to leave. For Erin, telling the story had felt good. She hadn't really been able to with anyone. Darcy knew, but Darcy was her child. Erin wasn't going to open up to her about all the details. And she hadn't told anyone else aside from the conversation with her minister.

She hadn't told anyone else. No wonder Jodi had been scared.

"Erin? Are you okay?"

She focused again. "I messed up. That's what happened." Things clicked into place. The probing questions her minister had posed, the fact that Jodi had never once given any sign she intended to move on. In fact, she'd built a relationship with Darcy. Would she have done that if she was not planning to stick around? Erin was sure she wouldn't have. It really was down to Erin rejecting her in front of Lindsey and Steve.

"How so?" Rhoda asked.

Erin told her. Told her about Jodi being there, about how good the visit was, about being in the kitchen and Lindsey showing up.

"I froze. I should have held Jodi's hand and told Lindsey. Keeping Lindsey in my life under false pretenses doesn't make for a real relationship."

It was true, true for everyone, not just Lindsey. It was like a switch flipped, and Erin forgot to be scared. If she wasn't living as her true and authentic self, who really had that relationship with Lindsey? Not Erin. Some person she was pretending to be. The same went for Brad, although she had an inkling he might not react badly. Grant would react badly, but the only way that affected Erin was if he tried to get custody of Darcy. That could be a battle, but it was a battle she was willing to fight. Darcy, too, would fight. It might be rough, but they'd handle it. Yes, her parents would likely not want anything to do with her. That would hurt, but it wouldn't impact her life in anywhere near the same way as losing Jodi.

Was it too late? Was it true that Jodi would have moved on anyway? After Erin had pushed her away with repeated public rejections? Shame washed over her. Her anxiety had been trying to tell her that her ideas of Jodi leaving were wrong. She should have listened. Now she was listening. She could claim her identity. She needed to learn from the shame but let it go. She could be a different person now. She could show Jodi she really meant it. Maybe it would be enough.

"I get not wanting to jeopardize your relationship with your daughter. It seems like Jodi could have given you some space."

Erin had nearly forgotten she was still in a conversation with Rhoda. So many things were running through her head. She took a moment to process her comment. "You're not entirely wrong. But I see where Jodi was coming from. You see, back in high school, I broke up with her because I was ashamed. I was torn between the expectations of my parents and church and loving Jodi."

And she had loved Jodi. She did love Jodi. She had to tell her. But first, she needed to put her house in order. "I chose my parents and church. I suppressed all those feelings, pretending it had just been a friendship that had gone too far. I realized last year that wasn't the case, that was who I really was, and it was like a truth bomb lit up all that flawed thinking. I knew it was okay. I needed to change my life and embrace my truth. And then, just when it was most important that I did, I went back to the old habit of hiding."

"Well, it sounds like you're very clear on what you want now."

"I'm sorry. I've kept you here practically ranting at you for so long."

Rhoda put a hand over Erin's. "What are friends for?"

CHAPTER THIRTY-ONE

Jodi's phone rang, pulling her out of the planning for the next *Books in Space* episode. It was Sal. She should answer, she knew. Sal kept texting, but all Jodi could muster the energy for was an occasional text back saying she was still alive. She hadn't called Sal on a lunch walk since she'd come home from Seattle three weeks ago. She hadn't even gone on her usual midday walks. Instead, she'd been starting work as soon as she woke up and going until it was dark, and she hadn't eaten. Although, it wasn't saying much that it was dark. It was winter in the Pacific Northwest. Dark came early.

When she came out of her work stupor, she put on shoes and started walking. She was accompanying those with audiobooks. She had to keep up her reading somehow. Basically, she'd come home and buried her nose in work. She couldn't bear to think about anything else. But she'd neglected Sal.

She hit the green button to answer the call. "Hi."

"Whoa. I really didn't expect you to pick up. I'm not sure what to say now."

Jodi didn't say anything. Normally, she'd banter back, but her brain simply would not produce anything to banter with.

Sal's voice softened. "Jodi, I'm worried. Brit is about to get us in a car and down there to stage an intervention. Please talk to me. Let me in."

One of the many things she hadn't done since she'd left Seattle was cry. She'd cried so much on Thanksgiving and the next day that at first, it had seemed she truly didn't have any tears left in her. Once she'd been dry-eyed for the whole train trip home, she'd decided she was going to keep it up until she felt ready to face being a full person again.

Instead of full personhood catching up with her, Sal had, with their insistence on checking on her. With their teasing turned into that soft caring voice, asking to be let in.

She started crying.

"Okay, listen. I think Brit is right. Do you want both of us or just one? It can be Brit. I know she's the more nurturing one. But one of us, at least, is coming down there. You don't get a say anymore. Except if it's one or both."

"No, no. It's not as bad as all that." Jodi pulled a tissue from the box she kept on her coffee table. She'd been working on the couch, as was her norm. She dried her eyes and blew her nose. She took a deep breath. "I'm okay. I've been fine. Just keeping busy with work."

"How busy can work possibly be keeping you? It's the holidays. Don't you take a few weeks off of new episodes this time of year?"

It was true. Both Jodi's podcasts took two or three weeks off, finishing the calendar year in mid-December and beginning again the second week of January. So did all of the podcasts she produced. Earlier this week, she'd done the last of the recording for the year, and the editing was already done. The last episodes of the year for the podcasts she produced were polished and ready for release. Jodi was doing work for episodes in January now. She'd been putting out her availability for taking on new podcasts online, hoping to keep busy, but it seemed no one wanted to focus on podcasts over the holidays. No one except Jodi, who wanted to concentrate so she could avoid her mess of a personal life.

"Yes, but there is work to do to prepare for next year," she said defensively.

"No, there isn't. I mean, yeah, sure, but you're avoiding."

This wasn't news. She knew it. She'd been doing it on purpose. Still, Sal's blunt evaluation stung a little. "I choose Brit."

"What?"

"If I have to talk to one of you, you're right. Brit is much nicer."

Sal laughed. "Okay, glad to hear you sounding more normal."

Jodi hadn't entirely meant it as banter, but she felt the ghost of a smile forming from Sal's laughter. She couldn't remember when she'd last smiled. Probably Thanksgiving. She sighed. "Fine. Yes, I've been working to avoid thinking about...anything."

"And how's that working out for you?"

"Ugh." Jodi sometimes hated all the time Sal had spent in therapy.

"Well, then. You avoided for, what, three weeks? And now you're all good?"

Jodi looked around her familiar living room, looking for an escape hatch. She didn't really want to think about it all. She didn't want to think about Erin. It hurt too much.

"I can tell by the lack of response that that's not the case. What are you going to do now?"

"What do you mean?"

"If what you're doing isn't working, then what now? Do you need therapy? A weekend with your best friend? Which is me, not Brit, by the way. I've changed my mind about offering her. I don't want to be replaced."

"That was a quick turnaround."

"Yeah, well, you're stuck with me."

"Well, that's about the worst thing I can imagine." Jodi kept her voice carefully toneless.

"I know. And yet, here we are."

"Here we are."

"Which, again, is where exactly? Are you mourning the loss of the one woman you've ever wanted to commit to? In waiting mode, hoping she'll come running? Preparing for a grand gesture?"

"Nowhere!" It was a wail. Jodi really had been avoiding all this. She truly didn't know. All she knew was that it hurt to think about.

"Okay. Okay." Gentle Sal was back, which nearly broke Jodi. "Listen. I'm going to get in the car. It'll be around eight when I get there. I'm staying for the weekend. We're going to figure this out."

It took Jodi a moment to remember what day it was. Right. Thursday. "Don't you have work tomorrow?"

"The usual nothing-to-do is even more profound in December, it turns out. I'll take the day off. Hardly anyone is in the office anyway. Are you going to be okay until I get there?"

Honestly, Jodi wasn't sure. Now that she was awake and thinking, she felt moments away from a breakdown. She wasn't sure she could go back into avoidance mode. But she was fifty-one and used to being on her own. Surely, she could hold out for three hours?

By the time Sal knocked on her door, Jodi was holding herself together with frenetic energy.

"Oh my God, you're here, I've been thinking I fucked up, what am I going to do?" Jodi said in a rush. Sal looked alarmed, but Jodi barely noticed. "Well?"

"You haven't, like, killed anyone, have you?" Sal peered into Jodi's condo.

Jodi crossed her arms. "No time for jokes. Seriously. I think I fucked up. I should have given Erin the time she needed to come out on her own terms. What do I do?"

"First of all, let me in. I need to put my bag down, and I have to pee like a racehorse."

Jodi paced the length of her condo while Sal was in the bathroom. She stopped when Sal came back. "Should I go to her right now and tell her that I support her, and she can come out on her own terms? That I'll wait patiently?"

Sal grabbed her by the shoulders. "Have you eaten today?"

"Um…no? Maybe?"

"We're going to go get some dinner. The fresh air and food will do you good. You can tell me on the way about your sudden change of heart."

By the time they got outside, the drizzle that had been going on most of the evening had turned to real rain. They walked with their hoods up, which wasn't a great setup for talking. They went to the Sweet Hereafter because it was close, and they could get their favorite drinks. With their raincoats hanging off the backs of the seats next to them, dripping on the floor, Jodi knew it was time to talk. The walk and Sal's presence had served to mellow her a little. She took a moment to collect her thoughts.

"I've been thinking," she said.

"I was worried you'd start doing that."

"Ha, ha."

"No, seriously, all that time not and then, bam, thinking. It could do a body some harm."

Jodi waved that away. "Yeah, okay. But listen."

"I'm listening."

The bartender called that their drinks were ready, so they were interrupted yet again by Sal going to retrieve them. Jodi had waited three weeks to even feel her feelings. A little over four hours ago, Sal had cracked her open. Four hours was nothing to three weeks, but the wait to finally talk this out seemed interminable.

Sal plunked Jodi's Hereafter on the table followed by their Mule. "Okay. I'm really listening. Talk."

"Here's the thing. People should be able to come out on their own time and to the people they want to. You're not out to your family. Brit chose to be with you anyway."

Sal looked troubled. "That...I think that's different. Brit and I can live out and proud to all the people who really matter to us. We can live together, walk through our neighborhood holding hands, and have friends over who tease me relentlessly about how Brit is the better half."

That last part was a direct tease at Jodi. As far as she knew, that wasn't something the rest of their mutual friends did. But more importantly, Sal had a point. While they would be able to be themselves inside the comfort of their own houses and on, say, vacation, actually living together would be a stretch if Erin's older kids didn't know. They could say they were roommates, but that would probably lead to a lot of speculation, essentially outing by a different name. And yet. The misery Jodi had been in since the breakup was signaling a problem. The problem was that she didn't want to live without Erin.

"I'm going to be really honest with you, Sal. I think I'm willing to do whatever is necessary to keep Erin in my life. It may not end up looking like other people's lives as couples, but I'm used to living on my own. I think we can make it work." Jodi took a drink and steeled herself for Sal's reaction.

"I do not want to be the sort of person who polices how other people live their lives. Consenting adults and all that. But are you really sure that you'd be comfortable living partially back in the closet?"

"Are you?"

Sal reared back in their seat. "No."

"Then why do you do it?" Jodi knew the answer or knew Sal's stock answer. Sal wasn't out to their family in Colorado because they wanted to be there from time to time, just in case one of their siblings' kids needed them. Just in case one of them was struggling under the expectations of their church and parents.

Sal narrowed their eyes and crossed their arms, the picture of closed off. "You know why."

"But will any of those kids actually know you're approachable? If you're not out?"

"I…" Sal opened and closed their mouth a few times. "I mean, I think I'm pretty obvious."

"So obvious that your parents and siblings have figured out your truth and stopped allowing you to visit the family home?"

"Wait." Sal held up their hands. "Why are we talking about this? This was supposed to be about you."

"We have all weekend, right? I can share time."

Sal squinted. "Weren't you the one who just said people should be allowed to come out on their own timeline to people of their choice?"

Jodi threw her hands up. "Yes. It's complicated. I don't know. But I wonder how happy you are going back there a couple of times a year and pretending to be something you're not."

Sal nodded slowly. "Not very. I hate going. And this is something I should think about, but also, isn't this what you're signing up for if you decide to get back together with Erin and she's never ready to come out?"

That sent Jodi's thoughts back into a swirl. She put her head on her arms. "All I know is that I am miserable without her."

Sal patted her head. "Maybe you'll get over it? I mean, people do?"

"It's been over thirty years since our first breakup. Have you seen me actually get over it?"

"Well, sort of? I mean, you've lived a life you seem happy with. Have you not been happy?"

Jodi straightened and just in time because a server was approaching with their food. Jodi had gotten a rice, tofu, and broccoli bowl while Sal had gone for a BBQ sandwich made with soy curls. The food at Sweet Hereafter wasn't bad, but it also wasn't Jodi's favorite. Even so, her mouth watered, and her stomach grumbled at the sight of the food. Hunger seasoning was real. She started eating.

After a few bites, she looked up to find Sal appraising her yet again. "What?"

"Just noting how hungry you were and hoping you're going to start taking care of yourself no matter what happens now."

"No promises," Jodi said around a mouthful of food.

Sal sighed. "Have you talked to her about why she doesn't want to come out?"

"I mean, she said back at the reunion weekend that she intended to but needed to do it at her own pace. And I promised patience, which I didn't actually follow through on." Jodi pushed her bowl away. Her appetite was dwindling. "She did tell Darcy. But stopped there. It went well with Darcy, and I don't get why she didn't keep going. I guess that's why it hit like a ton of bricks when she didn't take the opportunity to be honest with Lindsey."

Jodi was looking at her half-eaten bowl, but something about the way Sal was moving caught her attention. They were squirming. When Jodi looked up, they wouldn't meet her eye.

"What is going on?"

"I just realized that I think that might have something to do with me."

Jodi's head jolted back in surprise. "Why? Because you're not out to your family?"

Sal winced. "Because I told her that if she came out to her family as gay and then Darcy also did, she might be accused of being a groomer."

"Fuck." Jodi slammed her hand on the table. Heads turned in their direction, but it was late enough that there weren't any children. She lowered her voice. "Fuck. No wonder she didn't want to come out." She pinched her lower lip and worried it between her fingers. It had been a nervous habit in high school that still reared its head in times of stress.

"I'm sorry," Sal whispered.

Jodi didn't know what to say. Sal wasn't wrong that religious conservatives might see it that way, but also, Sal's intervention meant that Erin had gone from ready to tell the world, one step at a time, to scared. Maybe. Maybe there were other reasons, too, not just what Sal said. But one had to imagine that warning would stick with a person, particularly a person who already had reason to believe her family wouldn't be accepting.

But it was also true that, like Sal, maybe Erin needed to do it anyway. What was the worst that could happen? Well, the worst was that if Grant thought he had a case for child endangerment or worse, he could get custody of Darcy. That was bad, but it was also highly unlikely. The worst realistic outcome would be that Erin's parents and possibly one or both her adult kids wouldn't want to be a part of her life anymore. Jodi should have talked to her about this, to understand her fears. Instead, they'd veered away from the topic. Jodi knew why she'd done so. She was scared shitless that Erin would never come out and choose to break up with her again because it was too hard to live a lie. She couldn't be sure why Erin had shied away from the topic, but it could well be that she thought Jodi would overreact to her concerns.

What it came down to was that Jodi had promised that she'd be patient with Erin going at her own pace. And then, she hadn't been.

She needed to show Erin she understood and could both listen and wait. It wasn't easy, exactly. There was still the chance Erin would be fine with living partially in the closet and want to stay there. That would be difficult. Jodi didn't want to live that life. But she did want Erin in her life.

The question was, did she want that enough?

CHAPTER THIRTY-TWO

Erin had a new clarity of purpose. She needed to come out to her children. Then, she needed to go to Jodi and show her that she was in this, that she was comfortable with her sexuality and proud to be in a relationship with Jodi. If Jodi still wanted her. She hoped she did, but regardless of if Jodi did or didn't, Erin still needed to own her truth.

What she wasn't sure about was the details. She'd like to tell Lindsey and Brad in person, but that meant waiting for Christmas. Less than two weeks away now, but that felt like a long time to wait to tell Jodi how she felt.

She decided her first step was to tell Darcy that she was going to do this. That weekend, with one week left until Christmas, Erin made brunch for them. Breakfast was the meal they most often ate together, although that was on weekdays. But Darcy had been up and gone for practice before Erin had woken up that morning. She would come home starving.

Erin was full of nervous energy and had a couple of hours, so she baked cinnamon rolls and biscuits, made home fries, and prepped everything for omelets once Darcy was home. She'd need a shower, so there would be time.

"It smells so good in here," Darcy called from the living room. "Is it Christmas already?"

The question was a rough reminder that it was supposed to be. Or at least Christmas Eve. Jodi was supposed to be there for their pre-Christmas that weekend. Now the thought tormented Erin on two levels. One that Jodi wasn't there, but two that she'd thought throwing Jodi a bone about Christmas was enough.

"Oh, Mom. I'm sorry. I didn't think. Is all this because you're missing Jodi? Particularly this weekend?"

Erin had told Darcy about the Jodi Christmas plan. She'd been excited about having two Christmases. Erin mustered a smile for her. "No, Darce, this is just for you and me. A fun brunch. I thought you'd enjoy it."

"Oh, I totally will. Is there time for me to shower?"

"Yup, I'll finish up while you're in there." Erin hesitated. It had been on the tip of her tongue to say that she did have something to talk about, but it could wait.

Darcy, maybe sensing Erin had planned to continue talking, waited a beat. When Erin turned back toward the stove, she left.

It was so strange that there were butterflies in Erin's stomach. She'd already come out to Darcy. That was the hard part. This was just a team meeting to talk about next steps. There was no reason to be nervous.

Erin slid the omelets onto plates just a few moments before Darcy returned with damp hair.

"This looks great, Mom." She slid into her seat. "So…this is really just for fun?"

Erin waggled her head noncommittally. She set the pan in the sink to wash after and joined her.

"I knew it." Darcy picked up her fork and cut off a piece of a cinnamon roll. "You want something."

"It's not that I want something. It's that I have something to tell you."

"Are you going to Portland?"

"What? No." Erin thought for a moment. "Not right now, at least."

"So this is about Jodi?" Darcy took a large bite of the omelet, then waved her hand in front of her mouth. "Hot."

Erin was amused. "Yes. I did just take it off the stove."

"But good. Really good." Darcy took another bite. When she swallowed, she said, "But you still need to tell me what's going on."

"I'm going to come out to your sister and brother."

"Mom! That's huge. That's great."

"You really think so? You're not worried?"

"Well, Lindsey might not react well, but Brad will be okay."

There was such nonchalance in the statement. "What makes you think so?"

"About Brad?" Darcy shrugged. "I told him I was queer, and he was fine about it."

"What? When?"

"I dunno. We were texting. He said something about how his buddy's roommate dragged a bunch of them to a drag show. He said it was pretty cool. Seemed like the time."

It was a relief to know that Darcy had had a good coming out experience with at least one of her siblings. Erin didn't know if that acceptance would extend to her or not, but at least it had been okay for Darcy.

"That's good to hear." She took a moment to watch her youngest consume food with a speed only teenage athletes possessed. "I also plan on being out in general."

"That's good, Mom. I've worried a little that I shouldn't be because you weren't being. Like, you thought it would be gauche or something."

"No. Darcy, no. I think it's important to be true to yourself. I have said that before. You didn't think I meant it?"

Another shrug. "Well, no. Because that's not what you were actually doing."

She'd said something like that before. Each time, Erin heard it more. She'd been being a bad role model for her kid. She'd been performing the very actions she didn't want Darcy to have to perform, the very actions she'd divorced Grant to avoid for both herself and Darcy. And yet, she'd gotten stuck in thinking it was the only way.

"You're right. I've been scared that it will be a problem."

"How so? I mean, aside from Lindsey probably needing some time to come around."

"Do you think she will come around? She is very religious. That's been one of my main concerns." Erin couldn't quite believe that she'd put her blinders on so much that she had raised a kid who was homophobic.

"Our church is cool with LGBTQ+ folks. Why wouldn't she find a church that accepted both her mother and sister? At least, eventually." Darcy was still eating but had started to slow down. She was working on a biscuit she'd smeared with jam.

"She might." Erin wasn't at all sure she would. Lindsey had taken the most to church out of all three kids and had grown up to marry Steve, who was also devout. "How come you were able to see past what our old church said and accept yourself?"

"Well, as you've pointed out, our most recent church isn't as anti-gay as the one before, so I've had less exposure. But also? Before we switched to this church, I never paid attention. Church was always super boring."

Erin laughed. "I'm glad you were protected by boredom. I just wish…" She wasn't sure how to put into words what she wished. She wanted to have her children but also to have made completely different choices in her life. To have married a different person. To have parted ways with such conservative churches earlier. But here she was. And the important thing was that she made the right choices now, both for herself and as role model for Darcy. She shook her head. "Part of the reason I wanted to tell you that I'm going to come out is that I'm not sure how your father will take it."

Darcy frowned. "Why would he even care?"

"Because he might think I'm not a suitable mother. He might try to get custody of you."

Darcy pulled the corner of her cheek in between her teeth. "Can he do that?"

"He can try, but no. I called my lawyer to make sure. He said that no judge would take a teenager in their last years of high school who is clearly thriving and put them with another parent in a different state just because the custodial parent is gay."

"So I definitely wouldn't have to live with him?"

"No." Because the question still niggled at Erin, she felt compelled to add, "But even if he found a lawyer to take the case and somehow had a sympathetic judge who did give him custody... well, Darcy, you're nearly an adult. And I'll say that you always have a home here."

Darcy smiled. "Are you telling me to run away?"

Erin put a hand over hers. "I am telling you that you should never put up with being in a relationship with anyone who makes you feel bad about yourself."

"Thanks, Mom. But do you think he'll actually try?"

"I think your dad might initially want to fight for custody, but he would probably..." He'd likely lose interest. Looking back at the kids' childhoods, she remembered that he'd never been super into parenting. He'd wanted children. He'd appreciated the family man image, but Erin was the one who'd changed diapers, was up in the middle of the night, who'd gone to all the parent-teacher conferences, who'd sorted out disputes, and who'd read bedtime stories. He'd provided for them and sometimes showed up at games, concerts, and the like. He wouldn't really want to be a hands-on parent, would he? But also, Erin didn't want Darcy to think her dad didn't love her.

"He wouldn't want to do that much work just to have to really parent me, right? Believe me, I'm not blind about Dad. He was never here really. It wasn't a blow to lose him because I never had him." Erin's heart broke as she watched Darcy chew on the corner of her mouth for a moment before going on. "I think he was more there for Lindsey. She speaks fondly of him, but it's of a person I don't recognize. Maybe he was just tired of parenting by the time I came along. Or maybe he just liked her better."

Erin wanted to cry. She'd made all the right choices, according to her parents and church. She'd found a supposedly godly man who'd wanted a family. She'd had children and stayed married. And yet, this life had not only not served her, but it had also meant that this lovely person sitting across the table from her felt like she only had one parent who loved her. And had been raised in a church that had told her that she was wrong for even existing. But to Darcy's credit, she was such a mature, composed young adult. She taught Erin lessons every day.

"You know you're a great person, right?"

Darcy gave a half shrug, noncommittal.

"You are. You're brave and wise beyond your years."

"If you say so." But she looked pleased.

CHAPTER THIRTY-THREE

Everyone except Erin slept in on Christmas morning. The friends' party on Christmas Eve Eve had been a success. Rhoda had stopped by for a while and seemed to enjoy the energy. She'd left with a hug for Erin after they'd stood around the kitchen talking and watching the comings and goings of all the kids and no longer kids. Erin would have trouble thinking of any of them as not-kids for a long time, even though Lindsey and her friends were all well into their twenties.

Only a few of Lindsey's friends were in town. Many, like her, had moved away, but a couple had stayed, and a couple more were back in town to visit their parents for Christmas. Lindsey's group of friends had largely been formed from youth group, so several were married. Erin, having been a supposedly virginal religious young person herself, understood the drive to marry young. Not only did the church support it, but otherwise, you couldn't have sex. At least, not with a clear conscience. They had all gathered around the table in the dining room where they'd chatted and laughed for hours.

Brad, being a senior in college, had a proportionally higher number of friends in town. Most of them were home visiting parents. He was friendly with plenty of people, but his core group was, in an echo of Erin's high school friend group, four. All three of his friends had come over after picking him up at the airport. One had brought a projector that connected to his laptop. They'd taken over the office and had been in there watching movies on the wall all evening and well into the night, coming out occasionally to gather more food from the many offerings Erin had crowded onto the kitchen island.

That had left the living room for Darcy and her friends. Most of her fast-pitch team had come. They'd spent the day and again, well into night, talking and laughing, absolutely the rowdiest of the groups. They'd had the TV on but had rarely bothered to watch what was playing.

In the end, several of Darcy's friends had stayed over, crashing in the living room. Lindsey's group had stayed late but went to their respective homes, and Lindsey and Steve had retreated to Erin's room to sleep. Brad's group had all stayed, somehow working things out in the office. That had left Erin to sleep in Darcy's bed. It hadn't been exactly the plan, but it had all worked out. All three of Erin's kids had had a good time.

People had trickled out from early to nearly noon the next day. Then, there'd been evening church services to attend. Lindsey had opted to go to her childhood church with her friends while Brad had gone with Erin and Darcy to their new church. Everyone had been exhausted by the time Christmas Eve had drawn to a close. So it only made sense that everyone slept in.

Erin had woken early and couldn't get back to sleep. Her mind was swirling with thoughts of how she'd tell Brad and Lindsey that she was gay. Together? Brad first because maybe he'd be fine with it and give her another person on her side when she told Lindsey? Lindsey and Steve were leaving the next day, needing to get back for work. Erin had decided to tell everyone on Christmas Day in the evening, but she still couldn't sleep for fretting about it.

Her anxious thoughts strayed to Jodi. Her thoughts would always stray to Jodi, she expected. She wondered what Jodi was doing right then. She looked at her phone and saw it was only seven a.m. She hoped Jodi was sleeping. It was only five in Portland. Or Seattle. Jodi had said she usually spent Christmas in Seattle with Sal. Erin hoped she was there and was happy. Maybe not too happy. Selfishly, Erin hoped Jodi was pining for her, at least a little.

Eventually, she decided to get up and do something with her anxious energy. She padded across the hall to the bathroom. Still in her Christmas pajamas and with the addition of fuzzy socks, she crept past Brad in the living room. He did not so much as change his breathing pattern. Once in the kitchen, she preheated the oven and started mixing things.

Lindsey and Steve were the next to wake. They came into the kitchen with smiles and soft Merry Christmas wishes. Steve's eyes roamed the island. "This is so much food, Mom."

"It's Christmas," she said.

"Still, you've been up a long time, clearly. Is the office couch not comfortable? I feel bad we kicked you out of your bed," Lindsey said.

"No, no. The couch is fine. I just woke up and thought I'd get some Christmas morning treats going."

Steve rubbed his hands together in anticipation. "Well, I, for one, can't wait to dig in."

"Help yourself," Erin said. "Who knows when Brad and Darcy will make their appearances. No need to wait."

The kids helped themselves to coffee, then sat at the kitchen island. Steve snagged a cookie. It was Christmas. Why not start with a cookie?

"There's so much already, Mom. What even are you still baking?" Lindsey's eyes roamed over the cookies, breakfast sausages wrapped in biscuit blankets, monkey bread, and mini quiches already on offer.

Steve playfully swatted her arm. "Don't interrupt the woman. She's baking." His eyes danced, clearly indicating he was happy to eat whatever Erin wanted to make. He was a nice man who clearly loved Lindsey. Erin was glad she had him in her life. Her heart clenched to think that neither of them might want anything to do with her after she told them she was gay. That there might be a grandchild who wouldn't be allowed to know her.

Erin mustered a smile she hoped wasn't too strained. "It's just the bread to go with dinner. And the chocolate bear cookies are in the oven, too."

Lindsey bounced a little on her stool. "Chocolate bear cookies? Really? Oh my gosh, you haven't made them in years. They were always my favorites when I was little," she said to Steve. "But what're you still mixing, then?"

Erin looked down at the bowl. "Oh, yeah, um, sugar cookies. I thought we could decorate them together after we open presents." Sugar cookies had never been part of their family tradition. This thought was all about Jodi.

"That sounds fun," Steve said, snagging a sausage roll.

Lindsey looked more skeptical.

Because of the change in sounds coming from the kitchen or it just being time, Brad came shuffling in just a little later. He was wearing a pair of basketball shorts and a T-shirt, a uniform that he'd worn as pajamas since he was little. Between that and his unusually disheveled hair, Erin felt a pang of nostalgia for his five-year-old self. It was only magnified when, instead of making directly for the food or coffee pot, he shuffled right to Erin. He hugged her. "Merry Christmas, Mom."

She hugged him back. "Merry Christmas, Rad." It was a nickname he'd briefly tried to get them all to adopt when he was about eight.

Erin felt him laugh before he pulled away. She reached up and ruffled his hair.

As he poured his coffee, he extended Christmas wishes to Lindsey and Steve that they returned before Lindsey teased him about his fresh-out-of bed state. That led to him teasing back about her need to be put together all the time, and this was just family. They mostly playfully bantered back and forth while Erin puttered around the kitchen, listening to their comforting noise.

Darcy, sticking to teenager stereotypes, managed to sleep for another couple of hours. By the time she was up, the others were sitting around the dining room table playing Uno. Erin didn't notice her arrival until she heard her grumpily say, "Hey. You should have woken me up. I'm missing out on Christmas."

Brad stood and scooped her up. It was a feat because he was only about three inches taller, and she was built with solid muscle. "Merry Christmas, Merry Christmas, Merry Christmas, Darcy Larcy!"

She swatted at him without any heat. "Put me down."

Everyone joined them, enveloping Darcy in a group hug. "Merry Christmas."

"We didn't have any fun before you came in, I promise," Brad lied. "Except that I was about to win Uno, and you ruined that." Another lie. He had the most cards left. "Still, I will magnanimously allow the game to end so we can deal you in."

"Forget that," Lindsey said, ignoring the fact that she was the one who had just declared Uno. "Now that Darcy's up, it's time for presents."

The afternoon passed in a blur of presents, more food, more family games, cookie decorating, more cooking, and yet more food. They were sprawled on the couch in their loungewear, picking at the cookie offerings and debating which Christmas movie they should put on when Erin decided it was time to say what she had to say.

She set her mug of hot chocolate down and took a nervous breath. "I have something to tell you all."

They all looked at her with mild curiosity, likely thinking she was going to share an opinion about the movie choice or maybe say Darcy and she were moving—the apartment was small, and Erin could afford a bigger place now that all the finances had settled out—but Darcy looked anticipatory. She knew what was happening. She set her mug down, too, and nodded her support.

She took a deep breath. "I'm gay."

Darcy smiled. The other three just kept looking at her blankly. Maybe she hadn't spoken clearly or loudly enough? She decided to be more specific. "I'm a lesbian."

Steve started laughing. "That's funny, Mom."

Brad wrinkled his brow at Steve, then looked at Erin questioningly. Lindsey laughed a little, apparently also deciding it was a joke.

"I'm serious, you guys."

Steve and Lindsey both stopped laughing abruptly. Lindsey shook her head. "Mom. You can't be." She indicated herself, Brad, and Darcy as proof.

"Yeah, wouldn't you at least be bi?" Brad asked.

"She's not anything, Brad," Lindsey said angrily. "She's Mom. She's confused or messing with us or something."

"I am not either of those things. And, Lindsey, I am something. To say otherwise is hurtful. I do see why you would be confused. I was married to your father for a long time. I suppose on the spectrum of straight to gay, I'm not completely on the gay end, but I'm pretty close. I simply suppressed it for a long time."

Lindsey stood and put her hands on her hips. "Is this why you divorced Dad? Because of some perversion?"

Darcy looked hurt but stayed silent. Erin purposefully didn't look at her, not wanting to draw attention to her if she wasn't ready.

Erin opened her mouth to answer, but Brad beat her to it. "It's not perversion. It's unexpected, yes, but she's our mom, and we should respect that if she's telling us, she must know it's true. Also, you know as well as I do that Dad moved from here to Tami's house. Clearly, that was the reason for the divorce."

"Well, who can blame him if she's gay?" Lindsey shouted.

It was amazing that things had changed so quickly from family closeness to this. Or not really. Erin knew she'd dropped a huge bomb. She'd known that Lindsey was unlikely to take this news well. She'd hoped for better, but it wasn't exactly surprising.

Steve stood next to Lindsey with a hand on her lower back and glared at Erin. It was likely both in support of Lindsey and because he also thought it was wrong to be gay.

"We're not staying here with a lesbian." Lindsey's voice dropped when she said lesbian. It was clear she thought it was a bad word. "And neither of you should, either." She waved a finger between her siblings. "Particularly you, Darce. This must be a shock for you, finding out who you're living with."

Darcy folded her arms across her chest. "I knew. What's more, Mom isn't the only gay one in the family. And if you're going to be a bigot like this, then you definitely should leave."

Lindsey's mouth dropped open. She looked back and forth between Erin and Darcy, finally sputtering out, "I'm going to tell Dad." She stormed out of the living room, Steve in her wake.

This was as bad as it could have gone. Erin pushed her glasses on top of her head and covered her face with her hands. She felt the couch dip next to her and a hand go to her back. She expected it was Darcy, but when she looked, it was Brad.

"Mom? Are you okay?" he asked.

"Are you?" she asked in return.

He looked after Lindsey and shook his head a little. Then, he nodded. "I mean, no and yes. I'm shocked. I'm impressed. I'm worried."

That all made sense, but she wondered at the root of his feelings. "What worries you?"

He darted a glance down the hall. "That's she's going to run to Dad. And that he's going to try to take Darcy away."

She came to sit on Erin's other side. "But I won't go. This is my home, and I'm staying." The words were spoken with confidence. But she slumped and rested her head on Erin's shoulder. "Right, Mom?"

"That's right, Darce. We're sticking together. He can try, Brad, but he has no legal leg to stand on. We've got this."

CHAPTER THIRTY-FOUR

Driving home the day after Christmas in Seattle, Jodi's thoughts were going every which way. Christmas had been just as cozy and festive as always. Yet, Jodi had spent much of the holiday in her own head. She'd managed a brave face and enough participation that she didn't think she'd stood out in the crowd. When it was just her, Brit, and Sal, it had been different. They both knew she was struggling and were kind enough to be there for her, even though it was Christmas.

Although, Jodi reflected, the holidays were a hard time for a lot of people, particularly in the queer community, so maybe they just took it as a fact of the season. For Jodi, it wasn't about family. Not that she didn't miss her mom, particularly this time of year. That was in the mix somewhere, too, but this year, the reason for the seasonal disorder was Erin.

Jodi was sad that not only weren't they together for Christmas, but it seemed like they might not ever be together. Even if Jodi was to show up on Erin's doorstep, proclaiming her love and willingness to be in the closet with her, they wouldn't get to have Christmas together. That was part of what slowed her down when she considered attempting to reconcile.

And yet. She loved Erin. She missed her so much.

It was a mess.

But it was also true that Erin hadn't reached out. Maybe she didn't miss Jodi; in which case, what Jodi wanted didn't matter.

Jodi drove the three hours home without listening to music, podcast, or an audiobook. She'd tried, but as was true on the day she'd walked nearly all of Seattle, either her attention wandered, or she found it actively annoying. She gave up and spent the time thinking about what she wanted and what compromises she was willing to make. By the time she parked in her building's garage, she had decided.

She needed to go to Erin and be clear about her feelings. They could decide together what would work for them. Maybe Erin was done trying. Maybe Jodi walking out was too much. Or maybe they just needed to talk. The first step was clear communication, and that was best done in person.

Jodi pulled her laptop out, sat on the couch, and started planning.

Erin's phone rang at 8:06 a.m. Her heart leapt into her throat when she realized it was Grant. She'd been waiting on pins and needles for the shoe to drop ever since Lindsey had walked out the night before. She hadn't gotten a lot of sleep. If it wasn't worry about what would happen with Grant; it was Lindsey's shocked and outraged face floating behind her closed eyelids. Now, it seemed, she was going to face the Grant piece, at least.

She believed she and Darcy would come through this okay. She just needed to get to the other side. She took a deep, calming breath and answered the phone.

"What is going on over there, Erin? I had Lindsey showing up early this morning, knocking on my door, waking us up to tell me that you're a queer now?" The sneer on the word told Erin all she needed to know about him using it as a slur rather than as the reclaimed word many young people used these days. "What has gotten into you?" He sounded angry, unsurprising to say the least. The focus on being woken up this morning was a bit of a surprise, though.

"Good morning, Grant. I hope you had a nice Christmas." He hadn't even asked to spend time with Darcy. There hadn't been a gift from him under the tree. Erin wasn't sure if he'd even known Lindsey and Brad were in town.

"I got back late last night from a lovely week in St. Thomas only to be woken up with this news. So, yes, it was great until this morning."

Maybe by saying he'd been woken up early, he actually meant just minutes ago. Erin wondered if Lindsey and Steve were still standing there in the house he shared with Tami while he made this call.

Erin stayed quiet. There'd been no question there.

"Well, Erin? Answer me," he demanded.

"What question, Grant?"

"Are you a queer?" Again with the slur.

"I am a lesbian, yes." Erin's heart pounded in her chest. Aside from telling Lindsey and Brad, this was what had scared her the most about being out. Grant knowing and what he might do.

"With our daughter under your roof?" He was yelling now.

"Do you mean to ask if I'm gay when I'm at home and Darcy is also here?"

"You know what I mean, Erin. What kind of example are you setting for her? And poor Lindsey was so upset."

With the past tense, Erin had to assume that Lindsey had left. Had she shown up, Steve most likely at her side, knocked on Grant's door, looking for comfort, only to be sent away, still upset? Erin wasn't happy with her daughter and the way she'd reacted, but her heart still went out to her. She was hurting and apparently couldn't turn to either parent for comfort.

"The example I'm setting for Darcy is one of being true to myself."

"But what if she turns gay? Are you having women over when she's home?"

Ignoring the second question, Erin said, "People don't turn gay because they see gay people, Grant. That's not how it works."

"What happened with you, then? Erin, you were not a queer. Believe me, I'd know."

She was getting more and more hot under the collar, but she did her best to keep her voice calm, not only to try to defuse the situation, but so as not to awaken or alarm Darcy or Brad, who were still sleeping. "And yet, you didn't know, Grant. I don't blame you for not knowing because I was suppressing that part of me for a long time, but I've always been gay." That wasn't to say that people didn't realize it later in life. They certainly did, but they didn't turn gay because they hung around a gay person. If Grant was so sure that could happen, then Erin had to question the strength of *his* heterosexuality.

"I can't let Darcy live with you, not when you're living in sin."

"First of all, being gay isn't a sin. Second of all, you were having an affair and are now living with your girlfriend, unless you two have gotten married without telling anyone. If anyone has a case for proving one parent has set a bad example, it's me against you." And it was. Why hadn't that occurred to her before?

"We'll see about that." And he hung up.

After a few minutes, there was a gentle knock on Erin's door. "Come in."

She expected Darcy, but it was Brad who opened the door and stuck his head in. "Are you okay?"

She mustered up a small smile. "I think I am, yes."

He scooted all the way in and closed the door behind him. "Darcy is still asleep, I think, but I heard voices and figured it was Dad calling. It was him, right?"

"It was, yes."

"And?" He sat on the end of her bed.

"And he's making threatening noises, but I think it'll be okay."

"Lindsey went over there, huh?"

"It seems they went elsewhere last night, but she did go this morning. I think he might have been more upset about the early knock on his door than anything. He may try to get custody, but I kind of think he won't bother." She hoped that was true. It was such a big deal built up in her head, that he might try to get Darcy, but talking to him this morning reminded her of just how self-centered he was. He was upset at having been woken up early by one distressed daughter. Trying to get custody of his other daughter would be a lot more work than that. No, he was much more likely to just keep living his new childfree life.

CHAPTER THIRTY-FIVE

During the following week, Erin stuck close to home, especially when Darcy was home, just in case Grant showed up to make a scene. He didn't. She did get a call from the pastor of their old church who wanted to berate her for her "life choices," but she shut him down. She felt super proud about that. She called her lawyer again to let him know that Grant knew, so there might be action. He said he'd be ready.

Erin felt both relieved about all of that and a little angry. She was angry at herself for letting this strawman influence her decision to stay in the closet. Of course, it wasn't the only reason. She'd also been worried about losing Brad and Lindsey. The worry about Brad had been unfounded, but the worry about Lindsey had been spot on. Erin held on to hope that she would come around. And if not, well, that was horrible, but Erin couldn't stay in the closet for the rest of her life to appease her. It didn't even matter if Erin won Jodi back or not, she was still a lesbian, and she was proud.

She wished she'd realized all this before it had cost her Jodi.

But she really hoped to win her back. Maybe Jodi had moved on, maybe she wouldn't be willing to give Erin a second, or third, chance. Erin still had to try. And the best way she could think of was to go to her.

"Don't have any ragers while I'm gone." Erin smiled at Brad and Darcy to show she was joking. Neither of them was a big party type. Although Darcy might have several friends over and be a little loud later than the neighbors would be pleased with.

Darcy chewed the corner of her mouth.

"What? You don't think I should go? I thought you liked Jodi."

"I do," she said slowly.

"So…is it too desperate looking? I don't care if I'm dignified. I need Jodi to know how I feel. I just hope it's not too late."

"Mom, I think it's great," Brad said. "We'll be fine." He put his arm around Darcy. "I'll supervise the wild teen parties."

He was home for another week before his final semester of college. It was part of what made this a good time to go. Darcy would have built-in, semi-adult supervision. Adult. Brad was twenty-two now, almost a college graduate, and had shown remarkable maturity around all the events of the holidays. He'd also be there to support Darcy if Grant were to show up wanting to take her away. It hadn't happened yet, and it seemed increasingly unlikely that it would, but the worry wasn't entirely gone.

Darcy rolled her eyes. "Yeah. You know me," she said, deadpan. But she went back to chewing the corner of her mouth. Erin waited, hoping that Darcy would divulge more if given time. Instead, she asked, "Have you booked your flight yet?"

"I'm going to go do that now. I just wanted to talk to you two first and make sure you were okay with me going away for a few days."

"Go and get the girl," Brad said.

Darcy shot him a look and sucked the corner of her mouth again, but what she said was, "I am in full support of you and Jodi together. I think you're soulmates."

Erin pulled both kids to her. "Thanks, guys."

"Nothing to thank us for." Darcy's voice was muffled from the group hug. "We can live without you for a few days."

"I'm sure you can. You're both so big." Erin ruffled the tops of both their heads. She had to reach up to do it. They both dodged.

Darcy pulled out her phone. Her thumbs flew.

"Friend stuff?" Erin asked.

"Um, yeah. Can I go to Flo's for a bit?"

"Of course." While Erin did think that the phone call was the extent of trouble they were going to get from Grant, a niggling worry that just wouldn't die lived on in the dark recesses of her mind. But she was pretty sure Grant couldn't name a friend of Darcy's, much less know where one lived. Darcy was safe there.

For some sibling reason, Darcy dragged Brad down the hall. Erin was left looking after them bemusedly but only for a few moments. She pulled herself together and went to her office to book a flight.

"Mom?" It was Brad who came in to flop on the couch where he'd been sleeping since Lindsey left.

She swiveled away from her computer where she'd only just figured out which flight she wanted to book. "Yes?"

"I'm not sure where I should move after I graduate."

"I thought you wanted to live in Austin."

He let his head fall back until it clunked softly on the wall behind him. "Yeah, but what about moving back here? Or, I don't know, one of my buddies is going to live in Hong Kong. Wouldn't that be cool?"

She wanted to hear what he had to say. She really did. But her eyes strayed back to the computer screen.

He pushed her chair with his foot. "Mom? Are you too busy?"

She swiveled to face him. His timing was annoying, but he was her son, and she did want to know what was going on in his head. "I suppose the ticket isn't going anywhere. Tell me what you're thinking."

He was talking about what he'd loved about Austin when Erin's phone chimed. She ignored it. "Aren't you going to check that?" he asked.

"No. I'm talking to you."

"What if it's Darcy? What if she needs something?"

She hadn't even realized Darcy had left already. She hadn't stopped by to say good-bye, which she usually did. Erin picked up her phone. It was a text from Darcy. Erin looked up at Brad. "Kinda sus." It was a word the kids had been using with each other over the holiday.

"What? Is it her?"

"It is." Erin read the message. "Oh no. She got a flat."

"A flat tire?"

There was something in his tone that put Erin on high alert. She narrowed her eyes at him. "What's going on?"

He put on an innocent look. "I don't know what you mean. It sounds like she needs help."

"You should take my car and go help her put on the spare. It'll be good practice for you both."

He looked alarmed. "No, no. I, um, can't. I, um, promised I'd meet the guys for pizza."

She folded her arms. "What is going on?"

He took a moment, looking like he was considering his options. Finally, he said, "I think you should just go see."

What was happening? Were her kids conspiring to keep her from going to see Jodi? They both seemed so supportive. Brad hadn't met Jodi, but they'd talked about her. Quite a lot, in fact. Darcy was definitely on Team Jodi. Wasn't she?

Erin considered making Darcy wait while she got her ticket booked, but it was cold out. If she really was sitting on the side of the road, she needed rescuing. She texted, *I'm on my way*, and with one last suspicious look at Brad, she went to the front door and put on her coat.

"Will I see you when I return?" she called.

"Maybe later," he said evasively.

Something was most certainly up.

Another text from Darcy came while Erin was driving. At a red light, she read the message: Darcy would be waiting inside a coffee shop she'd been conveniently near. That was good. She wouldn't be freezing, at least.

But why hadn't she just called AAA? That was what Erin paid the membership for. Just this sort of situation. She should have just reminded Darcy of that and let her deal with it. It was part of the responsibility of being a driver.

By the time Erin got there, she was feeling disgruntled. She was pretty sure that her kids were up to something. Or if not, she should have handled this differently. She scanned the parking lot not seeing Darcy's car, then went inside.

She scanned the room. No Darcy. There were only a few customers. She scanned again and saw a familiar hairstyle.

"Jodi?"

Jodi stood, looking nervous. "Hi, legs."

Erin wanted to pull her into her arms but also felt off-center, which held her back. "What are you doing here?"

"I wanted to talk to you." Jodi looked around. A couple of people were looking at them curiously. They turned away, but it was clear people were watching. "Should we sit? Or we could go somewhere more private?"

Erin needed a minute to feel like she was fully in her body. Right now, everything felt surreal. She sank into the chair across the table. Jodi followed suit. Erin placed her hand on the table to feel its solidness. It was really there. This was really happening.

"Are you…" Erin began at the same time Jodi said, "I hope…" Then both said, "No, you first."

It broke some of the tension. Erin smiled at Jodi, who smiled back and looked a little less like she was about to jump out of her skin. "I was just about to book a flight to come see you tomorrow," Erin said.

"Really? Is that why…"

"Why what?"

"Why Darcy texted and told me that I had to meet you here right now."

"I imagine that is why." Erin felt tears form. It showed such support. They weren't trying to keep her away from Jodi. They'd been trying to help. She also wanted to laugh. It made her voice come out a little choked. "I knew those two were up to something. They seemed like they wanted me to go to Portland to talk to you *and* like they did not want me to book that ticket. It was the strangest thing." She stopped and looked around. "Wait. So Darcy doesn't have a flat?"

Jodi looked around, too. "Flat?"

"I think everything is fine, but I need to double-check." She pulled out her phone and messaged Darcy: *I assume you're fine?*

Who ru with? was the immediate response.

Jodi, as I believe you know.

Then, yes, I'm fine. I'm spending the night at Flo's, and Brad is staying at Carter's. Cu tomorrow.

Cheeky. She loved those two so much.

Erin tucked her phone away. "I'm all yours."

"Are you?"

Erin knew she meant more than, do I have your full attention? She'd flown out here and coordinated with Darcy to keep it a surprise. She must have had a reason. Erin hoped the reason was that she wanted them to be together. She took her courage in both hands and said, "Yes. No secrets. I told Brad and Lindsey. I want to be with you, and I don't want to hide it."

Jodi's face lit up like fireworks at midnight. Her eyes sparkled and danced. Her mouth curved into a smile. Her cheeks took on a rosy hue. Her spine straightened. She extended her hand across the table, seemingly without thinking.

Erin took the opportunity to show she meant it. She clasped Jodi's hand on top of the table, right there in public not twenty blocks from home. And it felt good. She felt triumphant. She wrapped her fingers around Jodi's and felt like her hand was finally doing what it had been created to do.

"I came here to tell you that I wanted to be with you and that if it was a matter of waiting for you to be ready, I could do that. I was hasty, I think, and reliving our past instead of seeing what was happening in front of me."

"What was happening in front of you was me repeatedly hiding us. It hurt, but I don't blame you. When you left, it forced me to really think about the choices I was making." Erin stopped, her voice constricted with emotion. "I'm not proud of my actions. I shouldn't have made you feel like a secret. I should have...I want to claim you, us." Erin felt shy and looked at the table. She was pretty sure they were on the same page, but there was a part of her that still thought maybe she was misinterpreting things. "That is, if that's what you want."

"What I want?" Jodi's voice rose a few decibels. "That's what I want more than anything, Erin."

Erin looked up, feeling a smile pulling hard at her cheeks. She leaned over the small table. Jodi leaned, too. They kissed. Erin didn't have time to revel because there were a few small noises around them that brought her attention to the fact that they were sitting in a public place, and people were watching.

It wasn't that she felt embarrassed. No, in fact, she stood and tugged Jodi to her feet as well. She pulled her in for another kiss, this time with a full body hug. She'd never been much of a public display of affection person, so she kept it brief. Even that was more than she'd felt comfortable with since…no, ever. "Can we get out of here?"

In answer, Jodi took her hand and led the way out.

CHAPTER THIRTY-SIX

O nce in the parking lot, confronted with both her rental car and Erin's SUV, Jodi stopped. As much as she wanted to have a beautiful moment, there were logistics to deal with. Erin, who had been trailing slightly behind, let go of her hand. Before she could miss the contact, Erin wrapped her in a hug from behind.

"Follow me to my place?" Erin's voice, husky with want, plus her breath tickling the shell of Jodi's ear nearly made her knees give out.

She leaned back slightly, wishing they didn't have to separate. "Or to a hotel?"

"If you're worried about the kids, they're both out of the house for the night."

"Then, I say we get moving."

Erin chuckled and held on to her for a few moments longer. Jodi both wanted to stay right here and to hurry and get in the car so they could be alone already. She wanted to be alone for obvious reasons. The appeal of right here was being in Erin's embrace and because of what that public embrace implied. Erin hadn't been blustering when she said she was ready to be all in and out to the world. It made Jodi's heart sing.

It was so much more than she'd hoped when she'd messaged Darcy to see if Lindsey was still in town or if it was safe for a visit. Darcy had said to come, which was encouraging, but Jodi hadn't been sure what to expect. Her flight had landed over an hour ago. Her plan had been to get the rental car, go check into a hotel, and then…well, she'd still been working out the exact details. Darcy had been pushing for a big moment of Jodi surprising her mom at a restaurant. Jodi hadn't wanted that because Erin had made it clear she didn't want to be out like that. They'd been in negotiation over the last twenty-four or so hours while Jodi made travel plans. Then, Jodi had gotten a message from Darcy just as she was getting into her rental car.

Pls say yr here. It has to be now!

So Jodi had gone to the coffee shop Darcy told her to go to and had waited to see what would happen. This happening had been beyond her wildest dreams.

Erin kissed her temple. "I don't want to let you go, but shall we?"

Jodi nodded, the back of her head rubbing against Erin's shoulder as she did so. "Yes." She set her resolve and straightened. Erin released her. She cupped Erin's cheek. "See you in a few minutes."

"Can't be soon enough. Let's get going."

With a chuckle, Jodi went the few yards to her rental and did her best to concentrate on the drive. Her thoughts were all on the woman in the car in front of her. On what she wanted to do to reconnect once they got to Erin's house, yes, but also on the possibilities for the future that now felt open in front of them.

At the apartment, Jodi pulled into a visitor's spot and considered leaving her bag in the car. She was in a hurry. However, not having to come back out later was also appealing. She grabbed it from the trunk. Erin was watching her with an intent look. Jodi grinned and considered leaning over the trunk again. Instead, she slammed it closed.

"Finally," Erin said, taking her hand and leading her to the apartment door.

Once inside, Jodi dropped the bag and put her hands into Erin's hair to pull her down for a kiss. She couldn't wait a moment longer. Erin was clearly in the same place. She pushed Jodi's coat off her shoulders before taking care of her own. They kicked off shoes between kisses.

At some point, Jodi realized she was only in her bra, and she focused enough to realize that so was Erin. She slowed down and made herself be in the moment. She wanted Erin, yes. But more importantly, she wanted this feeling to last. She wanted to explore all of Erin's skin. She wanted to remember the moment Erin's dark blue bra lifted away to reveal her tan nipples, already standing at attention. She wanted to look into Erin's eyes and watch them change as she slipped a finger into her folds. She wanted to taste her.

"What?" Erin asked. "Is something wrong?"

"No. Everything is exactly right. I'm just…taking you in."

They'd made it as far as the living room, which meant they were only feet from the door. The light was fading, but they were also in view of the window should anyone happen to look. Jodi took all of that in and was about to suggest they move to the bedroom when Erin took her hand and led her there.

Despite the fact that they had the apartment to themselves, Jodi closed the door behind them. Erin reached for a bedside lamp, then let her hand drop again, apparently uncertain.

"Turn it on," Jodi urged. She wanted to see the gorgeous woman she was about to make love to.

And it was love. Jodi was head over heels in love with Erin, no room for doubt.

She walked over, sliding her jeans off as she went. She stood before Erin in just her bra and panties. Erin's eyes roamed over her body. When they reached Jodi's eyes, her pupils were wide. She looked hungry. As they held one another's gaze, Erin's face softened. Jodi reached up, put her fingers into Erin's dark, silver-streaked hair.

"This is my favorite thing," Jodi said.

"Sex?" Erin quirked up the corner of her mouth.

Jodi went up on her tiptoes and kissed that corner. "No, well, yes, but, no. This. I've always loved this." She gave a little tug.

Erin gave a soft moan. "That was the move that got me in the hot tub all those years ago."

"And I love you."

Erin's eyes roamed Jodi's face as if looking for confirmation. When they settled back on her eyes, she said, "I love you, too."

Erin bent and kissed her. She could feel the love Erin put into the kiss, and she returned it as best she was able. She wished this moment would never end.

In some ways, it didn't. The moment extended as they maneuvered to lying on Erin's bed. Each moment of their lovemaking, when Jodi finally removed Erin's bra and lavished attention on her nipples, when she slicked her tongue across Erin's center, when she took her right to the edge, then moved up to look into her eyes as she took her to orgasm—and when Erin did the same for her—all those moments melded into one expression of love.

They lay together after, legs entwined, facing one another. Jodi wanted to be close, but she also craved the eye contact. Through their whole lovemaking, every time Jodi had looked into Erin's eyes, she'd seen love reflected back at her. She wanted to continue to bask in it.

"I love you." Jodi tucked Erin's hair behind her ear.

"I love you, too," Erin said. "How wonderful is that?"

"Pretty wonderful." Jodi bit her lip. She wanted to talk about what was next. Would Erin want the same thing?

"What?" Erin smoothed a thumb over Jodi's lips.

"I want to move here. I mean, to St. Louis. Not here, here. Would you be okay with that?"

Erin frowned. Jodi had clearly gone too far. She opened her mouth to quantify the statement, maybe with something like eventually or someday.

Erin laid her finger on Jodi's lips, stopping her. "What if I did want you to move here, here? Or maybe not here but into a place together, big enough for the three of us, big enough for the kids to stay when they came home." A look of pain flitted across Erin's face.

Jodi rubbed her hand down Erin's arm. "I'm so sorry about Lindsey. Is there anything I can do?"

Erin mustered a weak smile. "Just being here, loving me, helps a lot. I really hope she'll come around."

From what Erin had said about Lindsey, Jodi had her doubts. But doubt wasn't what Erin needed right now. "I hope so, too." She paused. "But Brad took it well?"

Erin smiled for real. "Yes. He's good people, Brad." She tapped Jodi's chin. "But don't think I didn't notice that I asked you to move in with me, but you haven't replied."

"Oh, right." Jodi felt a burst of happiness. Erin had asked her to move in. "I mean, yes, of course. I'd love to live with you. And we need space for your kids, for sure, but I don't need a lot of space."

"Excuse me, but recording your podcasts in my closet doesn't seem like a long-term solution."

"Closets have excellent dampening effects, making for good audio."

"But you have an entire recording room in your condo. You should have your own space. I've seen what you have hanging in there, at least what you can see from the camera angle. You need room to express yourself."

Jodi considered her recording room. It was a room she loved. She had a couch for sitting on with her laptop. It was the sort of couch that had a spot to put her feet up, which was particularly nice with short legs that dangled. She had her desk and microphone, of course, but what gave the room character was all the things she'd put on the walls to break up sound waves. It wasn't soundproof by any means, although there were a few squares of soundproofing material hanging on the walls. She'd also hung things like the baseball cap with a unicorn on it that her mom had bought her at the flea market when she was eleven, shelves with her favorite books, character art, and an assortment of stuffies. She'd collected some because they were cute and some because they were favorite characters, but there were four special ones.

She wondered if Erin had noticed. Could they be seen from the camera angle? Jodi often did video chats with Erin from her living room, but she'd taken a few in her recording room. If she'd been at her desk, she was pretty sure at least a couple of the special ones were visible. Aside from the unicorn cap, they were the only childhood things she still had.

"You're right enough that I'd like a room, but I'd be willing to put up with the closet for a little while."

"I think I've made you endure the closet enough for one lifetime." Her tone was mostly joking, but there was a note of seriousness.

"Well, when you put it that way, sure. You owe me a whole room."

"A room where you can proudly display Dip, Pip, Mip, and Bip."

Jodi planted her face in her pillow in mortification. Erin had seen them. She had given Jodi a stuffed animal for each of her birthdays in high school. It had been a bit of a joke because Jodi hadn't been much of a collector of anything except books. Bip, the senior year one, had been Erin's gift the night of the practice kissing in the hot tub, the night Jodi had realized she was gay, the night they'd shared their first real kiss. The other three had become special by association. "I…don't know what to say about them."

"I think it's sweet that you kept them."

"Or tragic. I was clinging to a doomed high school romance." Her voice was muffled in the pillow.

Erin gently pulled Jodi's face away from the pillow and looked at her intently. "High school wasn't the right time for us to be forever, but I think we can clearly see it wasn't doomed. At least, I hope not."

"I'm sure I'd have fucked it up, but I think I wanted forever even then. I honestly think that's why it hasn't worked out for me with anyone else. My heart was taken this whole time. I love you, Erin, and I'm not sure I've ever really stopped." Erin's eyes got shiny. Jodi ran her thumb under one. It came away wet. "I'm sorry. That was a lot."

"I just…" Erin's voice wavered. She took a breath and tried again. "I just wish it hadn't taken me so long to come around."

Jodi shrugged the shoulder that wasn't against the mattress. "I think it happened when it happened. I'm just glad we're here now."

"Me too. You're amazing."

"You are. Just think of everything you've overcome to be true to yourself."

Erin shook her head. "Agree to disagree on who's more amazing."

Jodi pretended to be put out. "I suppose."

Erin rolled on top of her. "I guess I'll just have to show you, then."

"I mean, you have to do what you have to do."

EPILOGUE

C an we watch *A League of Their Own* tonight?" Darcy asked.

This time, everything was different. Darcy was wearing a two-piece swimsuit instead of her practice gear, they were on the beach in San Diego rather than in their home in St. Louis, and of high importance, Jodi was sitting on a beach chair on Erin's other side.

"Of course. I believe it's tradition at this point. You'll have to go to a college with quarters instead of semesters next year, so you'll still be home to celebrate our annual *A League of Their Own* night."

Darcy kindly ignored the fact that she'd be choosing a college based on who recruited her for softball rather than her mom's preference for having her home in late August. "And we'll always have pizza and ice cream."

"This is a holiday I can get behind," Jodi said as she dangled her e-reader from one hand. Darcy had the same e-reader on Erin's other side, a gift from Jodi for her birthday.

"It's a good one," Darcy confirmed.

Erin looked at her phone to check the time. "How about we head back to the rental in an hour to shower and order pizza?"

"Sounds good." Darcy pushed to her feet, dropped her e-reader on her chair, and picked up her boogie board. "I'm going to go catch a few more waves."

"I have to say that I appreciate the water being warm enough not to wear a wet suit." Erin tilted her face to the sun.

"It does make life easier."

Jodi was sporting a lazy grin. She looked happy and content. Erin wanted to bottle the feeling she got from looking at her in such a state. Instead, she leaned over and kissed her, nearly toppling her beach chair in the process. Jodi caught her.

"Pretty worked up for a public place, throwing yourself at me like that."

"Ha, ha." Erin righted herself.

Jodi took her hand. "I mean, I don't blame you. I'm pretty hot."

Erin laughed for real this time. "I mean, you are."

Jodi's cheeks turned even redder than they already were from the sun. She brought their clasped hands to her mouth and kissed the back of Erin's hand. "Thanks, legs."

"No problem, tot."

Erin watched as Darcy successfully caught a wave. Her daughter was happy and healthy. She had the woman of her dreams by her side. After vacation, they'd go home to the house they shared. Life couldn't be much better.

As happened frequently, a small wave of sadness washed over her. Jodi must have noticed because she said, "Thinking of Lindsey?"

"Yes. I can't help but wish things were smoother there. It's the only fly in the ointment, you know?"

"I do." Jodi squeezed her hand. "At least she sent you the announcement."

It was true. Lindsey had sent a birth announcement. It had made Erin incredibly sad not to have been there to help with her first grandchild. But it also gave her a glimmer of hope. Maybe someday, Lindsey would find it within herself to reconcile. All she could do was hold the door open.

Jodi got to her feet and pulled Erin up, as well. "Come on, let's go catch some waves while we still can."

They walked to the water holding hands. They caught a wave side by side and rode it into shore, laughing.

"That was a good one," Jodi said, eyes sparkling.

"The best one." Her eyes were locked on Jodi's. Erin's chest filled with love. She'd found the very best one. And this time, she was keeping her.

About the Author

Sage is a board game enthusiast and occasional hiker who enjoys reading and writing books about women. When the weather allows, she's further distracted by her stand up paddle board.

She always makes time to snuggle with her beloved dog and chat excitedly about books with her daughter. Sage lives in Portland, Oregon.

Books Available from Bold Strokes Books

All This Time by Sage Donnell. Erin and Jodi share a complicated past, but a very different present. Will they ever be able to make a future together work? (978-1-63679-622-2)

Crossing Bridges by Chelsey Lynford. When a one-night stand between a snowboard instructor and a business executive becomes more, one has to overcome her past, while the other must let go of her planned future. (978-1-63679-646-8)

Dancing Toward Stardust by Julia Underwood. Age has nothing to do with becoming the person you were meant to be, taking a chance, and finding love. (978-1-63679-588-1)

Evacuation to Love by CA Popovich. As a hurricane rips through Florida, so too are Joanne and Shanna's lives upended. It'll take a force of nature to show them the love it takes to rebuild. (978-1-63679-493-8)

Lean in to Love by Catherine Lane. Will badly behaving celebrities, erotic sex tapes, and steamy scandals prevent Rory and Ellis from leaning in to love? (978-1-63679-582-9)

Searching for Someday by Renee Roman. For loner Rayne Thomas, her only goal for working out is to build her confidence, but Maggie Flanders has another idea, and neither are prepared for the outcome. (978-1-63679-568-3)

The Romance Lovers Book Club by MA Binfield and Toni Logan. After their book club reads a romance about an American tourist falling in love with an English princess, Harper and her best friend, Alice, book an impulsive trip to London hoping they'll each fall for the women of their dreams. (978-1-63679-501-0)

Truly Home by J.J. Hale. Ruth and Olivia discover home is more than a four-letter word. (978-1-63679-579-9)

View from the Top by Morgan Adams. When it comes to love, sometimes the higher you climb, the harder you fall. (978-1-63679-604-8)

Blood Rage by Ileandra Young. A stolen artifact, a family in the dark, an entire city on edge. Can SPEAR agent Danika Karson juggle all three over a weekend with the "in-laws," while an unknown, malevolent entity lies in wait upon her very skin? (978-1-63679-539-3)

Ghost Town by R.E. Ward. Blair Wyndon and Leif Henderson are set to prove ghosts exist when the mystery suddenly turns deadly. Someone or something else is in Masonville, and if they don't find a way to escape, they might never leave. (978-1-63679-523-2)

Good Christian Girls by Elizabeth Bradshaw. In this heartfelt coming of age lesbian romance, Lacey and Jo help each other untangle who they are from who everyone says they're supposed to be. (978-1-63679-555-3)

Guide Us Home by CF Frizzell and Jesse J. Thoma. When acquisition of an abandoned lighthouse pits ambitious competitors Nancy and Sam against each other, it takes a WWII tale of two brave women to make them see the light. (978-1-63679-533-1)

Lost Harbor by Kimberly Cooper Griffin. For Alice and Bridget's love to survive, they must find a way to reconcile the most important passions in their lives—devotion to the church and each other. (978-1-63679-463-1)

Never a Bridesmaid by Spencer Greene. As her sister's wedding gets closer, Jessica finds that her hatred for the maid of honor is a bit more complicated than she thought. Could it be something more than hatred? (978-1-63679-559-1)

The Rewind by Nicole Stiling. For police detective Cami Lyons and crime reporter Alicia Flynn, some choices break hearts. Others leave a body count. (978-1-63679-572-0)

Turning Point by Cathy Dunnell. When Asha and her former high school bully Jody struggle to deny their growing attraction, can they move forward without going back? (978-1-63679-549-2)

When Tomorrow Comes by D. Jackson Leigh. Teague Maxwell, convinced she will die before she turns 41, hires animal rescue owner Baye Cobb to rehome her extensive menagerie. (978-1-63679-557-7)

You Had Me at Merlot by Melissa Brayden. Leighton and Jamie have all the ingredients to turn their attraction into love, but it's a recipe for disaster. (978-1-63679-543-0)

All Things Beautiful by Alaina Erdell. Casey Norford only planned to learn to paint like her mentor, Leighton Vaughn, not sleep with her. (978-1-63679-479-2)

Appalachian Awakening by Nance Sparks. The more Amber's and Leslie's paths cross, the more this hike of a lifetime begins to look like a love of a lifetime. (978-1-63679-527-0)

Dreamer by Kris Bryant. When life seems to be too good to be true and love is within reach, Sawyer and Macey discover the truth about the town of Ladybug Junction, and the cold light of reality tests the hearts of these dreamers. (978-1-63679-378-8)

Eyes on Her by Eden Darry. When increasingly violent acts of sabotage threaten to derail the opening of her glamping business, Callie Pope is sure her ex, Jules, has something to do with it. But Jules is dead…isn't she? (978-1-63679-214-9)

Head Over Heelflip by Sander Santiago. To secure the biggest prizes at the Colorado Amateur Street Sports Tour, Thomas Jefferson will do almost anything, even marrying his best friend and crush—Arturo "Uno" Ortiz. (978-1-63679-489-1)

Letters from Sarah by Joy Argento. A simple mistake brought them together, but Sarah must release past love to create a future with Lindsey she never dreamed possible. (978-1-63679-509-6)

Lost in the Wild by Kadyan. When their plane crash-lands, Allison and Mike face hunger, cold, a terrifying encounter with a bear, and feelings for each other neither expects. (978-1-63679-545-4)

Not Just Friends by Jordan Meadows. A tragedy leaves Jen struggling to figure out who she is and what is important to her. (978-1-63679-517-1)

Of Auras and Shadows by Jennifer Karter. Eryn and Rina's unexpected love may be exactly what the Community needs to heal the rot that comes not from the fetid Dark Lands that surround the Community but from within. (978-1-63679-541-6)

The Secret Duchess by Jane Walsh. A determined widow defies a duke and falls in love with a fashionable spinster in a fight for her rightful home. (978-1-63679-519-5)

Winter's Spell by Ursula Klein. When former college roommates reunite at a wedding in Provincetown, sparks fly, but can they find true love when evil sirens and trickster mermaids get in the way? (978-1-63679-503-4)

Coasting and Crashing by Ana Hartnett Reichardt. Life comes easy to Emma Wilson until Lake Palmer shows up at Alder University and derails her every plan. (978-1-63679-511-9)

Every Beat of Her Heart by KC Richardson. Piper and Gillian have their own fears about falling in love, but will they be able to overcome those feelings once they learn each other's secrets? (978-1-63679-515-7)

Grave Consequences by Sandra Barret. A decade after necromancy became licensed and legalized, can Tamar and Maddy overcome the lingering prejudice against their kind and their growing attraction to each other to uncover a plot that threatens both their lives? (978-1-63679-467-9)

Haunted by Myth by Barbara Ann Wright. When ghost-hunter Chloe seeks an answer to the current spectral epidemic, all clues point to one very famous face: Helen of Troy, whose motives are more complicated than history suggests and whose charms few can resist. (978-1-63679-461-7)

Invisible by Anna Larner. When medical school dropout Phoebe Frink falls for the shy costume shop assistant Violet Unwin, everything about their love feels certain, but can the same be said about their future? (978-1-63679-469-3)

Like They Do in the Movies by Nan Campbell. Celebrity gossip writer Fran Underhill becomes Chelsea Cartwright's personal assistant with the aim of taking the popular actress down, but neither of them anticipates the clash of their attraction. (978-1-63679-525-6)

Limelight by Gun Brooke. Liberty Bell and Palmer Elliston loathe each other. They clash every week on the hottest new TV show, until Liberty starts to sing and the impossible happens. (978-1-63679-192-0)

Playing with Matches by Georgia Beers. To help save Cori's store and help Liz survive her ex's wedding they strike a deal: a fake relationship, but just for one week. There's no way this will turn into the real deal. (978-1-63679-507-2)

The Memories of Marlie Rose by Morgan Lee Miller. Broadway legend Marlie Rose undergoes a procedure to erase all of her unwanted memories, but as she starts regretting her decision, she discovers that the only person who could help is the love she's trying to forget. (978-1-63679-347-4)

The Murders at Sugar Mill Farm by Ronica Black. A serial killer is on the loose in southern Louisiana and it's up to three women to solve the case while carefully dancing around feelings for each other. (978-1-63679-455-6)

Fire in the Sky by Radclyffe and Julie Cannon. Two women from different worlds have nothing in common and every reason to wish they'd never met—except for the attraction neither can deny. (978-1-63679-573-7)